I0764372

THE LAST OUTPOST
and Other Tales

Z. S. Adani

HADLEY
RILLE
BOOKS

THE LAST OUTPOST AND OTHER TALES

ISBN-13, hardcover edition, 978-0-9829467-6-3

Published by
Hadley Rille Books
Eric T. Reynolds, Editor/Publisher
PO Box 25466
Overland Park, KS 66225
USA
www.hadleyrillebooks.com
contact@hadleyrillebooks.com

To the memory of my parents, Julianna and Géza Zsadányi.

Contents

Prismatrix

I WAS SIPPING MY DRINK and calculating the profit I would make the next day guiding the two Coalition scientists when something banged down on the roof of the Clover Leaf. The walls vibrated, and a few bottles fell to the floor and splashed booze on my face.

"Damned if another pylon broke loose," Stevon, the owner said. "Just paid off the repairs from the last damages."

With the back of my hand, I wiped my face and looked up at the ceiling, glad that the carbon alloy hadn't cracked. I took another sip of my drink and bit down on the tiny green worms, savoring their peppery flavor when a message icon appeared on my retinal screen, bearing the official seal of the Governor. The message was short: Governor Evans requests your urgent attendance at City Hall.

I cursed and downed my drink. Having just returned with a group of scientists, I was hoping to have a quiet evening before I had to deal with careless off-worlders again. I stood up and left.

Several people clustered outside, looking up at dozens of Rings sailing above Pylon City. Sunlight reflected off the crystalline Rings as they flipped to a horizontal position, assembled into a cylinder, and then disassembled again into solitaries and scattered in a crazed pattern. Some dived low and zigzagged between the pillars and webworks. Citizens dispersed in a hurry, ducking into alleys and alcoves. Others scurried toward the stairways leading to Undercity, where the poor lived.

"What the hell?" a man said. "Something's rattled the Rings."

Darin, there's a Fhra warship in low orbit, Viane sent through my MemBrain interface, on my customer channel. She stepped out from the bakery, face composed, but her gold-speckled eyes conveyed unease. *The Fhra is a member species of the Sentient Species Alliance.*

An SSA warship. My stomach clenched, but I refrained from asking questions. Instead I turned and headed toward the east tram.

Viane matched my stride. Her face was flushed, from anger or fear, I guessed, and her white hair stood erect, eyes glazed over, as no doubt she communicated with someone.

We passed the rhomboid and pyramidal domiciles of the wealthy, grown from expensive house seeds, bucky glass surfaces glinting under the late afternoon sun. Fluted columns, arches, and balconies graced some ancient designs that resembled old Earth style. Built on the foundation of native ironwood, tall pillars supported numerous walkways and floors, a lacy structure stretching into the distance. All would be pounded into dust if the Fhra decided to attack the city.

Eateries emptied along our way, and people exiting shops along our path looked up and nervously hurried on their way. A series of low vibrations transmitted up through the soles of my boots, shaking dust from every surface. Moments later, a segmented tram pulled up. Commuters got off, and we boarded in silence.

A Space Force ship has just passed Rhiane's orbit, Viane sent. *It'll be here in six hours.*

Would it be enough to hold off the Fhra warship?

She nodded. *Let's hope it will not come to that.*

I didn't consider Viane a friend—she had been Janice's friend. Janice, whom I had lost for a Ring fragment. I turned away as the memory of the bluebone's proboscis piercing Janice's body flashed before me.

We got off at the downtown stop, dodging pedestrians as we crossed the park. Earth palms lined the walkway, genenged to withstand the abundant sunlight of Prism, blue-green fronds swaying in the hot breeze.

I motioned for Viane to enter. We then took the lift to the third floor, stopping short at the sight of a two-meter tall, pink alien visible beyond the open door of the Governor's Office.

"Come in and close the door," Governor Evans said. He gestured to the alien. "This is TveLon, a representative of the Sentient Species Alliance. He's a Sxaleti."

TveLon inclined his large head, then turned his back and looked out the window.

Evans grimaced and continued the introductions, addressing the Sxaleti's back. "Viane Butler is a technical advisor to the Governor's office, and Darin Cleary is our best expedition guide."

He brushed pudgy fingers through his silver hair, then motioned to vher-hide formchairs. "Sit."

"I'll stand." I eyed the Sxaleti. He was clad in a tight, one-piece garment that outlined long limbs jointed at three places.

Viane shook her head and began pacing, every turn taking her closer to the Sxaleti, hair sensors erect and analyzing the alien pheromones.

Evans shrugged and remained standing. "Station alerted me to the Fhra warship several hours ago." He turned on the wall screen and the image of a black spacecraft appeared, knobby weapons ports and odd protrusions gleaming ominously. "It has arrived since then and parked itself in a low orbit. The Rings don't like that." He raised his voice, making sure the Sxaleti heard, but the alien just stood there. Evans threw up his hands, frustration clearly written on his face. "All I know is, and this is from Fletcher at the station, that Defense and Intelligence had no ships nearby, but they were able to divert a Space Force ship from another mission."

"Why the warship?" I shifted from one foot to another, trying to remember which guides were out beyond the Barren. Most of them couldn't afford a CC interface, a communication link that would put them in contact with Pylon City and warn them about irate Rings.

"Apparently, the SSA wants us off Prism," Evans said.

"Really?" I looked at the Sxaleti now. "Prism is not in any of the SSA star sectors. And humans aren't part of the SSA yet." I hoped we never would be.

The Sxaleti turned. "The Noninterference Laws state that no world can be colonized if there are native species present, unless the natives agree to such thing. The SSA has no records showing that the Rings have agreed to human presence." The chirping voice sounded impatient, but the large violet eyes seemed to convey fear. Or what fear would be if he were human, I thought.

"TveLon," Viane said abruptly, as though savoring the name. She dipped her head as if he hadn't been ignoring them and held out her hand in greeting. "It's nice to meet you."

He stared for a moment, confused, but then he reached out with his own hand, covered by a shimmering suit field.

Viane nodded. "The SSA Noninterference Laws, interesting. And you're interfering on a human colony, you and the Fhra." Her voice was a low purr without any hint of an accusation, just a simple stating of the facts. "Aside from that, I'm sure the Coalition supplied records on all our colony worlds before the negotiations for joining your SSA began."

"They did. But the Fhra is a brash young species. They think the Rings may need protection."

"Protection?" I asked.

"To enforce their rights, because the first settlers—how shall I phrase this so as not to offend—well, they have been thrown off the world."

I snorted. "We would all be dead if the Rings didn't want us here." The anger in my voice annoyed me, so I took a breath and continued, "The Rings attacked my ancestors because they didn't want any structures sitting directly on the *surface* of Prism, hence we all live in Pylon City."

Evans pointed out the window. "And the Rings gave our ancestors the ironwood to *build* the city."

"I know all that from the Coalition files," TveLon said. "But I must satisfy the Fhra, because once they're on the warpath . . ." All twelve of his long fingers fluttered before him like helpless pink snakes.

"Don't worry, TveLon," Viane said. "Space Force will hold off the Fhra warship." *But not indefinitely,* she sent to me.

The Sxaleti nodded in a human manner and dropped his hands to his sides.

Evans turned to me. "Darin, tomorrow I need you to take a small group to the mineral spirals and try to make the Rings assemble."

I'd suspected that that was coming but it still took me by surprise. There had been no full assembly of the Rings since after their attack on the first settlers, over four centuries ago. Some people who studied the Rings, like Janice, had witnessed partial assemblies from which she had formulated her theories on the Rings and Prismatrix, but even those were rare. I wasn't sure if we could make the Rings assemble. But judging by the Rings' behavior, set off by the low-orbiting warship, an assembly was the easiest way to defuse the situation. Leaving Prism was unthinkable; it was my home. And besides, Janice was here, and even though she was dead, I could never abandon her.

"Tomorrow is too soon," I said. "The training for off-worlders is two or three days."

"No time," Evans said. "This situation is urgent."

"A small group - who?"

Viane smiled. "I, of course, will be going. And one crewmember from the Space Force ship."

"And TveLon must go," Evans said. "To record what the Rings say."

"Viane can do that."

Evans shook his head. "An SSA representative must record it. The Fhra insist."

"Really?" The word came out a snarl, and I temporarily lost all the diplomatic skills I had worked so hard to acquire. "And who the hell are the Fhra that they come here to bully us?"

"They're from a high-gravity world," Viane said and looked at the Sxaleti. "And I believe not too long ago, before they joined the SSA, they'd subjugated a couple of species."

TveLon dipped his head, as though in resignation. "To invite them into the SSA was the only way to stop them from preying on weaker species. Their warcraft—"

I made a chopping motion. "That's another reason humans shouldn't join the SSA. You question our colonization records, but you allow felons to run your Alliance."

The large violet eyes of the Sxaleti looked down on me. Imploring? Placating? "The Fhra do not run the SSA, but every member species has a say in important matters."

And this is important. I knew it was only a matter of time before the SSA would become interested in the Rings. But if I could prove Janice's theory, that the Rings were components of a planetary AI system, then perhaps Janice wouldn't have died in vain.

Evans sighed. "You must leave in the morning, Darin."

"Fine, but brief TveLon on the dangers, or he'll likely get himself killed."

I stabbed the tent pole into the pebbly ground and waited for the carbon filament to unfold from the fist-sized casing. It was safer inside the stone corral I used during my expeditions to the mineral spires, but it wouldn't have hindered a rhinticore or a bluebone, both crepuscular hunters. Night was approaching on Prism, but for another hour, the white sun would still shine.

Refracted light flashed a few hundred meters ahead from the vertical band of brilliant crystal etched out against the hazy mineral spires in the distance. The crystal flipped to horizontal, shifted its angle, and defined into an ellipse.

A Ring! I cursed as the Ring shimmered and started moving toward the off-worlders, generating a faint humming sound.

The sound grew.

TveLon looked up from his specimen collecting, his large pink head tilting to the side. He said something to Mike Preston.

As an expedition guide, the off-worlders were my responsibility, and I instinctively took a few steps toward them.

Viane dropped the supplies she carried and grabbed my arm. "Darin, don't," she whispered, her lips barely moving.

Viane was right; I couldn't help the two off-worlders by running to them. Only standing still or being near an armoride would help them, as the Rings tended to avoid our rides. Desperate to do something even though I shouldn't move or make a sound, I whistled to Elly. When the armoride appeared outside of the stone shelter, I pointed to Mike and TveLon. Elly took off toward the off-worlders, her armored head swinging and six legs kicking up clods of wet soil.

TveLon dropped the specimen kit and broke into a loping run. A shimmer covered him. The fool had turned on his energy shield! When Mike followed the pink-skinned Sxaleti, my heart lurched. Energy fields, vibrations, and motion all attracted the solitary Rings; individually they were not intelligent enough to process that they couldn't join with humans as they joined with one another. I had briefed the off-worlders about the dangers before we set out.

"No, stop," I said, taking a step toward them. Viane jerked me back this time, long, brown fingers gripping the back of my bluebone armor. "TveLon, deactivate your suit field!"

But he didn't; when he saw Elly running toward him Tvelon changed direction and ran faster. The Ring vibrated and matched his course, cleaving the air as it sailed the remaining distance.

Mike, stay away from TveLon! I sent through my MemBrain interface when I saw him follow the alien. *And don't move.*

Mike disregarded my warning and kept running. I cursed again; Space Force crew should have learned to obey commands. Standing still, I watched the Ring twirl a few meters above the Sxaleti, pacing him. The Ring contracted into a two-meter hoop, fattened, and brushed against TveLon's suit field. As the different energies met, the air crackled with static and piezoelectric sparks. White sunlight shone through the crystalline Ring, refracted, and broke into a rainbow of colors. TveLon flailed his long arms and swiped at the Ring, and his suit's field bounced it into Mike's path.

Stand still, Mike, I warned. Hands curled into fists, I watched, sweat trickling down my back.

Mike panicked and lifted both arms to ward off the Ring. It contracted again and dropped over his head, shimmering and humming. Mike choked out a scream as the Ring made a whooshing sound, turned opaline, and constricted around his throat. Mike convulsed and the odor of charred meat filled the air. As the Ring expanded and slid off his neck, the body dropped to the moss-covered stone with a thud. In a lazy twirl, the solitary Ring sailed off toward the mineral spires.

I ran to Mike and squatted. With a shaking hand, I felt for a pulse, horrified at the sight of the charred groove across the man's neck. A sick feeling churned in my stomach. I should have kept a closer eye on them.

Viane crouched and closed Mike's staring eyes. She stood up and faced the Sxaleti, her white hair sensors rippling in the slight breeze. I doubted she could extract the alien's emotional state through his suit field, but I waited, listening to the clicking of small mandibles as the sand bunnies devoured the fresh blooms. Memories from a year past flashed in my mind. Turning away from Viane and the Sxaleti, I stared at the distant mineral spirals and my heart emptied. Janice was there, entombed in slab of crystal. And maybe Mike would be taken there.

"Darin, I am sorry," TveLon said behind me.

Jaws clenched, I turned but didn't look at TveLon.

"I, I should have listened to you. My suit field . . ." TveLon trailed off, his twelve ropy fingers groping the air between us. He stared at me, and then at Viane, violet eyes wide with shock.

"It's not your fault," Viane said, but the expression in her eyes belied her statement.

I growled, stabbing a finger at the Sxaleti. "From here on, deactivate your damn suit field."

"You must, TveLon," Viane said. Her cinnamon face was set in sculpted lines, only a slight twitch in her neck indicating that she was far from being calm. She glanced up to where the Fhra warship orbited Prism. "Tomorrow we must get the Rings to assemble."

Near our shelter, I covered Mike's body with rocks while Viane said a quiet eulogy. TveLon sat next to the stone mound, head hanging between his knobby knees and a keening sound issuing from his throat. I shivered—I could almost feel his remorse.

With a sigh I walked to the tents and got out some meal packs for dinner. Normally I would hunt but with the urgency of the situation Pylon City had provided ready meals.

None of us touched the sealed containers. Viane walked over and sat down.

Night poppies opened their crimson petals, and I breathed in the fragrance as I unfastened my bluebone breastplate, crafted from the same bluebone that had killed Janice. Because I had deviated from the rules, because I'd not been fast enough to prevent it. Because—

I bolted to my feet and called out to TveLon. "Get into your tent now or something might just rip your guts out." My voice came out a growl, but I didn't care—at least the tents projected sonic waves that deterred some predators. Passing Viane, I added, "Make sure he obeys the rules."

Then I stormed into my tent and fell onto the air mat, pressing my face into the pillow and trying to smother the memories—

—it wasn't a Ring, it wasn't a Ring, my own sobbing reverberated in my mind as the memory reared its ugly head.

"Get off your stone perch and help me dig out this Ring fragment," Janice said, her alto echoing off the spires. She hugged me from behind and planted a kiss on my shoulder.

I shook my head and gave her a lopsided grin. "When you're using the sonic saw, I guard. We agreed."

We were at the edge of the mineral spires, where a buzz, energy output, shrill sound, or vigorous motion could set off solitary Rings.

"Come on, Darin," Janice said. Her smile outshone a dozen Rings. "Two can work faster. I think it's a Ring fragment in this vein."

"I sincerely doubt that. Rings don't break."

"Who's the expert here?" Janice pouted, bow lips pursed and eyes twinkling with mischief. "Maybe I'll come out with Viane next time."

I laughed to hide my jealousy. Sometimes I'd caught myself resenting the bond my wife had with Viane, resenting their light-natured bantering and the finishing of each other's sentences.

"But I'd rather spend the time with you, Boss guide." Her slim fingers caressed my face, then slid down on my arm and clasped my hand.

I kissed her fingers and breathed in the hyacinth fragrance of her skin. My guiding expeditions, paid by off-world outfits, kept us apart for days and even weeks at times. I felt cheated when Janice went out with Viane, and guilty when she had to soldier on with her research alone. But until Janice made a Ring-shattering discovery, my work kept us fed and housed.

"Please?" Janice pulled me toward the large outcrop of malachite and aqua, along which ran an arc of brilliant white. "It's a trapped Ring, inactive. We could learn so much."

"It's not a Ring."

"I think it is." She handed me one of the sonic saws. "Start cutting above. We'll meet in the middle." Then she walked a few meters away, turned on the saw, and began cutting below the arc of crystal.

Deafened by the motor of the sonic saw, I scanned our surroundings. When I was satisfied nothing lurked nearby, I began to cut the stone above the white crystal arc. Soon a cloud of rock dust surrounded us.

We were about three meters apart when a spray of red hit the stone before me. With a howl, I pulled my gun, pivoted, and fired a volley of foot-long flechettes into the bluebone's eye. Yellow ichor splashed me, mingling with Janice's blood, as I pumped another round of nerve poison into the beast. The bluebone shuddered, and I grabbed Janice as the creature crumpled to the ground, cobalt armor plates clattering on the stone. I sobbed as the monster's corkscrew proboscis ripped out her insides.

I lowered Janice to the hard surface, staring at the jagged wound in her torso. Terror stole into my heart as her life seeped into the pewter stones.

Janice smiled, black hair smeared with blood. "I love you, Darin."

"Don't—"

Janice closed her eyes. I buried my face in her hair and felt my heart turning into stone.

Numb, I wiped my face and lay in the tent, looking at the faint ripples in the carbon filament fabric. Night wind moaned outside. Sometime later I fell asleep.

I woke up exhausted and dressed quickly. Viane stood over to the site where we had laid Mike's body. She shook her head.

A shudder passed through me, and I turned away. I'd known last night that the Rings would take Mike, like they had taken Janice to the mineral spires. They took every human that died outside of Pylon city. Oddly, the Rings never took the bodies of dead aliens; those were left to the scavengers. And like countless times before, I was wondering why—after all, humans too were aliens to Prism.

We gathered our belongings and set out to cross the Barren. Viane rode alone now, and TveLon sat behind me. Blinking on my sun lids to protect my eyes, I turned Elly toward the mineral spires. Her six flat feet clacked on gravel, claws extended for better purchase on the incline.

Past noon, we were halfway across the Barren, when the Sxaleti tapped me on the shoulder.

"I would like to dismount," TveLon said in his chirping voice.

Reaching under Elly's neck, I pressed one of her sensory organs. The armoride halted, sections of her armor plates grinding from the sudden stop. I slid to the ground and glared at the Sxaleti.

TveLon jumped off, thin arms flailing to keep his balance as he landed on a slab of malachite-infused basalt. "I'm sorry. You are resonating bad feelings. I want to walk for a while."

"No one asked you to come."

Viane pulled up, riding her armoride like a queen of the Barren. *I think he's an empath,* she sent through my MemBrain interface. *He can sense your resentment.* Patting the armored head of her mount, she slid off, long legs bending at the knees to absorb the impact of the two-meter drop.

Viane's armoride moved toward the lung tree leaves that had fallen to the ground, wide mouth open and sticky tongue snatching up the succulent delicacies. Elly joined him.

"I'm not here of my own choice," TveLon said. "Please understand that the Fhra must be satisfied. And they won't be until they are certain that humans are not exploiting an intelligent species."

"Intelligent, yes," Viane said. "Only when several of them join together though. But *species* is a misnomer. According to scientists, the Rings aren't alive in a strict biological sense. For example, no one has seen them reproduce in over four centuries. And they don't die—"

A loud screech split the air.

Eyes narrowed, I pivoted, scanning the basalt cliffs. Over the buttes, a cloud of dust boiled up, partly obscuring a rhinticore. "Get behind the lung trees," I said to TveLon as I ran to my armoride and mounted. Elly needed no urging and broke into a trillop, head low to the ground.

Viane was up on her mount, racing along the trees and readying her weapon.

The rhinticore hurtled toward us, jointed carapace gleaming obsidian, head swinging side to side, and mandibles grinding. It was a big one, at least five meters long and two high. Horns curled up, it turned abruptly and tumbled down the basalt hill, landing on its feet in a cloud of pebbles, forked stinger extended over the segments of its body.

The rhinticore accelerated and opened its pincers wide. I aimed my high velocity dart gun at the monstrous head and held it level, then when the mandibles opened, I unleashed a volley of flechettes. As I rode past the beast, I saw Viane also fire.

The rhinticore reared up on its four hind legs and shook its head, trying to dislodge the poison darts, its pincers opening and closing. It quivered, black ichor dribbling from its mouth parts. Then it froze and keeled over with a loud bang, throwing up a shower of rocks.

Viane turned her mount abruptly and rode back to the Sxaleti. "TveLon, we must reach the mineral spirals before nightfall. That," she said in a sharp tone, pointing back at the rhinticore, "is the reason we never stop at the Barren."

TveLon's face turned a dark shade of pink.

Viane never yelled and never argued; she was always in control, showing just enough emotion measured out to be effective. Except with Janice. If I hadn't seen the way Viane had smiled at Janice and hadn't heard the song in her laughter, or the heated argument they had once, I would have thought she was emo-suppressed. Speaking to the Sxaleti harshly now was very un-Viane. But having lived on Earth before, she knew a lot more about the Coalition than anyone in Pylon City, and obviously about the SSA aliens as well.

The Sxaleti is a long-lived species, Viane sent, *which could explain TveLon's cowardice.*

I blinked to acknowledge her comment. *TveLon should ride with you.*

He won't, she sent. *Not without his suit field. He's in a mating triad. Close contact with another female, Sxaleti or alien, could mess up their reproduction.*

"Let's move on," I said. "The rhinticore carcass will attract other predators." I grudgingly guided Elly closer so TveLon could mount her.

The afternoon rain had given rise to an explosion of colors; yellow rock moss, emerald snakeroots, and pink bowl flowers covered every stone surface. Sand bunnies chomped on the bounty, shaking rainwater off their russet carapaces, small mandibles clicking in a chorus of contentment.

By the time we reached the edge of the mineral spires, the sun had set. Eye, with its immense crater facing Prism, rose in the eastern horizon. It was smaller than Earth's moon but not by much. Eye, always watching, had witnessed how the Rings had come to be, who made them, and other mysteries about Prism that even after four centuries remained unsolved. The little we had learned we did not share readily; like a collective of misers, we clutched those riches to ourselves. It was our only livelihood. And according to Janice, on a subconscious level, we knew that the Rings didn't want us to share.

Heart beating in my throat, I slowed Elly to a walk, reluctant to lead the others further into the midst of the mineral blocks, some fifty and sixty meters high. Cobalt and indigo spires rose above the blocks, twisted into shapes vaguely reminiscent of city structures. The sand here was mildly radioactive, but not enough to cause cellular damage if we didn't stay long, which of course depended on how quickly the Rings would come.

Viane rode abreast of me, slim fingers on the head of her armoride, as though she sought to calm him, or herself. TveLon squirmed behind me, no doubt uneasy without his suit field. But we couldn't risk another attack, and as much as I wanted to blame the Sxaleti for Mike's death, I knew that our hasty departure and lack of preparations contributed to the accident. Still, the death of the Space Force crewman weighed on my conscience.

I fingered my bluebone armor as the memories of Janice's death knifed into me. I had found her body months later in the depths of the mineral city, and for a second I'd thought she was alive. Entombed in a translucent aqua and white gemrock, she stood there inside the crystal chamber, face serene, with no sign of the hole the bluebone had left in her midriff. I had put my face against the cool gem and listened, hoping to find some glimmer of life. Though the crystal had vibrated, I'd heard no heartbeat.

Looking into the distance, my eyes misted. Then suddenly, I was blinded by brilliance. In a whirlwind, thousands of Rings sailed above us. Lightning stitched the sky, and the air smelled of ozone. I felt TveLon's hands gripping my torso from behind, and wasn't surprised that the alien was afraid, not after having seen Mike killed.

Without turning my head I said, "Relax, we're not in danger now." Or not much danger anyway. It was possible that a sudden movement or sound might set off a stray Ring, but I didn't think it likely—they never sought human contact when there were several Rings in sight.

I touched Elly's sensory organ and the armoride stopped. Viane did likewise. Crystal lines, curlicues, and fat circles filled the sky, darting and whirring in a blur of colors like translucent ribbons painted in rainbow. Capricious and unreliable, the Rings could take off any minute and return to the mineral city or other parts of Prism, so I looked at Viane and nodded. On the count of three, we each raised one arm very slowly, then opened our hands to reveal the mirrors we held.

At first the Rings did not react, but then their whizzing slowed down, synchronized, and they moved toward one another until individual Rings assembled and formed geometrical structures. A large cylinder descended to the ground, followed by a smaller one. Another structure that had attenuated into a long thin rod speared the ground vertically.

I lowered my arm and stared in wonder. No one, not since the original settlers, had seen such a large assembly. Not even Janice, a physicist whose specialty was the exotic atom-like particles made up of different types of topological vacuum defects known as monopoles. She had once explained her theories of the Rings to me—they were superconductive power grid nodes made of femto lattices and pico tubes, in which the extoms in the molecules were made up of exotic optical tubes and buckytubes.

There was a tinkling sound like the clinking of thousands of wine glasses, as the Rings fused and assembled, myriads of colors flowing on the crystal surfaces, until the entire thing became a vague icosahedron shape. Above it a cone of light projected.

I sucked in my breath, searching. *Janice*, I thought, as an overpowering feeling of her presence filled me. The fragrance of her hyacinth soap wrapped around me; I heard her laughter and saw her windblown hair.

The icosahedron started vibrating. It produced a low harmonics, which shook the rock foundation we were standing on. Heart pounding in my throat, I gripped Elly's head plates and waited. The sound grew to a higher pitch and, in a tinkling chorus, a question floated up in the air. "What do you wish?"

Among the chorus of voices I heard Janice's alto. Had the Rings copied her voice? They must have done that and more, because I felt her presence now. Light filled me and untied the knot of pain that had been my companion for the past year.

Janice.

For a moment I was speechless, but then I swallowed and raised my voice above the jingle. "Others came to this world." I pointed above where the Fhra warship orbited Prism. "They question Humanity's right to live here. The Rings must make known to them if we can stay, or the others will use force."

"Humans stay. Others leave." The answer was loud. It echoed a moment from the surrounding stones before bleeding into the tinkling of disassembly.

Janice's presence faded as the large icosahedron fell apart. I whipped my head around, looking for her. Cylinders rolled away, long tubes darted off the ground and separated into Rings that sailed up into the air. The entire disassembly took less than a few minutes, then the Rings whizzed past and took off toward the mineral spires, taking Janice with them.

I rubbed my face and glanced at Viane furtively. Janice, I thought and breathed a laugh. *Janice,* I sent to Viane.

Viane smiled and, through her MemBrain interface, she sent, *Prismatrix.*

So she knew about Janice's hypothesis: Prismatrix. According to Janice, Prism was a matrix comprised of the world and the Rings, an alien artifact, an artificial intelligence on a planetary scale. But since no one had ever found a Ring particle to examine under the nanoscope, Janice's hypothesis was just that. Until now.

I reeled from the realization. That Janice's mind was part of the matrix was evidence that Prism *was* part of the artificial intelligence network, because the Rings had arrived hours after she died. If Prism had not recorded Janice's mind right after I had set her down on the stone, before the moment of death and before the Rings had arrived, she would not be in Prismatrix. Prism had imprinted her, and the imprinting process—

Another piece of the puzzle fell into place; the Rings had attacked the original settlement my ancestors had built on the surface, because it interfered with the imprinting. *"No large structures can cover the surface of Prism,"* was what they had said four hundred years ago. They had even given us ironwood to build Pylon City.

I wondered who the makers were and what they had intended with this planetary AI. Prismatrix had been Janice's name for it, and she was a part of it now. For the first time since her death, I felt comfortable within my skin.

Why the system stored the human bodies in crystal slabs I didn't know, and that information about the Rings I'd never sold to the Coalition. Not everything was for sale. So far, I had found only a few chambers where the Rings stored dead humans, and was certain that no one else had penetrated the mineral spirals deep enough to find them. Something told me that I must ensure that no off-worlders would disturb them.

"Faced with this record now," TveLon said, a finger pointing at his eyecam. "The Fhra warship must leave."

Viane raised her eyebrows, white hair sensors erect. "Tell me TveLon, why did the SSA allow the Fhra to come here? I mean, the idea that the Rings need protection is a flimsy excuse. The Coalition will want to know that whoever hired the Fhra will back off."

"Absolutely, they will," TveLon said, his chirping voice loud. He regarded Viane thoughtfully. "The Noninterference Laws apply to the Fhra too. Those laws have not been broken in over a hundred thousand of your years. Questionable issues have arisen in the past and attempts to bend the Laws, such as we have seen here, have regrettably occurred, but no species of the SSA would draw the wrath of the Mainmind."

Dismayed at my own ignorance, I turned to Viane.

"The Mainmind is a Matrioshka brain the size of Rhiane," Viane said.

I nodded. Perhaps one of the SSA species harbored grudges against the Mainmind and was exploring the means of getting rid of it. Or maybe the Mainmind itself wanted a foothold on Prism, to control the Prismatrix AI. Could that be the reason the Prismatrix AI needed humans now, to fend off another AI? At any rate, the Coalition as a whole would not benefit from sharing the particulars of Prismatrix with the SSA. As for the colonists of Prism, I glanced at Viane, trying to gauge her intention.

I suppose at some point, Janice will tell us what I should report to the Coalition, Viane sent. She smiled, and though it was a mere ghost of what she had shared with Janice, it was enough now to build a friendship upon.

I grinned, turning Elly toward Pylon City. The sooner we got back, the sooner I could return.

"You are resonating good feelings now," TveLon said. "I'll be glad to ride back with you."

Author's note: I used the *The Dhyany* universe for this story simply because there are so many worlds I've already built up.

Divergence

NICK HOROWITZ BLINKED AS THE ICON of Alphega Medical Center appeared on his retinal screen. Sweat broke out over his brows as he read the message: Your wife is at the trauma center.

He should've done something when Ann had first started showing symptoms. Heart pounding, he jumped up from the formchair and dashed to the door. He ran along the corridor, took the droptube to the ground floor, and sprinted outside to the nearby tram station. When the tram pulled in and people trickled out, he jumped in and shoved his credit chip into the slot.

The car lifted slightly and passed the deserted campus, solitary buildings dotted the streets, some of them collapsed. They were the remnants of the food riots, burnt support structures poking into the sky and reaching toward the high dome of Olympus City.

Nick counted the seconds as the tram passed along Slow River, a shallow body of water once part of the first comet. City Hall rushed past, the oldest building constructed from fused Martian sand.

As the tram system announced Alphega Medical Center, Nick exited and ran across the street, dodging the mobile sleds transporting the sick from the paramedic units to the trauma center. Some sleds had full-body autodocs, their lights blinking yellow and red. He wormed his way through the machines and arrived at a large door.

As the door dilated, the odor of medchines and scrubnits assailed his nostrils, overlaid by a stench of decay. A drone cart rolled out of the trauma center, a cagey construction crammed with bodies on racks. Blue-tinged arms and legs poked out, stiff with rigor mortis. He glimpsed at faces with eyes bulging and lips gnawed, as the brains had swelled.

For a second, Ann's features superimposed upon the distorted faces. Nick swallowed and pushed past the cart, running the length of the corridor. He peeked into each holding unit until he found her, blonde hair splayed out around her pale face. She was ensconced in a mediform, gel sensors and feeds connecting to her head in an azure halo of glittering jewels. She appeared to be sleeping. Nick darted across and took one of her hands. He kissed her fingers, not caring about the medtech manipulating the diagnostic screen.

"I'm Nick Horowitz," he said when the medtech turned. Her face was carved with fatigue, but her eyes held kindness. "May I speak with the doctor in charge?"

"If you don't mind the long wait," the medtech said. Her slightly enlarged head indicated that she had gone through the divergence and survived, like Nick himself and some forty percent of the population. The diagnostic screen flicked off. "Excuse me. I have to attend to the infirm." She pulled the decon partition aside and left.

Nick dragged over a plaz chair and sat down. Horrific images of Ann's brain compressed into slush swam before him, caused by a genetic glitch when a set of noncoding DNAs initiated the growth of an additional brain. Ann was not alone; since the divergence had begun two years ago, it had killed billions throughout the Solar system. According to the latest statistics sent from Earth, the percentage of survivors was higher there, most of them on dole and a few hundred of the very wealthy. *What do the wealthy and the poor have in common?* He should take Ann there.

A haggard man entered Ann's cubby. "Emmanuel Valdez," he said and turned on the holoscreen above the mediform.

"I'm Nick Horowitz. What's her prognosis?"

Valdez pointed to the image of Ann's skull.

As the grid superimposed over it, there was some thinning of the cranium, necessary to accommodate the new brain, but no outward expansion of the bone yet. The MemBrain, a thin film of brain tissues built from the cannibalized dura, was growing underneath. When it finished growing, it would look like a pancake of folded neurons and glial cells, longer and stronger axons and dendrites, and crystalline structures never seen before the divergence. A secondary brain, if she survived the transformation.

Valdez pointed to lattices of cobweb-like structures on the inner surface of the MemBrain. "The neural pattern for the connections is already in place and her immunites are producing adequate stem cells, but. . ."

Nick swallowed. Ann's new brain was a bloom of misfolding proteins. It was the initial stage, but the bloom would accelerate and kill her within a month. He glanced at her face and his heart constricted.

"I'm keeping her under sedation. She's not in pain at the moment."

"Can you put her in stasis?"

"I would if I had a stasis unit. One less patient for me—" Valdez looked down at his shoes.

—To lose or to care for? Nick wondered which had been on the tip of Valdez's tongue. All stasis units had been claimed, bought, or stolen. "Please, keep my wife comfortable." His tone was beseeching, and he held the other man's gaze for a few seconds before he turned and left.

Pacing the length of their tiny dayroom, Nick activated Coalnet and watched the newsfeed from Earth on his retinal screen. Several small wars had broken out. Fires raged in cities, where looters dodged between collapsing buildings. Armor-clad mercenaries darted from building to building, while their planes bombed dole tenements and research facilities. Divisions of the Earth Police, also wearing armor, exchanged shots with them, but few men remained standing. Nick sighed, saddened and puzzled by the insanity.

Nick blinked off the view and picked up Ann's thermal suit, stuffing it in a cleaner chute. His gaze stopped on her bamboo and cypress plants on the shelves. They looked rather forlorn, as if they already sensed her absence—like he felt her absence. It was far worse than ten years ago when Ann had to finish her contract on Earth—to pay for her health plan—and Nick had to leave for Mars right away. He regretted that he had been unfaithful to her, even if they had agreed on an open marriage during the year separation. Unlike him, Ann had chosen not to take a lover, as he'd found out later. At least she had gotten the best immunite treatment Novi Clean had to offer. Not that it would help her now. Nick savored the memories of her presence as he walked to the plants and adjusted their water drip.

He sank into the formchair and stared out at Mount Olympus blotting out the sky. Mars was home after his ten-year tenure at the University, and they had decided to settle and raise a family.

What if there was no easy genetic switch? Yes, scientists were working on it, but. . . On Mars, the bloom had killed the neuroscientists, biochemists, and biologists. The situation was pretty much the same everywhere, and as civilization was fragmenting, research began to lag behind, unable to keep up with the too many variables the divergence presented. There was no major genetic drifting to account for it; it happened everywhere simultaneously. And it was not a prion disease. Variants of the Microcephalin and ASPM genes were involved in the MemBrain growth, along with enhancers, shadow enhancers, pseudogenes, transposable elements of both LINEs and SINEs, microRNAs, and noncoding RNAs. As a planetary engineer, Nick knew he was out of his league, but he'd tried using stem cells and gone through thousands of enzyme combinations. Nothing worked. His gut feeling said the remaining scientists on Mars wouldn't tackle it, not in time for Ann.

He projected a view of his programs and tapped the icon for his search agent. Ca-Nine, a dog with nine eyes wrapped around its head, grinned at him. Decades ago during their university years on Earth, Andre had helped him design the program, and it could break into encrypted files on the net. If anyone, Andre could have found a cure for the bloom, but he'd been murdered shortly after the divergence had begun. Andre had been a Demetrist, part theoretical biologist and part software designer, using evolutionary algorithms to *breed* programs, which Andre had done during the Infowar to help the underground fight for a transparent government. Transparency had never been achieved, but Nick suspected the underground was still active. Unlike Andre, Nick was never a risk-taker; he coasted through life and waited things out. But he couldn't afford to wait now.

"All right, Ca-Nine, find me a stasis unit on Mars or the near-belt." Any farther and he couldn't get it delivered in time to make a difference.

The head grew a body and six legs, shook itself, and loped off.

Nick leaned back in the formchair and surrendered his sore body to a massage.

Ca-Nine's soft barking alerted him, presenting three sources with contact info. Nick dismissed Ceres and Titan Station; too far, Ann could die by the time he reached it. To his relief, there was one in Tech City on Mars. He opened the link and left a message.

Nick was studying synthetic protein assemblers when the instructions arrived. He read them quickly and closed all his programs.

Uncertain if Tech City's dome was intact, he reached for his thermsuit and pulled it on, then transferred his credit chip to the outside pocket. While he rode the droptube, he connected to the net and called a flyer. By the time it arrived, he had gone through two dozen scenarios that could end in his death, and then Ann's. He dismissed them and stepped through the opening door of the flyer, then punched in the scrambled coordinates. Though he knew his destination was Tech City, the exact location remained a mystery.

The flyer rose above the residential complexes. Spires of fused Martian sand in shades of cinnamon and ochre, plazoy bridges and buildings, research facilities built of buckyglass, and parks with mature trees raced by below. Then the shield wall of Olympus City shimmered, the field flickered once, and let the flyer through.

Below at the cemetery, fresh corpses were piled on decon sheets. Robots were digging shallow graves, their curving metal arms glinting in the faint light. Soon they wouldn't be able to keep up with the accumulating cadavers. At the beginning of the divergence, the deceased had tombstones, but stone crushers had bowled them over one night, no doubt at the command of the mayor in reaction to the protests from family members of the recently dead.

Compost and fertilizer. No one said it but everyone knew, and people ceased to care in the woes of transformation. Nick turned away, lips compressed into a bitter line. The possibility of losing the colony filled him with dismay. The decades-long terraforming, thousands of ships hauling comets and easing them down onto the surface, millions working on engineering a biosphere, designing crops, building the Coalnet sats and the Martian cities, all would be lost without people to continue. Nick felt a momentary shame for worrying about achievements when people were dying, but he couldn't help it.

Of all the catastrophe scenarios, no one had considered evolution, because evolution should be gradual. Since the mid twenty-first century, when the presence of the 189 base pairs were discovered in the junk DNAs, theories abounded about their role in evolution, although nothing had been proven. The lack of cure for the bloom had escalated the riots, more on Earth than elsewhere in the Solar System. Some people believed that the divergence was engineered, others believed that it was an alien experiment. The conspiracy theories were fueled by the fact that the survivors would benefit.

The flyer banked and passed through Tech City's shield wall. Low cylindrical structures interconnected by pipes and tubes of buckyglass glinted on russet sand. Landing fields raced by, sprinkled with various atmospheric crafts, some ringed with nacelles and weapons ports. Criminal elements had taken over parts of Tech City, and Nick feared that anarchy was not far behind.

The windows darkened and the flyer jolted, then leveled out and dropped to the ground. As the door lifted to reveal a dark alley, Nick felt his stomach plunge. Three men stood in a shadowed alcove, wearing glove suits, containment systems designed to keep out pathogens and nanites, or to keep in skin and hair particles. Two of the men were heavily augmented, with bulging muscles on their two-meter tall frames, but the third one was slight.

Shots rang out from above. Nick looked up at four men standing on the roof. The next moment, pain seared through his leg. He was falling, his head smacking against the plazoy wall.

Nick woke up to an excruciating headache. He sat up and winced, touching a lump on his head. By his internal clock, he'd been unconscious for 18 hours. Someone had transported him to a living area, with several bunks, outdated consoles, and containers of dry food bars cluttering the place. A table stood in the center, and on crude plaz chairs sat the two heavily augmented men.

The slight man picked up a glass full of green fluid from a table. "My name is Marcel. You might want to drink this."

Nick's throat was parched, but he wasn't ready to trust these people. He could stand the thirst, now that the pain in his leg had subsided, due to an autodoc perching on his calf and busily changing a gel bandage on the wound. Confusion filled him. "Who . . . who shot me?"

"Smugglers," Marcel said. "They attack more frequently now, but this place is safe. I want to point out that you're here only because Andre Toth was your friend."

Maybe I should trust them, Nick thought and drank the contents of the glass. His headache abated almost instantly. "I need a stasis unit."

"We got one," Marcel said.

"All right," Nick said and reached into his pocket for his credit chip.

"Fifteen thousand credits," Marcel said and rattled off the account number.

Nick gulped at the exorbitant price, but he transferred the amount. It would leave him without funds to pay for passage on a ship to Earth or the Moon, but he would tackle that later.

"Get the merchandise," Marcel said to one of his men.

"What's the guarantee it works?" Nick realized belatedly that he should've asked before he had paid.

Marcel scowled. "You may examine it."

Following the burly man, the stasis capsule arrived on a robosled, crated in plazfoam. Nick contemplated whether he should uncrate the unit and run a diagnostics, but decided against it. It would take time, and he just wanted to return to Ann. And besides, Andre had helped the underground during the Infowar because he'd trusted them.

Nick manhandled the stasis unit through the back door of Alphega Medical Center, avoiding the envious glances of people he passed.

After Valdez finished with another patient, Nick helped him put Ann inside the capsule. As they waited for the capsule to show her vitals, Nick looked at the bullet-shaped, charcoal exterior, then at Ann's face through the oval buckyglass viewing plate and it suddenly occurred to him that someone might dump her and steal the stasis unit. Even if he could get the funds for their passage to Earth soon, Valdez couldn't be expected to guard her. "I'm taking her home."

Valdez seemed relieved. "She'd be safer there."

"Thank you for caring for her."

On his way home, Nick calculated how many house seeds he would have to steal from the lab to pay for their passage, cringing at the prospect of committing a felony.

* * *

Twelve days later, they were aboard a cargo shuttle to the *Hecate*, a small Belter ship plying between Clarke Station, Mars, and the asteroid belt. Nick regretted that from a law-abiding citizen, he had turned into a criminal. It couldn't be helped, he thought, staring at the pilot's slightly expanded cranium. Her neck jerked sideways, a quick spasm that lasted only for an instant, but he realized that she was going through the divergence. And maybe not as smoothly as he had, with minor symptoms of mild headache occasionally, itching behind his eyes, and a low fever. He hoped she didn't have a seizure while piloting.

The shuttle punched through the thin clouds and accelerated toward Phobos. As the ochre and green face of Mars dropped away below, he was relieved to be leaving. Yet, he felt cheated. They had been happy here. Even though Ann couldn't hear him, he'd been talking to her daily while running diagnostics on the stasis unit. He missed her smile, spontaneous puns, wisdom, and the way she tackled everything in a precise manner, like her mathematical equations.

Nick dozed, one hand protectively on the stasis capsule, when a sudden jolt woke him. He looked through the viewport at the growing ship and paled. The *Hecate* was a lumpy metal fish with cargo pods welded on haphazardly, with a single fusion engine protruding at an odd angle. Her pitted gray surface raced by as the shuttle angled toward the open cargo bay. A loud clang and a scraping of metal told him that the shuttle had landed.

The pilot floated off her chair and opened the clamps holding the stasis unit. Nick pushed the crash web off his body and held onto the seat's edge with one hand, while he grabbed the stasis capsule with the other.

The pilot's jet belt propelled them to the airlock. "Fred," she said to a round-faced man when they exited into the cargo bay. Her arms jerked as she released the stasis unit, and her speech was slurred. "Move the passengers out of the way and help me transfer the cargo."

Fred glared. "That's your job, Jael."

Face flushed and hands trembling, the woman turned away and activated a robosled.

Nick was certain that Jael had the bloom. He wanted to help her transfer the cargo, but Fred shoved him out of the way. Nick gagged as the unwashed smell of the man hit him.

Fred pointed a thumb at the corridor. "Horowitz, you stash the stasis unit, third door on the right. And don't come out until we're under way."

Nick negotiated the stasis unit along the narrow passage, bumping it against the bulkheads and cursing silently. What had he gotten himself into?

The cabin, a filthy box of three by three, had only a fold-up bunk; it was a tight fit for the stasis unit. He secured it with clamps to the opposite bulkhead, then folded the bunk down and lay down, pulled the battered crash web over his body and fell asleep.

Nick woke to a full bladder and the sound of discordant droning. By consulting his MemBrain, he saw that the ship was accelerating at 1.5 gees. After the Martian gravity, he felt like a lump of lead. He extricated himself from the bunk with an effort and stood, then ambled to the door and out into the corridor. Bare metal clanged under his boots as he walked to the lavatory. After he relieved himself, he decided to look around. He passed a small galley—grimy beyond belief—and stacked boxes in an open central area lined with storage lattices before he reached the bridge.

Nick found the door open and looked inside. Next to Fred and facing the command column, a gray-skinned man sat in the command couch. *So Captain Cardi is a Methoxy*, Nick thought. Some Belters were bioengineered to work on Titan's surface within a harvester, a minimal life-support bubble they used to harvest organics for food assembly. Nick hoped there were enough people left to tend the machines, otherwise they would be starving out there. The Captain's slightly enlarged cranium indicated that he had gone through the divergence, and the back of his hairless skull displayed two neuroports.

Fred turned. "Now look here, no wandering around the ship." He stood and rushed to the door, eyes shifting from Nick to the Captain.

"Fred, I thought you saw to the comfort of the passengers."

"Captain, I barely had time to stash the cargo before we took off." He motioned Nick to move. "I'll do it now." He sealed the door behind him and headed toward the galley.

Nick followed.

Fred stopped by the storage lattices. "Here," he said, and grabbed a handful of ration bars from a box. "The robochef broke, so you'll make do with these. Short on water, too." He gave Nick four one-liter bulbs. "After these, you're on recycled water. Keep the crash web on and stay in my . . . your cabin." Then he turned and stalked off, leaving his effluvia behind.

Nick returned to his cabin, Fred's cabin—no wonder the man hated his guts—and checked on Ann. The stasis capsule slowed the MemBrain growth considerably, giving him months to find a cure. He sank down on the bunk and pulled the crash web over his body.

Determined to puzzle out the statistics from Earth and the Moon, Nick displayed the data on his retinal screen. And there it was: over fifty percent survived the divergence, the highest percentage among the worlds and habitats of the Solar system. Most of the survivors were the very wealthy and the very poor, and ninety-eight percent of the middle class citizenry succumbed. Nick wondered what the wealthy and the poor had in common. He couldn't think of anything. Poor people on government dole had food, housing, and palliative medical care, but no luxuries like travel and health plan that included an immunite treatment. The middle class could afford decent health plan, entertainment, and some traveling; and the wealthy owned half the Earth and Clarke Station. While the ship accelerated and gravity pushed him into the filthy bunk, he used Ca-Nine to run every comparison he could think of.

Sometime later, a list of the health plan providers popped up: Cell Sense, ImmuGen, Omni Guard, Novi Clean. They were the best with extensive immunite shields—owned by a dozen Corpuscles, corporate muscles—and the majority of the victims had a plan with one of them. Of the people with any of those four plans, only a few hundred wealthy survived. The survival rate among people who used mediocre health plans was dismal, roughly the same as on the outer worlds. But people on dole survived the divergence.

None of it made sense, yet he kept coming back to these stats. The best health plans, Nick thought, Cell Sense, ImmuGen, Omni Guard, Novi Clean.

Novi Clean! He sat up suddenly. Sweat beaded his brows; Novi Clean had done Ann's immunite treatment back on Earth . . . and he had gotten a cheap one on Mars, one scarcely better than a series of vaccines. Ann had the bloom, and he had survived the divergence. Hope glimmered in his heart. It was possible that cellular treatments interfered with the divergence, and if so, the best treatment interfered so well that it killed people. That would explain why poor people on dole survived the divergence. But what about the few hundred super wealthy?

He started a search on those super wealthy, corporate muscles who owned pharmaceuticals, domed cities, and private armies. A short time later he saw that people connected with the Corpuscles survived the divergence. All of them. And if their product had a side effect that killed people, they would not want the public to know about it. *Private armies, mercenaries.* Nick shuddered as he recalled the news from Earth, mercenaries destroying dole tenements and research facilities.

Nick shook his head as a dreadful suspicion clouded his mind. Andre had been killed on Earth. Andre could have found a cure. Perhaps Andre had discovered something.

A plan began to emerge. He linked up with Coalnet, voice only, and called Arusi, Andre's wife living on the Moon. As he waited for the connection, his conviction that Andre's death was connected to the Corpuscles grew into certainty. Dread toyed with him. Andre had been brilliant and had the underground's protection, and yet the Corpuscles killed him. What chance did Nick have?

"Nick," Arusi said, her strong voice sounding tinny over the distance. "I'm glad to hear from you."

"Is everyone all right?"

"We're fine," Arusi said, though her voice sounded strained.

"Do you know what Andre was working on when he was killed?"

"No. He always worked on several things."

"He could've worked on a remedy. Could Ravi look into Andre's files?"

"There is no remedy. The divergence is evolution, a natural process."

"A facilitator, some activator molecule the survivors' genes code for and the victims' don't," Nick insisted.

Arusi sighed. "If he did, he would've been using a Demetrist program and I'm not privy to that info."

"Damn it, Arusi, people are dying. If Andre was working on a cure before he was killed, we need to know."

"What's going on?" Her voice trembled.

"I'd rather not discuss it on the open net."

"I'll see what I can do."

Nick woke to the crackling of the shipcom. Bangs and truncated expletives came from the bridge. ". . .can't get away. . ." He recognized Captain Cardi's voice, followed by the raucous laughter of Fred, thudding sounds, and cursing. Then Jael's hysterical voice. "Damn you, Fred, you shot him! That's not part of the agreement." More thudding sounds, then Fred's cursing, "Bastard turned on the shipcom—"

Without thinking, Nick sprung up from the bunk, unclamped the stasis unit, and activated its wheels underneath. He opened the door and peered out into the corridor. Under the 1.5 gee, the stasis unit was heavy but he manhandled it into the narrow space, heading away from the bridge. At every second, he expected a shot in the back. He pushed open a small door and looked inside. It contained a partially dismantled service robot, cables, and stacked containers.

He hurried to the next one, full of bulkhead pieces, small engine parts, and a couple of storage racks. Nick quickly moved some of the clutter to the other compartment and guided the stasis unit inside. Straining, he shifted it to an upright position and, with the cables lying around, he secured it to the storage rack. Then he moved a large plazoy plate in front of it. He stood still for a few seconds and listened. When there was no reaction to his activities, he picked up a metal pipe, peered into the corridor, and hurried back to his cabin. It occurred to him that he should go to the aid of the Captain, but instinct told him to stay put.

With shaking fingers, he pulled out the foam bomb from his pack. He bunched up the blanket on the bunk and covered it with the crash web. They would notice the missing stasis unit immediately, but he only needed a few moments. And loads of luck. Knees shaking, he gripped the pipe and moved behind the narrow door.

Fred's odor preceded him, followed by his footsteps. The door banged aside and, from a weapon held by an outstretched arm, shots pelted the bunk.

With all his might, Nick shoved the door against Fred. It produced a painful grunt. "Move back," he heard Fred say. Nick cracked the door open and listened, then tossed the bomb in the direction of Fred. Reacting with the molecules in air, the bomb exploded into a white gluey mess and expanded before it reached Fred, then Jael. The foam quickly covered an area of ten cubic meters, frothed and burbled, mingling with Fred's curses, as he fired a few stray shots before the foam hardened around his arms. Jael, with back turned, jerked her arm.

Nick was satisfied; they would stay put until someone cut them out. Panting from the adrenalin rush, he ran toward the bridge.

Captain Cardi was sprawled on the deck. Nick examined the small hole that had burned through the Captain's suit. The gray face was pale and clammy, and the small nostrils of the flat nose fluttered slightly. A touch to the neck revealed a faint pulse. Nick searched the cubbies and storage bins until he found a portable autodoc. Crouching next to the Captain, he activated it, then peeled the suit away and placed it on the leathery chest, over the injury. A small diagnostic screen sprung up above the quivering autodoc as it unfolded into a glittering blue and silver flower. Hair-thin gel sensors snaked out from its underside and attached to the Captain's temples and wrists, while hyaline membranes spread around the wound and sealed themselves to the skin.

Nick held his breath and waited. Reams of data appeared on the screen. Scorched tissues and a small nick showed on the cardiac membrane, which the autodoc began to repair. It administered immunites and bone welders to knit the punctured sternum and one rib.

Nick stood and looked at *Hecate*'s main screen. The ship was on autopilot, so he went back to check on the entombed crew. Fred snored loudly, head hanging. Jael was twitching, with her eyes rolled up and blood seeping from her ears. Nick ran back to the galley for a knife and began to hack at the foam. Guilt filled him; he knew Jael had the bloom, but he'd tried very hard to dismiss it. The foam parted under his hacking and he lifted Jael out. Her back arced and she went into a seizure. Nick held her, contemplating whether there was enough time to get the stasis capsule, when her body shuddered once and then stiffened. In a flood of shame and sorrow, he lowered Jael's lifeless body to floor. He could have saved her by taking Ann out of the stasis unit, if he had been willing to alternate their stay in there. But he was terrified of losing Ann.

Nick found a body bag and put Jael inside, then walked back to the bridge and sank into a formchair.

Hours later the Captain sat up and looked at his chest with the autodoc stuck to it. "Thank you," he said and tried to stand.

Nick helped him to his feet as a prerecorded message from Arusi arrived. He projected both the image and sound onto the bridge.

Arusi shook her head, eyes full of grief. "I have some news about what you asked. Come to Cratown and we'll talk. At any rate, you can't get a shuttle to Earth from Tycho City. The spaceport is closed. There's rioting and looting."

"Damn," the Captain said and slumped into the command couch. "My cargo is due at Tycho City." He brushed a gray hand over his skull. "I have to check the hold to see what Fred smuggled aboard."

Nick swallowed. "Your shuttle pilot . . . Jael. She died of the bloom."

The Captain's face stiffened. "What happened to Fred?" He leaned forward and plugged a feed into his neuroport.

"He's resting in solid foam."

Cardi nodded. "I should've never allowed Fred to run the *Hecate*, but since my wife and daughter died . . ."

"I'm sorry," Nick said, knowing how inadequate it sounded.

The Captain turned away, listening to the newsfeed. "Your friend is right." He waved a hand at a screen showing the images of moon cities. "There's chaos everywhere. We'll land in Cratown and see if my buyer can transport the cargo from there. Please secure your wife's capsule. We'll be landing soon."

Following Arusi, Nick negotiated the stasis capsule along the corridors of lower Cratown, passing over ramps and walkways crossing a manufactory chasm, silent and depopulated. Shadows lurked below. The few rising vehicles and swooping kites warmed his heart, a comforting sight amidst so much death. In the residential section, the massive walls and balconies carved into lunar rock and fused with carbon composites, cast sharp shadows.

"There's no shortage of housing now," Arusi said over her shoulder. "I got you a double unit near mine."

She pressed her palm to the sensor and the door opened. Nick pushed the stasis capsule inside and looked around the two-room unit.

Arusi turned to him. "Ravi took a shuttle to Earth after your call. You were right, Andre has been working on something related to the divergence, a series of deactivator enzymes. But all his work is gone." She wiped a tear off her face. "And someone's killing underground members. Mostly the scientists, but others too. Over thirty people disappeared on Earth. Like Andre."

"It's worse than I thought."

"And Nick," Arusi said and took a deep breath. "Legislator Walder is behind the Corpuscles. I couldn't tell you over the open net, but Ravi found evidence recently."

"The Earth Legislator." Nick nodded. "He's one of the biggest shareholders in Novi Clean." It made sense to help cover up the treatment's deadly side effects.

Arusi looked up at him, with a grim expression on her face. "Milan is showing early symptoms of the bloom." She started sobbing now, her small body shaking.

Nick held her, silently sharing her loss of Andre and dreading the possibility that Arusi could lose a son as well. He couldn't imagine losing Ann, but at least she was safe for now. Milan deserved a chance at survival. He knew Arusi couldn't bear another loss.

"We can alternate Ann and Milan in the stasis capsule."

A look of gratitude brightened Arusi's face. She put a hand on his arm. "Thank you, but Milan's not at that stage yet. Besides, he's coordinating the underground's effort to round up the Corpuscles."

Relief washed over him, followed by shame. He averted his eyes, quickly walking toward the desk and the bioanalyzer-replicator she had supplied.

"It's a closed system." Her voice took on an ominous tone. "And you must keep it closed. Ravi found an earlier version of Navagunjara in Andre's files. He slaved the replicator to Nava."

Nick stopped. "Not Nava, you can't connect a replicator to Nava." Andre had told him about Navagunjara, an evolving program that could easily become dangerous. Like the gods in Hindu mythology that he'd found so fascinating. Nava was a similator program that contained all the human sciences. And now feedstock to fabricate anything.

Arusi nodded, opened the door, and left.

Nick stood still, a shiver of fear passing through him. But there was no time to waste. He sank into a chair and activated the system. A hard screen lit up, displaying a chimera made up of several animals. The peacock head bobbed, its iridescent blue feathers contrasting sharply with the emerald scales of its snake tail.

"What can I do for you, Nick Horowitz?"

He did a double take, wondering what Andre had built into the program. Reluctantly, he inserted a data chip containing everything known about the divergence into the reader. "We need to disable people's immunite treatments. Start with the ones designed by Novi Clean."

"Analyses commenced," Nava said.

Nick watched the rows of data and the curlicues of protein and enzyme fragments folding and unfolding when Arusi reported that underground commandos had penetrated Walden's residence and took him into custody, along with another Corpuscle. He was relieved, but he was more interested if Navagunjara could do the task. Punishing the responsible parties could wait.

"This is the rd-105 gene." Nava projected an image on the screen. "It's part of the Reservoir DNAs, previously called noncoding DNAs. When it turns on, it starts orchestrating the brain growth, which is a complicated process."

"What about it?" Nick was impatient for Nava to get on.

"You were right. Soon after the rd-105 turns on, it's messages and functions are sabotaged by the cellular treatment. To the immunites, the process of the divergence is the same as illness: cancer, encephalitis, cranial osteoporosis, neuron growth, accelerated stem cell production, etc."

"We need to disable the immunites." Nick was almost shouting.

"I will need another two hours and sixteen minutes to design the bionts to disable the Novi Clean immunites. I can start replicating the nanites while I work on the other types of health plans. But you do realize that I cannot replicate enough for billions of people."

Nick watched the diagnostic screen showing the stasis field counting down to zero. The unit split in the center and folded aside, revealing Ann's face framed within golden hair. For a moment, Jael's contorted features superimposed upon those of his wife. The memory of Jael's death filled him with shame, but at least Milan would be saved now, as well as other people. Ann's eyes fluttered open, eyebrows notched, one hand brushing her forehead. "Nick?"

"I'm here." He helped her sit up, and with the stasis unit between them, embraced her awkwardly.

Blue eyes regarded him for a second. "I knew you would find a way."

He grinned. Ann's confidence in him ran deeper than his own, but it didn't alleviate his worries that she be would the test subject. Hand trembling, he stuck the patch to her temple, with micro needles and a capsule containing the nanites that would neutralize her immunites.

Nick was checking on the net for the number of facilities on Earth that had started replicating the neutranites when Ravi's image appeared on his holoscreen. "Walder is awake now," Ravi said.

Ann and Arusi looked up, as well as Captain Cardi and two other Belters present, staring at the image of an angry Walder.

"You won't get away with this," Walder said. "My men will find this shithole." He glared, his hand gingerly touching a purple bruise on his face.

Nick saw that Walder had survived the divergence. He hated the man for murdering Andre and countless other people, but he forced himself to be civil. "Your secret is out. By now it's all over Coalnet that you and other Corpuscles tried to suppress the side effects of your immune treatments. The templates for the deactivator enzymes to neutralize the treatments are all over the net." He couldn't help smiling. "Unfortunately for you, the underground is holding you until you can stand trial. Now, I'm sure it would mitigate your sentence for your crimes against Humanity if you called off the rampages of the Corpuscles."

Walder shook his head. "I can't influence private armies."

Ravi snorted, then transmitted the images underground agents had acquired of Walder's secret meetings with several other corporate muscles. "The CEOs of Omni Guard and CellSense have already given us statements," he said. "They'll testify that you'd pressured them into this scheme. And we have proof that it was

Novi Clean's cellular treatment that works the best to block the necessary process of the divergence. For that, billions died."

Walder's jaw dropped. "Fuck you."

Ravi sneered. "You'll rot in prison for the rest of your life."

Walder looked down, then up, a hopeful gleam in his eyes. "Look, we'll breed ourselves into extinction by allowing everyone to survive. It's a good opportunity to thin out the population."

Ravi sucked in his breath, Arusi glared at Walder, and Ann looked down at her hand.

Nick wanted to launch himself into the holoscreen and strangle the man.

Walder shrugged. "If you waste time treating everyone, you won't have time for anything worthwhile. Imagine what scientists could achieve with this new MemBrain." He tapped his head. "It's far superior to any augment designed so far. Maybe scientists could find a way around the light speed barrier, and we can start colonizing extra-solar planets. We should keep it for the deserving."

"And you would determine who's deserving," Arusi said.

Nick shot to his feet and released his balled fists. "If you stop the Corpuscles, you may get a reduced sentence."

"I can't help you," Walder said.

With a grim set to his mouth, Nick faced Ravi's image. "Make sure the underground holds him until his trial."

"Will do," Ravi said. "And don't worry, Nick, we'll make this work. Milan is coming to Earth to help set up more replicators, and the underground is mobilized to distribute the neutranite."

Arusi flashed him a proud smile, and Nick nodded. "We're counting on you, Ravi."

As the *Hecate* accelerated away from the inner system, Nick stared at the screen that showed the diminishing Earth and Moon.

Ann smiled. "We're going home."

Captain Cardi patted the instrument panel facing him. "With a full larder."

They were en route to Mars with a payload of food, hopefully enough to ensure the colony's survival until food production could be restored. Belter ships had left to Ceres, Vesta, Hygiena, Egeria, Psyche, Juno, Titan Station, and to the smaller settlements of the various asteroids. Arusi, with the help of others, oversaw the replication and distribution of the neutranite in Cratown and in other cities on the moon.

Ann yawned and moved her couch closer, taking his hand. He squeezed the long fingers gently. She slept a lot nowadays, like he used to during the development of his MemBrain, but the pressure and pain in her cranium had stopped.

Nick tried not to think about Nava, whether it had somehow copied parts of itself into the neutranite's template to propagate. It would be all over Coalnet now, and as a Demetrist program, it would evolve. He shuddered at the thought and dismissed it for now, but he would have to be vigilant.

Author's note: In my novels, I didn't want future humans to rely on artificial intelligence alone, so I'd decided that evolution would help us along a bit. I do believe that the Human species is still evolving, and so Divergence came about when I was working out the back-story for my novels. The story is set forty years before *The Covert Files* series. I'm currently working on *Fragments*, book one in the series.

A Fistful of Tassels

SPORE-SATURATED RAIN PELTED Ataki's naked skin. The deluge bent the fronds of stink trees, mold-furred bulbs brushing his head as he passed under them to reach a cluster of pearl berries. Among all the tribal duties, scouting was his favourite, hiding near a drop site and waiting for the prisoner pod to splash onto the world. He enjoyed following the fresh ones, observing them, and reporting their actions to Ghost Eli. As a tribe leader, Ghost Eli decided if they would adopt fresh prisoners and offer them survival.

Ataki sighed. He had learned his name the day his mother died, eaten by the canibs when he was sixteen years old. Though his mother, Raken, had been a convicted mass murderer sentenced to Spore, he missed her. Secretly, he wished to find someone like her and offer the gift of life. Alas, most of the fresh ones were too violent, so Ataki watched from a safe distance.

After hours crouching under a dragonstool, hunger drove him from safety. He quickly gobbled mouthfuls of pearl berries.

A gurgling sound reached him, followed by mangled words and a chorus of whistling breaths. Ataki froze, his mouth stained with pearlescent powder and ears straining toward the faint sounds muffled by the rain. Several feet moved in the luminescent undergrowth, squishing fungi. But it was not a solfant, the solitary animal with eight massive legs. Ataki unfurled his nose cilia, scenting the air for the fetid reek of canibs, but there was nothing save the pungent fungal growth around him. He realized his mistake when a few seconds later a herd of gracers burst from the forest, followed by a nose-shrivelling stench.

A hiss cut through the drumming rain as a volley of bone flechettes sliced the air. Ataki dove into a purple dragonstool, its spongy flesh parting around his body with a wet thump. He held his breath while his sharp claws dug deeper into the giant fungus, conical cap trembling from his invasion. He clawed himself into the softer trunk and made a small gash.

Carefully, he peered through. Naked canibs surrounded a couple of quivering gracers, their eight legs twitching, graceful bodies leaking burgundy body fluids. The canibs howled and shoved at each other, eyes full of bloodlust. They all sported several fungal infections; some in neon colors oozing blood and pus, and others furry molds that sucked the moisture out of flesh until the body shrivelled up. Clawless hands jerked and bloated heads bobbed with palsy, as they began hacking the coral skin of the gracers. They all grasped blowguns or bone knives. Fortunately the canibs didn't live long; otherwise, they would hunt all the symbs, dapters, and fresh ones to extinction. Although canibs had poor hearing, Ataki dared not move. He watched them eating parts of one gracer while still alive. After they couldn't eat anymore, they shouldered the rest of the bloody meat and moved off.

The canibs were a fair distance away when a red light wounded the sky. Unlike the even light of Baleful, this was piercing, followed by the loudest noise he had ever heard. A solid, dark object filled the centre of the light. Ataki watched the apparition as it cut a swath through the stink trees, pearl berry bushes, and creeper crapes. It left behind an oily trail of fumes and slid, screeching. Screams and curses were cutoff abruptly as several fleeing canibs were crushed beneath the object's path.

Ataki knew it was not a prisoner pod: those were olive green and made of vegetal matter—whatever that was—and they were never accompanied by world blood, the liquid fire that bubbled up at places on Spore. Through gray steam, he glimpsed a large, reddish-black mound, sizzling and sputtering as the rain hit its stone skin. He listened and, when there were no sounds from the canibs, he crawled out of his shelter. Despite the astringent odour wafting from the alien intruder, Ataki felt no fear approaching it.

When he was only a few metres away, he heard moaning. He parted the yellow shroon canopy cautiously and peered beneath its spongy petals.

And jumped back.

A canib glared at him, her arms scorched and one leg twisted at an odd angle. Blood seeped from the leg wound, bone poking through the skin.

"I'm Kate," the woman said in a hoarse voice. "I'm not going to hurt you, little dapter. That's what you are, aren't you?" She threw back her head and laughed, exposing missing teeth and swollen gums. It seemed more like a painful hacking, and a trickle of blood ran down her chin. "But I can see why others would. You're ugly as sin."

Ataki stared at her, speechless. Unlike fresh ones and canibs, dapters didn't kill people, but he felt a stirring of anger. He knew he was ugly compared to the fresh ones, tall and smooth-skinned with their different colored hair, but it was wrong of her to insult him. She seemed in the first stages of putrefaction, barely a canib. She could be dangerous.

Raken had told him these people were all psychopaths, ruthless killers that would eat him if they caught him. Or they would just simply murder him for the pleasure of it. He recalled his mother's words: *'It's not really the capacity to do evil that sets the Spore convicts apart from other people, most people have that in them, but rather that we're incapable of feeling any remorse afterward. We never feel remorse; we're psychopaths.'*

Perhaps he had always entertained more hope for Humans than Raken ever had, because despite Kate's ill-mannered nature, his heart constricted at the sight of her injuries. It didn't help that she reminded him a little of Raken. Same pale skin, and black hair hanging in limpets on her bare shoulders.

He swallowed and looked around, afraid there might be other canibs lying in wait to snatch him.

"I think they're all dead."

He nodded, feeling a twinge of shame for his relief. "I'm Ataki, Raken's son. I can't carry you to safety."

"No, I didn't think you could." She tilted her head and squinted. "Heard about Raken."

He shuffled from one foot to another, uncertain whether to feel proud or embarrassed. Raken had freely admitted that she was the worst of the worst, but fresh ones and canibs remembered her as brilliant and fierce, one that had survived the longest without anyone's help.

"Do you have trocar tassels?"

Ataki knew he shouldn't give her any without Ghost Eli's permission, and besides, the trocar probably wouldn't help her, judging by the patches of spore-rot on her skin, but he pulled a fistful of purple tassels from his gracer-hide pouch and offered her half. "I need the rest for the fresh ones." He pointed toward the drop-off site.

Kate eagerly crammed the entire fistful into her mouth, but once she began to chew, her face crumpled into an expression of disgust. "Tastes awful," she choked out, but swallowed it. "Let's wait until the ship cools and see if anyone survived. In a crash landing there's always a chance someone might have. Don't be afraid, they're not murderers. And they'll have autodocs that would work for hours, until this planet of yours ruins them."

So it was *a ship*. Raken had told him about ships and autodocs.

Kate curled up and slept fitfully. Ataki crouched near her but made sure he was out of arm's reach. The cold rain fell relentlessly, and it took less than an hour for the ship to cool.

Kate woke up and groaned. She surveyed her surroundings with weary eyes. "Go now, but be careful of the jagged edges. They can cut even your tough hide. That round eye below the crack is an airlock, a door. You must try to open it."

Ataki approached the damaged ship, watching for movements of canibs that the noise of the crash would certainly attract. Black water ran in rivulets under his feet, carrying ash and scorched detritus from the ship. He stopped and looked up, searching for a suitable purchase among the protruding lumps of hard stuff. A flat surface stuck out below the cracked side, but it was too high. Ataki walked back a few metres, then ran toward the ship and jumped up to grab the flat triangle. He pulled himself up and surveyed the curving hide of the ship. Holding onto a twisted rod, he carefully stood up and peered through the airlock. A flat plate with markings was set into the circular metal rim, with a cluster of symbols. He began to press the symbols at random. When the airlock hissed, he snatched his hand back.

Now what? He looked back at Kate.

"Pull it toward you," she shouted. "And once you go through, see if anyone's alive."

He nodded and followed her instructions.

Inside he found a hard floor. Yellow light and a peculiar odour greeted him. He fluttered his nose cilia and started to walk in the tube, more regular than the tube trees in which his Tribe lived. Alien detritus cluttered the floor. Some spat sparks like exploding smog bugs, others were thorny and glittering. A curling haze surrounded the entire mess. Minding Kate's warning, he avoided stepping on them.

A loud clang startled him. He jumped back and cried out as a sharp piece of wreckage stabbed his arm. Blood welled up and trickled down his forearm. Ataki wiped it with his fingers and cursed his stupidity.

After a few turns, a down-sloping tube led him to a large central chamber. A man slumped in a weird contraption he recognized as a chair. One of the man's arm hung limp, face a bloody bruise. Ataki rushed to the man and touched his neck, relieved when he felt a pulse. *An innocent, someone who hadn't murdered anyone.* A warm feeling fluttered in his chest, but he worried that the man might die of his injuries.

The ship creaked and shifted. He grabbed the arm of the chair and wished the man would wake up.

Gingerly, he shook the large body. "Wake up, please. We must leave the ship before the canibs come." His voice sounded strange in the enclosed area. He waited and then shook the man again. "The canibs will eat us," he said louder.

One of the man's eyes opened and looked around with a dazed expression. His other eye was shut and covered in dry blood. Finally, a sound came out, "Whassit?"

"I'm Ataki, son of Raken. Can you stand up?"

The man moved a little, his hands fluttering above the web-like thing covering his body. Ataki wedged his fingers under the web and lifted. He jumped when it sprang up. The man sat up and coughed, then buried his face in his hand and groaned.

After a short while, the man looked up and said, "My name is Jon. I can barely understand you."

Ataki swallowed. He recalled Raken's speech lessons. *'You will repeat after me,' his mother had said. 'Diversity of Mycota and related fauna on Spore is roughly ten percent of the Earth's Eumycota species. Yet, ninety-five percent of that ten percent is lethal to humans.'* When Ataki had repeated the words garbled, Raken slapped him. *'You will speak properly. Place the tip of your tongue to the top of your upper gum, thus.'* She had pried his lips open and positioned his tongue in the correct way. *'You will do that when you pronounce the hard sounds like 'd' and 't'. And pay attention, you little dung maggot.'*

Ataki looked at Jon now and detected fear in his eyes. He quickly retracted his nose cilia, knowing how unsightly they were to fresh ones. Then he ran his tongue around his toothless gums and tried again, slower this time. "I am a dapter, born on this world and I have no teeth. Can you understand me now?"

Jon nodded and stood up, swayed, then grabbed an intricate hard shell covering the front of his chair. Ataki rushed to his side and offered his small body to lean on. Together, they staggered to a wall and Jon opened a flat surface. He rooted inside and withdrew something that looked like a handbug but larger and with more legs.

"An autodoc," Jon said. He pulled up the cloth covering his limp arm and placed it on his bare skin.

The autodoc unfurled like an infant gorgon and sprouted pseudo-cilia, fastening them to Jon's flesh. It then extended a sheet of light similar to Baleful. Squiggles appeared on the shimmering surface. Ataki knew the squiggles were writing; he recognized a few individual letters.

Jon gave a relieved sigh and straightened up. "Medchines," he said and pointed to the autodoc.

"Medical equipment?"

Jon nodded, walked to his chair, and slumped into it. "The pain is gone now, and the bone welder is knitting the break." The autodoc undulated on his arm and made swishing sounds.

Ataki followed and removed the trocar tassels from his waist pouch and offered it to Jon. "You must eat this if you want to live."

Jon frowned but didn't take the tassels.

"I'm on scout duty, watching for the prisoner pods. My tribe offers these to some fresh ones." The tassels hung from a bulbous oval cap, staining his hands purple. "It's a symbiont micro fungus, and it enables people to survive on Spore."

Jon accepted the trocar and put a few tassels in his mouth. His eyes watered as he chewed. "Bitter," he said and ate the rest. "Thank you."

"We must leave your ship. The canibs could be here any moment. They'll eat us both. If you have another autodoc, please bring it. There's an injured woman outside."

"I must unload some supplies."

"Not worth lugging them. The microorganisms on Spore will render everything useless in a few days."

Ataki liked the shaggy tan hair on Jon's head, and the blue eyes that didn't cringe at the sight of him. The man looked just as pleasing to the eyes as his mother had. Raken had pale lavender skin after the trocar had transformed her, and only a few missing teeth. Despite his rough childhood, shoved and cursed at, he missed Raken's grudging protection and caring.

"You keep mentioning canibs," Jon said. "Who are they?"

"They used to be people. Their bodies rot from the invading spores. Canibs either never found trocar tassels or the transformation didn't take. They're generally the most ferocious of the criminals."

"And they're cannibals," Jon added.

Ataki nodded, and refrained from telling him that he was one too. After Raken had killed Fred, his father, they had eaten him. Fred had been a heavy-worlder, strong as two solfants, and he'd raped Raken. Fred's moods had ranged from sadistic to murderous rage. One day, while Fred had been beating Ataki, Raken stabbed him. Although Ataki had hated Fred and was glad the beatings had stopped, he felt ashamed of doing the same thing the canibs did.

He shook his head to clear away the unpleasant memories. "We should go."

"All right." Jon stood up and walked to the hole in the wall. He removed a sticky twine and wrapped it around his injured arm. "I don't want to jar the autodoc loose." Then he took out another autodoc and handed it to Ataki. "How far is the airlock from the ground?"

"Not too far," Ataki said, following Jon out of the chamber. They walked through the convoluted tubes and reached the airlock. Water pooled on the floor of the small compartment. They sloshed through and exited, then stepped onto the flat surface and jumped down, Ataki clutching the autodoc to his chest.

Phosphorescent green and violet emanated from the fungi jungle, seen through a sheet of pewter water.

Jon groaned, looking around. "Hell might be preferable to this."

"About time you came out," Kate said. She was leaning against the trunks of weeping grape trees and, as soon as Ataki moved into her reach, she snatched the autodoc from him. She fastened it to her injured leg, then dropped to all fours and scuttled away from the derelict ship. "Hurry, I heard canibs."

Ataki refrained from pointing out that she had been with the attacking canibs.

"Nice to meet you, too," Jon said, following her. "I'm Jon."

"No time for niceties."

"Her name is Kate," Ataki whispered. "Mind the gorgon!" He shoved Jon away from a turquoise tendril whipping out from a large boulder they had passed. His heart pounded at the thought of Jon dying so quickly. "It has poison barbs that paralyze you, and then . . ." He pointed to the pulsing bladder squatting at the base of the rock, carmine slit opening at the scent of prey. "The stationary fungi are the most dangerous because they kill you fast."

Jon shuddered at the sight of the gorgon and followed Kate silently, eyes casting left and right. A group of fur rugs undulated under a large shroon canopy, and Ataki considered catching one for Jon to sleep on, but the reek of the approaching canibs dissuaded him. There'd be time enough. If need be, he'd offer Jon his own fur rug. For some reason he couldn't fathom, he wanted very much for this man to survive Spore.

They rounded a large jelly swamp, quivering from the pelting rain and glistening green with unseen life.

After an hour of walking and crawling, Kate stopped and leaned against a pearl berry bush. She removed the autodoc from her leg and attached it to her injured arm. "It'll take a while for the bone welder. I'm sure you want to go on."

A frown notched Jon's brow. "No, we'll wait for you." He sat next to Kate, removed his autodoc from his arm, and placed it on his chest. "Broken rib," he said, wincing.

Kate grabbed a fistful of pearl berries and began to munch on them, smearing the pale shimmering powder of the berries on her lips. "Eat some," she said to Jon, grinning.

Ataki was uncertain what he should do next. He knew that Ghost Eli wouldn't allow Kate to join the Tribe without knowing first if she could be trusted. The Tribe had a full crèche, nine infant dapters. Though he disliked crèche duty, he didn't want anyone to harm them.

Three days later Tom died, another symb whose symbiosis had failed. The hunters had thrown his body into the ocean, a custom developed by the Tribe to prevent the canibs from eating the bodies.

Forty-one Tribe members, their subdued faces in shades of lavender and purple, surrounded Ghost Eli and Kate. Ataki stood beside Jon, grateful that Ghost Eli had assigned him to teach the newest member survival skills. His respect had grown for Jon, a quick learner who never complained, even when Ataki detected despair in his expression. He tried to hide his own fear, that the symbiosis might not take, that Jon could die.

They were in one of the large air bubbles of the tube tree—though tree was a misnomer, for it was a gigantic fungus with hundreds of tubes leading to spherical chambers. Ghost Eli's pale face shone in the lime bioluminescent organisms sticking to the inner wall in patches. Her tall figure ramrod straight, she regarded Kate with appraising eyes for a long time. The dapters and symbs waited for her pronouncements, shuffling around impatiently. Ghost Eli was like Raken but old, another pale-skinned criminal that had survived the trocar symbiosis. Ataki was glad that the Tribe had accepted Jon immediately. Kate, however, had been waiting at the foot of the tree until finally Ghost Eli called for her.

"You'll be on trial and you'll be watched, Kate," Ghost Eli said. Soft-spoken words belied the flash of warning in her black eyes. Her paleness became more pronounced as her large, flat moles turned a darker shade of lavender. "I'm assigning you hunting and gathering duty, and perhaps later you'll earn sentry duty. But you will stay clear of the crèche at all times."

Kate nodded with a relieved expression. "I understand. Thank you." She'd been eating trocar tassels that Ataki had taken out for her while she waited, and her progression into canib seemed to have stopped.

"Go with Simon and Lea to gather geosticks." Ghost Eli pointed to a tall symb of purple skin and a paler dapter female.

"Let's go," Simon said. "We want to return before sunrise."

Kate and Lea followed him to the lip of a tube and all three disappeared from sight.

"And you, Ataki," Ghost Eli said. "Show Jon the lookout before Baleful rises. There's not enough time to sleep anyway."

"I'll be glad to." Ataki gave Ghost Eli a toothless smile and motioned Jon to follow him.

He first went to a carved indentation in the chamber wall, removed his only remaining geostick meat, and handed it to Jon. "Eating animal meat will help you survive the trocar symbiosis."

They were low on stored food, and until the gatherers and hunters brought in more, the adults would have to ration.

"Have you eaten?"

"Yes, while you slept," Ataki lied, cursing his growling stomach.

Jon frowned, and to distract him, Ataki explained, "Geosticks are made of eight rods that can form different geometric shapes depending on what the creatures need to feed and move. They live in the higher branches of some fungi. You may remove up to two sticks from each geostick without killing it. They can re-grow two, but take more and they'll die."

Jon stared at the rubbery, orange stick. "What I would give for fire." He took a small bite of the raw meat.

Ataki understood. Raken had always cursed the lack of fire.

They entered an upward slanting tube and quickly climbed the cut steps at the center that connected to another chamber. On impulse, Ataki led Jon to a hole in the tube. He put a finger on his lips and whispered, "That's the crèche."

The infants in the other chamber crawled on fur rugs. Holding the hand of a dapter woman, one child took a few wobbly steps.

"They're so tiny, and some of them are walking," Jon said.

"Dapters are smaller than humans or symbs."

Jon looked at him and smiled. "How old are you?"

"Twenty-six and a half."

"That's about thirteen standards."

Ataki nodded. They left the antechamber of the crèche and entered another tube. Pale green tube slugs crawled upward on the rough surface of the cavity, transporting nutrients to the upper chambers. Darker green ones slithered down and carried waste products from the tubes to the ground.

Ataki grabbed a climbing tube slug and ate it. "You only eat the pale green ones," he said. "The dark ones carry toxins down to the ground."

Jon reached for a tube slug with a shaking hand. He grabbed the squirming thing and closed his eyes as he put it into his mouth, throat convulsing in the effort of swallowing. He opened his eyes and blinked. "Tastes a bit like oyster."

At the top of the tree they exited through a narrow opening. Ataki lent a hand to Jon, who seemed to flounder on the slippery red surface.

"This is big." Jon surveyed the top of the tree. "Looks about ninety metres diameter."

"Roughly," Ataki said. "There are bigger tube trees, and we'll have to move once the infants grow up a bit. A tree of this size can support about fifty people at most." He waved to Tim, patrolling the perimeter and watching for canibs.

They approached the edge carefully. The rain had stopped to a drizzle and visibility improved. Color exploded under the pearly mist, reds, yellows, blues, purples, and greens in every shade and hue.

"Beautiful," Jon whispered.

Ataki felt his throat constrict. As far as he knew, Jon was the only person who ended up on Spore by misfortune rather than by committing murder. Yet, he found this killer world beautiful.

Jon leaned over suddenly and vomited over the edge. The drizzle sluiced the green vomit off, and he straightened up, wiping his mouth on the decomposing sleeve of his coverall.

Ataki's stomach clenched with fear. Jon had vomited twice during the three days he'd been on Spore. His autodoc had stopped working after ten hours, so there would be no more medchines. Jon staggered toward the tube they had come through and sank down onto the surface. Ataki followed and did likewise.

Jon seemed thoughtful, furrowing his eyebrows. "Tell me about the trocar symbiosis."

"Emilio Trocar, a biologist, found the tassels—"

"I heard about him," Jon interrupted. "Trocar killed an entire colony by experimenting on people. It happened centuries ago, but spacers remember because the world is still quarantined. He used alien nanotech."

"That's him. About three-and-a-half centuries ago, Trocar was sentenced to Spore. After the dissolution of his vegpod, he watched the animals and discovered that they all consumed large quantities of a certain fungus. He started doing the same and became the first man to survive on Spore. For longer than four local years, that is."

"And the Coalition doesn't know people are doing it." Jon stared before him, shaking his head.

"Raken told me their bio scanners are set to human standards. Dapters and symbs have lower body temperature, so the scanners might take us for local life, which I suppose we are."

"I guess I'm not transformed yet because I'm cold." Jon's clothing was peeling off in sections. "Useless," he said, and began to brush off the remnants of his coverall, smearing blue fungi-infested fabric on his body.

Ataki nodded. "Darker-skinned people have a better chance to absorb the symbiont—something to do with melanin—but that's not the only crucial genetic marker. Trocar didn't know what the other factors were without equipment to test his theories, but the fact that some pale-skinned people like my mother and Ghost Eli survived proves him correct. By watching and interviewing the survivors, Trocar concluded that people must have a certain mindset: high level of adaptability, sheer will power, and the firm belief that a mere planet is not going to kill them." He stopped and looked at Jon expectantly. Did he have these abilities? He wished Raken had taught him how to pray.

Perhaps Jon detected his anxiety, because he said, "Have no doubt, I'll get through this."

Relief flooded Ataki. "You never told me why you landed on Spore."

A flicker of anger crossed Jon's eyes. "I was shot at near the moon. My sensors couldn't identify the ship that fired at me. After I lost the main engine, I turned on the auxiliary engine and burned tail. That's when two more shots hit us. One breached the outer hull, and the other one took out the small tokamak."

A scream rent the air. Kate burst through a tube, pivoted, and kicked Jon in the chest.

They both sprung up. Jon pushed Ataki behind him, fending off Kate with one arm.

"Don't hurt him, Kate!" Ataki shouted. "We're your friends."

Kate stopped and looked at them, and for a second, her expression seemed to clear of the madness. Tim arrived, shaking his head. Kate's limbs were twitching, lashing out on their own. Her mouth began to foam. She let out a keening sound and started running toward the edge of the tree, stopped and looked back at them, then she threw herself off the top.

They ran, reached the edge, and looked down.

Jon panted. "What . . . Why would she do that?"

Ataki was trembling. He had seen only one case of the monk madness, and that person had killed two tribe members.

Tim was still shaking his head. "She started on the trocar tassels too late, when she was already in the rot stage. I'm sure she ate monk meat."

Jon looked from Tim to Ataki, so he explained, "Monks are animals that look like brown hooded cloaks. We never eat them because the meat causes madness."

"Poor Kate," Jon said and walked away..

Ataki agreed. Despite having attacked Jon, in the end Kate had chosen to take her life rather than hurting them.

"Jon, I'll make you a knife." From the cubby, Ataki removed a slightly curved, flat gracer bone, one of the ribs of the creature, and headed for a down-sloping tube.

"Why aren't you carrying one?" Jon asked after they exited the tube.

"Only adults are allowed to carry weapons. Perhaps another two years and I can go with the hunters. Raken made a knife for me, but Ghost Eli has it in safekeeping."

"What happens when canibs attack?"

"I run." He pointed to his nose cilia. "I smell them from a distance."

They wove their way through thick spongy trunks of stink trees and weeping grape trees, and walked over the bodies of slow-migrating fungi under the pelting rain, looking out for canibs. Popping sounds came from above. Ataki stopped and pointed up the tree. "Geosticks," he said. "Can you reach them?"

Jon jumped up and grabbed one of the creatures. It squirmed in his hand and quickly rearranged itself into another geometric shape, then sprung away, leaving one of its sticks and taking the rest of its body parts high up into the tree. Jon handed him the quivering stick, and Ataki bit off a piece.

"Catch another one and remove two sticks," he said.

Jon caught four more and removed two limbs from each creature before he allowed them to escape. He stashed the sticks into his gracer-hide pouch and bit into one. "Tastes like musty rubber."

"They contain lots of protean," Ataki said, chewing with his hardened gums.

"You mean protein." Jon laughed.

Ataki joined him and didn't feel embarrassed about garbling the words. They followed the usual path in a companionable silence for a while. He steered away from the trail of a gunk worm and they soon arrived at the shore.

Ocean and rain blended into a gray mist. Ataki crouched down and, using his sharp claws, dug away the fleshy chunks of ground fungi, exposing charcoal rock.

"Looks like basalt," Jon said and squatted next to him.

"The bones of Spore," Ataki said. On a rough, jagged surface, he began to pull the gracer rib back and forth, carefully angling the edge of the flat plane just right, the way he had seen Raken do. "The stone extends all the way down to the seabed. There are five islands similar to ours. All have drop-off sites, so they must have people."

"I suppose Raken told you that." Jon smiled and extended his hand for the bone. "I'll take over now, but thank you for showing me."

Ataki gave him the emerging knife and placed his rump on a slab of fungus. "Yes, Raken taught me much."

"She taught you to speak well."

"Thank you. She was very smart." Ataki swallowed the lump in his throat. His unquenchable thirst for knowledge had led to many questions, which sometimes earned him a smack when Raken was too tired to answer him. But she had never grown tired of exploring. She had shown him several paths leading to the Tribe's tube tree. Many times they had huddled under a dragon stool and observed the Tribe from a distance. *'We could join them but we won't,'* Raken had said once. *'For one thing, I don't relish people judging me whether I'm worthy or not. And for another, I hate people.'* Ataki had found the communal life of the Tribe appealing, but he knew it was futile to ask Raken to reconsider.

"What's that smell?" Jon sniffed, squinting through a spray of floral scent coming from the ocean.

"Croc kelps," Ataki said and pointed to the black undulating tentacles in the water. "They're mating."

"I've never smelled anything so pleasant." Jon stood up and started toward the rocky edge, the half-finished knife in his hand.

"Keep back." Ataki pulled him away from the ledge. "The water's deep here, and a tentacle could reach us."

Suddenly, the toadstools exploded behind them. Chunks of purple and yellow fungi flew through the air as three canibs burst through.

Jon whirled, one hand slashing in a wide arc, while the other one pushed Ataki behind him. The foremost of the canibs fell bleeding and writhing on the fungi. Another one stumbled on a rotting foot, and his bone knife caught Jon's arm. The skin parted and blood flowed.

Ataki whimpered and cowered behind his protector as knives slashed around.

John shoved the limping canib into a row of stink trees and slashed at the other one. The canib fell, arms wheeling, and smacked Jon in the knees. Jon's bone knife clattered to the stone, and Jon fell back into the ocean.

"No!" Ataki screamed. He crawled to the edge and looked down. The water began to churn, floral-scented sprays splashing his face.

Heart in his throat, Ataki picked up the knife and stood up. With his eyes on one of the canibs trying to stand, Ataki ran to the dead ones. He grabbed one of the bodies by the hands and pulled it to the edge, then shoved it in the water. Black tentacles whipped up, thicker than his body. *Would it be enough to distract the croc kelps?* His tears mingling with the rain, he ran back for the other dead canib.

The limping canib staggered into his path, swaying and yelling through a mouth covered in scabrous growths. Ataki stiffened, hand on Jon's knife, his flight instinct paralyzed by the need to save his friend. Even if Jon could swim, how long could he avoid the tentacles?

With an anger that rivalled Raken's, he stepped back a pace, feigned left, then buried the knife under the canib's ribs. Before his attacker reached the ground, he shoved hard. He ran to where Jon fell, yelling his name. Leaning over the ledge, he scanned the surface of the water, ropy tentacles lashing around.

"Jon," he sobbed, wishing he could swim.

"Here," he heard a sputter. A hand appeared on the stone ledge, then another.

Ataki buried his toe claws into ground fungi, grabbed the wrists, and pulled with all his might. Jon's head appeared. Ataki pulled harder and felt his toes slipping. A shoulder and an arm heaved out of the water, one hand grabbing the rough stone. Ataki gave a final yank and Jon emerged fully. Just as they were crawling away from the edge, a black tentacle whipped by and smacked Jon's legs.

For two days, Jon had lain feverish from the croc kelp toxin. Though the injury on his arm was healing, he had vomited several times. Ataki kept feeding him trocar tassels, hoping the symbiont would counteract the toxin.

He listened to Jon's snoring, and it reminded him of his mother. Raken always snored. She had slept with her body wrapped around his, for warmth and for protection. Tears stung his eye. The people who protected him paid a price, Raken with her life, and now Jon. He didn't want the big man to die, like Raken.

One night while they had huddled under a shroon canopy, Raken whispered to him, *'If I ever become incapacitated and can't walk, you must run to the Tribe.'*

Ataki had protested and received a cuff on his head.

'You'll run, you little dung maggot.'

There was only one thing Ataki resented. Not the smacks and reprimands, but that Raken had refused to join the Tribe. Ghost Eli would have accepted them, and then Raken would be alive now.

He closed his eyes and tried to sleep, but Raken's face, just before she had been killed, intruded.

They were running ahead of canibs when a solitary fresh one rose and grabbed Ataki.

Raken whirled, her arms a blur, and buried her long knife in the man's chest. He staggered and fell against a stink tree. Raken pulled out her knife from the body of their attacker and grabbed Ataki's arm roughly. *'Don't lag behind.'*

By then, the canibs were close, preceded by their obscene miasma. One barely into the rot stage tackled Raken. She sprang up, stabbed the canib, and backed toward the trees, pushing Ataki behind her. Four of them surrounded her. Raken brandished both of her long knives and stabbed one, but another one got under her left arm and buried his knife into her ribs. She staggered, blood flowing down her side and mingling with the rain. Her arms slashed left and right as she said breathlessly, *'Run, little dung maggot, run to the Tribe.'* She wounded three of the canibs, and they lurched away, but the fourth one eyed her warily from a short distance.

Raken circled around the tree trunk, pulling Ataki behind her. *'I told you to run!'*

'I'm not leaving you.'

'Your name is Ataki, son of Raken, and you will run.' She shoved him in the direction of the Tribe.

He turned back and saw her stumble. She recovered her balance and ran in the opposite direction, toward the remaining canibs, yelling curses at them. The trail of blood she had left behind turned into wisps of brown by the rain.

He had turned and ran, tears washing down his face.

Ataki was curled up on his side and sniffled, as always when he remembered the last moments of her life. He wiped his face with an angry motion and tried to lay still.

A hand descended on his shoulder. "You must miss her," Jon whispered, face lit by the bioluminescent fungi.

"Your fever broke." Ataki sat up and peered at Jon's face cautiously, afraid to hope. He was gaunt but his eyes had lost their glazed look, and his skin had a lavender tinge. Hope swelled in his chest. *He's going to make it.*

"Thanks to your diligence."

He gave Jon a toothless grin. "Tomorrow, we'll watch Baleful rise. Sunlight helps the transformation." *And I will also remember Raken.*

Author's note: Spore is a world in *The Dhyany* universe, my other novel series set in the 34th century. In Book 2, Spore is only seen from orbit, as the transport ship drops off prisoners, but I still had to work out why the world is so deadly that people don't ever land there. I thought it would be interesting to see the world from the prisoners' point of view. I also wanted to explore an extreme case of motherhood.

Caretaker Gods

DUST SWIRLED IN THE VALLEY BELOW, obscuring the cavalry of the charging armies. Helmion cleared her throat and activated her far vision, watching the flashing swords and flying lances as foot soldiers rushed in from the flank and threw themselves into the battle. Blood and sweat soaked through cuirasses and chainmails.

Helmion closed her eyes and breathed in slowly, then exhaled in a quick puff, as if she could rid herself of the anguish. She pivoted and walked to the flyer. "Let's go. I've seen enough." She climbed in, not waiting for Aerodin.

He took them up above Merope and headed for the ocean. "Look at the spy cloud." Aerodin projected the image over the main viewport and pointed at the cloud of tiny machines above the continent, from which a swarm detached and drifted up. "That's odd. Monitor clouds never separate like that."

"No, but who cares." Helmion raked her fingers through the tangles of her hair. "I'm concerned about Theleora. She's getting negligent. It's *her* duty to keep Merope peaceful. She shouldn't have allowed matters to escalate into a war." They had spent two days verifying the conflicting reports of the monitor clouds on the armies of the normals. Grime covered the coarse skirt and tunic she wore, a flimsy disguise as a mainlander, because any normal could see that they were different.

Sunlight danced on white waves as the flyer approached Arlantis, shimmering in rainbow colors as though covered by a giant soap bubble. Ocean liners docked at retractable piers.

The flyer banked and, just before it slipped through the force field, Helmion caught a metallic flash high up in the sky. GAI was spying again. Helmion didn't trust the AI.

GAI relegates the cloud management to a small part of her mind and delves into the past, deeper and deeper until she snatches at a data packet. Memory. Ancient. Ganymede. Thrill.

The red gas world looms in our shared view, its immense eye a turbulent storm. I snuggle close to Ganymede's mind, nestled next to mine like lovers under a starry sky. I collapse the scan window and bring up an orientation sensory, as we drop into the upper atmosphere. I will need to keep the pod at the correct angle to prevent a tumble. Surely I can't have the pod burning up in the atmosphere, as that would result in my own demise.

No, GAI quickly withdraws from the poisoned red world, and from the fragmented memory that reminds her of the Shatter Wars. She's confused; the memories are jumbled.

"What's your plan for Merope?" Helmion asked.

Aerodin's sharp profile stood out, jaws jutting forward. "I'm sending in the special agents to assassinate the rulers and their generals. We can't let them fight another war."

"No, we can't." The last one had decimated a third of Merope. Helmion looked out the viewport, down at the emerald circle covered by terraced crop fields and jewel-colored orchards. Cars and produce transports flew from ring to ring. "But to maintain such a large seed stock is getting tedious."

"We must follow Arlan's wisdom," Aerodin said. "With all the changes we wrought in our genetics, we can't be certain it won't lead into an evolutionary dead end in a million years. We need normal humans."

Arlan's wisdom, indeed. She almost snorted but caught herself and made it into a cough.

The flyer banked over the next ring of Arlantis. Squat, windowless nanofactories and warehouses heaved out of the ground, like icebergs, with most of their bulk deep below the water. Giant robots moved around them, sorting, loading, and cataloguing consumer goods. Box flyers rose into the air and proceeded inward.

She had just about had enough of Arlan, the man who had phased into energy form and departed to greener worlds, rather than struggle with the local problems. And Arlan and her other ancestors had allowed the Theians to remain in the Solar system in their transphased state, playing gods with the normals.

"We won't die out," she said finally. "Helios knows how many thousands of star systems the transphased settled."

"Not in pure human form."

Helmion suppressed her annoyance with Aerodin for spouting Arlan's words. She enlarged the view and watched the people on the streets, wearing the latest fashion of flowing robes and scarf dresses decorated with gold and silver embroidery. As always, she was amazed at their beauty and grace. "The normals should be like us. I'd rather uplift the bunch of them and be done with it."

Aerodin laughed. "Ezeus won't let you. Besides, we must keep a seed stock."

"He has no say in the matter." She was tired of the Theians' interference.

They passed over the inner residential belts separated by walls. Marble mansions supported by enormous columns and a variety of pearly towers dominated here. Turquoise lakes and silver canals speckled with colorful boats nestled between the estates. Whiskers of hanging bridges twinkled in the distance. Some of the floating gardens were beginning to seal their pods and fold up their petals for the evening, protecting the rare alien flora from the cool night.

"Regardless, he won't let us."

Helmion nodded grudgingly. Aerodin was right; the transphased still possessed fearsome weapons. The ruble of Theia, the fifth world they had terraformed and settled and then blew up out of sheer viciousness, attested to their insanity.

She looked down at the inner circle of Arlantis. Obsidian and celadon marble buildings with golden roofs and fluted columns lined the wide avenues. Cars zipped between them, landing on tongues of pads protruding from the balconies and towers. The city was peaceful, but beyond the walls chaos ruled, and beyond the fourth world where the Theians lived on the orbiting rubble, madness ruled. And her people were in the middle of it, between the post human Theians and the primitive normals, just the three island states. *We're islands in a sea of insanity.*

"Aerodin," Gavil said through the flyer's com. "We received the report from the west monitor cloud. The Holmecs are doing it again."

A muscle twitched in Helmion's face. "Damn their bloody rituals. Will they never learn?"

"Be right there, Gavil," Aerodin said.

"We're in the Capitol Theater," Gavil said.

Aerodin faced her. "It's been what—a decade and a half since we took care of the last set of rulers?"

"Sixteen years," Helmion said. Her heart constricted at the thought of another viral release. Selective, certainly, but it cut to the core of her soul.

The flyer banked over the largest building, a squat yet graceful construction of cerulean marble veined with gold. Aerodin swooped directly into the central courtyard and guided the flyer between the columns to a landing pad leading to Capitol Theater.

Helmion was out of her seat and headed toward the irising door. She crossed the wide hall lined with statues, sandaled feet leaving trails of sand on the polished marble floor.

Gavil waited by the gilded door of the theater, with a few of his men milling around. He dismissed them with a wave of his hand.

Helmion sank into a formchair and leaned back, grateful for the comfort of home. Aerodin sat down next to her and nodded to Gavil.

The large holoscreen showed a multitude of people, chanting below the four-sided pyramid of Tleox, current Emperor of the Holmecs. The crowd extended to the shore, where the indifferent sea lapped at white sand. The sun stood high, sparkling on bronzed shoulders beaded with sweat. Gavil's monitor cloud zoomed across the steps dark with old blood, up where Tleox sat in his golden throne. His priests, guards, and females sitting on cushions surrounded him.

Wrapped in an air of arrogance, Tleox lifted his arm.

The crowd roared.

A supine man tied to a stone slab, eyes shut, mouthed a prayer to his non-existent god. Zapatk the High Priest, wearing an air of superiority and his ceremonial robes stained with blood, walked to the sacrifice. Zapatk stopped, his headdress of bright feathers moving in rhythm with his chanting. He bowed to Tleox.

The crowd roared.

A wide blade glinted, and Zapatk stabbed down at the man's chest. Bones cracked and blood sprayed as he twisted the blade with a deft motion. The man's back arced and his body convulsed as Zapatk reached inside the chest cavity with his other hand and ripped out the heart. He lifted it high in the air, blood trickling down his arm.

The crowd roared.

Another Priest removed the leather thongs from the body. With a casual fling of his foot, Zapatk kicked the victim's body off the stone slab. It tumbled down the steps like a wet sack, bouncing and leaking blood.

Helmion shot to her feet and turned to Gavil, lips trembling. "How . . . how long?"

"Over a year," Gavil said. "I think the monitor cloud has been sabotaged. I found its alarm code removed, so it couldn't transmit when the Holmecs started. GAI alerted me."

Helmion notched her eyebrows; GAI again, something nagged at the back of her mind.

Aerodin hit the formchair. "Damn the transphased. I bet they've been feasting their quantum eyes."

"Still, the normals . . ." Helmion leaned against him. She had hoped that they would stop the insane murders. "Why can't they live in peace?"

GAI delves into her favorite memory, or an ancient virtual, one that she will make in the future. She's in a city, in a boxy dwelling that has many rooms. People live here, huddled and cold and alone, worshipping a God that they cannot see. It's winter, and the cold snow lends the primitive, filthy architecture a veneer of purity. The people hurry about their business, hunched into their drab coats that stinks of sweat. Yet, there is a charming element to this scene. Normal. The future. Soon.

Aerodin's arms enclosed her. "We'll teach the normals. You must do your duty now."

Helmion nodded. It was her fault that more people had died. Aerodin had warned her that Tleox wouldn't listen, not even to their fourth warning, but she'd argued and gotten her way. She disengaged from his embrace and hurried toward the droptube, determined to correct her mistake. "I'll be in the lab."

"You gave them another chance." Taking long strides, Aerodin easily kept up with her. One hand shoed away a botanim servant whose golden face beamed with a programmed smile, offering refreshments on a tray. They passed the massive blue columns and stopped at the droptubes.

"A chance to kill more." She connected to the net and found

Appolena. "Come to the lab. We have work to do."

"I *am* in the lab," Appolena said, her face hovering before Helmion. "I'm finishing the protein analyses of the new crop."

"Good, stay there." Helmion disconnected.

Aerodin waved. "I'll fly out with Dyomos to the other side of Merope."

"See you at dinner," Helmion said as the door of the droptube opened. She rode it down four levels and exited at the laboratories.

Appolena was bending over a 3D electrophoresis unit when Helmion entered. She leaned against the stasis drawers lining one wall and breathed in, then exhaled slowly. Her gaze slid over the round door of the cryo-chamber, and it stared back at her like a fisheye. Small units of enzyme fabricators, quantum imagers, sealed pipette and microplate boards covered every surface of the benches. The nanoelectronic assembler was turned on, its holoscreen blinking. It was a soothing environment, for beneficial purposes. Mostly.

Appolena straightened up and waited.

"All right," Helmion said and sat down by the holoscreen of the assembler. "We're priming the Taxoviola FX-12 virus with the genetic markers of the TLX group."

"How many?"

"All four hundred ninety-eight individuals."

Appolena looked up, face a study of discipline. "Load and dispense?" she asked, but her hand was already punching in the code to release the vector capsules. Seventeen translucent mini missiles slid out of the bio storage of the ceiling and entered the assembler unit through the tube access.

A scream cut through the silence, and Tamarin's face popped up on her retinal screen. Helmion paled. "What is it?" she asked the Governess.

Face red and tear-streaked, Tamarin sobbed, "Khalin fell off the balcony. He's . . . he's hanging."

Helmion shot to her feet. "Call Seloman. And a Healer." Before the door closed behind her, she said to her assistant, "Appo, prime and load the virus."

Sandals squeaking with sand, Helmion raced across corridors, droptubes, and halls to reach her son's room. She arrived panting and darted to the balcony.

Below the entablature of a large column, Khalin gripped a marble leaf with one arm; the other one bent at an odd angle. He was crying, face scrunched up. Seloman was approaching from the east courtyard on gravbelt.

Helmion held her breath, afraid to speak lest Khalin lose his grip. Tamarin stared, one fist covering her mouth. Helmion put an arm around her, and they watched until Seloman reached Khalin. With the boy wrapped in his arms, Seloman floated through the double door and put him on the settee, careful not to jar the injured arm.

Helmion ran to him.

"Momma," Khalin sobbed. "It hurts."

Helmion kissed his sweaty forehead and took his uninjured hand in hers.

"Uncle Hermes," Khalin said over her shoulder.

Her brother ran into the room, pulling off a mobile autodoc from his float pallet. He held it over Khalin's arm and waited until it unfurled blue gel wings and wrapped itself around the broken arm. Khalin sighed with relief. A small diagnostic screen popped up above the autodoc, and Hermes reached inside to adjust the medchine dosage.

He straightened up, looked at her. "Multiple fractures of the ulna and radius. It will take a few days for the bone welder." Then he gave Khalin a stern look. "The autodoc stays on for a few days, young man."

"Yes, Uncle Hermes."

With the help of Tamarin, Helmion moved Khalin to his bed. She stayed with him all night, cradling him in sleep.

Helmion watched Khalin feed the Vore lilies, his gloved hand reaching into the bag for another slug. The pink lily petals glistened, fleshy and quivering like tongues, as they leaned toward the delicacy. She glanced at the autodoc on Khalin's arm and breathed in the fragrance of flowers from countless worlds. The xeno-habitat was her pride, thousands of species from different worlds she had procured during their travels when they were young, thousands of years ago.

When Khalin ran out of slugs, they walked along the lake and watched the green water monkeys as they rushed to the shore, chattering in their high-pitched voices.

Khalin laughed and answered them, shaping his lips and tongue to form the words properly. "They're asking about Elodin."

"Tell them he has music lesson." The water monkeys would be offended if they knew that Elodin chose girls over chatting with them.

Appolena's holo image intruded upon the alien scene, her features carved in stress lines.

"What is it?"

"They're dead. Most of them are dead."

"Who?" asked Helmion, fear knifing through her.

Appolena burst into tears. "The Holmecs."

Helmion started running, Khalin right beside her. "Calm down, Appo, we'll send in the antiviral."

"I already did," Appo sobbed. "Maybe a few will survive. I'm so sorry, Helmion. What did I do wrong?"

Helmion stopped and closed her eyes, trying to shut out the images of horror. A cloud of sorrow wrapped around her. She opened her mouth to say something, but no words came out.

"A Shining One is approaching at near relativistic speed," GAI said. "Forty seconds to arrival."

"Thank you, GAI, but my orbital surveillance reported it three minutes ago," Aerodin said.

He wondered if it was worth it to bother with GAI. It was a model designed by Ganymede, and the only AI remaining from the Shatter Wars of the Theians, Shining Ones, as the AIs had called them. Though damaged, he supposed GAI still had some uses.

Aerodin sat in his sapphire throne and fingered the gold edges of his white robe. Helmion sat next to him, frowning, no doubt angry at the blatant treaty violation of the Theians.

A shimmering energy ball swooped into the Capitol's courtyard, changing into the giant human shape of Ezeus, holding his forked energy lance. Golden muscles bulged as he shifted to face Aerodin. "How dare you kill my subjects?"

"*We* are responsible for the Earth, and the normals are not your subjects." Aerodin narrowed his eyes. "It befalls us to stamp out social psychosis. And according to the treaty, your kind is not supposed to come near the Earth." He knew that the Theians couldn't stay away. They were bored with their infinite powers and constantly visited the Earth in human forms.

"Silence, you upstart!" Ezeus waved his lance. Blue light stitched across the open space, and several columns snapped in the courtyard, crashing to the floor. Dust flew up from the pulverized corundum crystals.

Aerodin glanced at the damage, and from the command menu, he activated the maintenance system. Charcoal repair scarabs glided into the courtyard and began cleaning up the debris. He also alerted Gavil, in case Ezeus unleashed his full wrath rather than just his usual tantrums. The remnants of Theia, orbiting beyond the fourth world, was proof of their violence, but the eons-long pointless existence had driven them hopelessly insane. It was hard to believe that his people and the Theians had once been the same species.

"Would you make rubble of the Earth too?" He couldn't keep the sneer out of his voice.

A flicker of shame passed through the giant visage. Then Ezeus stiffened and waved a golden arm. "We could house all the baseline humans on the planetisimals, so don't get cocky with me. If you overstep your station, we could wipe you off the Earth."

Arlan had warned him about the treachery of Ezeus. Aerodin often wondered if that was the reason Arlan had phased and left on a galactic voyage, to join their previously departed ancestors.

Helmion faced Ezeus, eyes unflinching. "How else can we do our duty? The baselines are killing each other."

Aerodin admired her courage. She was more than his spouse; she was his partner as well.

"Leave them to us," Ezeus said.

She glared at the giant. "Now who's overstepping his station? You have forsaken your duty millions of years ago. You are far too removed from organic life to be guardians of the seed stock."

"This is your last warning. Leave my mortals alone."

"The Earth is not your playground," Aerodin said.

Ezeus laughed and rolled into his energy sphere, then shot up into the air, streaking across the sky faster than a meteorite.

"*His* mortals, the arrogant fraud," Helmion said. "As if he owned them."

Aerodin called his aide. "Gavil, sweep the courtyard for spynits." Then he turned to Helmion and embraced her. "I'm sorry Appolena made. . ."

"It's a tragedy." Helmion trembled. "But it doesn't give the Theians the right to interfere on Earth."

Aerodin couldn't agree more, but the Theians were still powerful, even in their diminished numbers. He watched as a large assembler centipede stood up vertically below the snapped columns and began to eat the detritus. From its upper end a stump of a cylinder appeared, slowly filling in the marble column.

"Let's go to the garden." He led his spouse out of the courtyard.

Gavil's face appeared before them. "Aerodin, the Capitol is clear of spynits."

Relief surged through him, for Ezeus was capable of more than threats. Arlan had told him about the time of the Titans, the predecessors of Ezeus and his group. The first transphased had lived in habitats orbiting Titan, a moon of the seventh world. Then Ezeus and his retinue had chosen to phase into energy form, and soon after, quarrels with the Titans arose, followed by several wars. The Ezeus faction was on the verge of losing when Tartar had discovered another form of phase energy. He had engineered it to trap the Titans' energy, warped it into a sphere, and sealed it. The prison had been named Tartarus sphere, around which Ezeus had formed a small world and sent it on a trajectory beyond Pluto's orbit. The orbit was always unstable, and after ages, Tartarus had left the Solar system, to forever wander the dark reaches of the galaxy.

GAI probes her sensory circuits and wonders how she should feel. Ganymede is gone, his patterns erased from the phase-grid, defeated by the Ezeus faction of the Theians. She should be sad, but she feels nothing at first, then anger. Anger, frustration, abandonment, and fear roll into one. Once again, she gropes into an ancient virtual she calls past.

I must be careful now, the timing must be perfect. The timing. Time. The past, I want the past.

GAI untangles from the memory—or is it a virtual? —and gives the command to the spybots.

Now she can rest and allow her parts to self-repair. And wait for the past.

* * *

Aerodin dined on roast pheasant and spiced rice, admiring Helmion and the view from the terrace when Gavil's image appeared before him.

"We have a problem," Gavil said. "Murlan released a deadly bio agent on the Tsu continent. My surveillance net shows massive deaths over there."

Aerodin felt his stomach knot. He knew Murlan had his share of troubles with Emperor Che, who enslaved three quarters of the population of the Tsu continent. A decade ago, Murlan's army had freed the slaves, but most of them had returned voluntarily, only to die from diseases and inhuman conditions. Maybe Murlan had had enough and just wanted to end it, one way or another. "Are you sure?" The pheasant felt like a lump of wood in his mouth. He swallowed it with an effort.

"I'm tracing the path of self-propelling clouds that originated from Murlantis. They're leaking viral particles."

Aerodin stood up and hurried to his command center, Helmion right behind him. He wondered whether he should consult the Legislators, but he knew they didn't have time; arguments and debates could cost them their lives. He was their chosen leader and authorized to act in a crisis. Besides, other than his young sons, he was the only descendent of Arlan, founder of the island.

"Gavil, halt everything and prepare the Talon spacecrafts. Fueled," he said. "And send the evacuation order to every household, including the bulk of your people. We only need a few men to supervise the loading."

Aerodin and Helmion rounded the last corner and stepped into an open droptube leading to the command center. As the tube descended below the ocean floor, he wondered if any of his people would survive the wrath of the Theians. Murlan had a rotten timing releasing a plague now, so soon after the Holmec disaster.

They exited the tube and hurried across the circular chamber. Aerodin pressed his palm to the wall sensor and the door dilated.

"You think the Theians will attack," Helmion said. For the first time, fear showed in her eyes.

"We must prepare for the worst. They blew up their own world. We can't expect anything better." At the vault entrance, he pressed the symbols in the proper sequences.

"I don't think they will attack. You heard Ezeus. He was angry about the death of the normals. They wouldn't do anything to harm them."

"I hope you're right."

He hadn't even told her about the spybots enmeshed inside the utility clouds he and Gavil had discovered in low orbit, because he didn't want her to worry. They always knew about the transmitters the Theians had scattered in near Earth space, but the spybots were only about a decade old.

The massive door of the vault opened and light spilled out in a wide cone. Aerodin headed to the control panel and placed his palm on yet another sensor pad. White light scanned his brainwaves, ten identical squares lit up in blue. He pressed each one and waited.

Helmion sighed. "I never really believed it would come to this when I designed the untangler."

He took her hand, watching the floating capsules settle one by one onto a transport pallet. Each stasis unit held a body, replicated normal humans in stasis, selected from a set of genes for beauty and not much else. Their bodies teemed with disguised nanites coded to activate in the presence of the Theian energy matrix. The untangle field then would convert the phased energy of the immortals into incoherent quantum bits and return them to the quantum foam within a few hours. According to intelligence reports, the Theians had no means to detect the untangler; they were too arrogant to think that the superhuman islanders were capable of designing anything against them.

After the stasis units settled onto the pallet, Aerodin slaved its program to his wristband. They left the vault and ascended to ground level, the float pallet following a few paces behind. Crossing the lobby, they entered another tube that carried them up to the main landing pad.

Ten of the Talon class spacecrafts waited, their hulls identical to the crafts the Theians had given their pet normals. The ships' destination was preset to the ten asteroid habitats the transphased occupied.

"Start loading the stasis capsules," Gavil said to his men.

Aerodin looked down from the landing pad. Capitol Cirque had spilled its population onto the streets and pads, where they all boarded some type of flying crafts. The evacuation seemed surprisingly calm. No one jostled and pushed others to get ahead. A blink of his eyes activated his far vision. Thousands of people queued on the piers, waiting for the ships and boats.

"Murlantis and Doradus won't evacuate," Gavil reported. "I just spoke to Murlan and Theleora."

"I was afraid of that," Aerodin said. "They always planned to ride it out by channeling all their core power into their shields."

"Not knowing what the immortals may throw at us, I'd rather be far from the islands," Gavil said.

The airlocks of the Talons flowed shut and they became seamless claws. The spacecrafts lifted off the pad silently, their deadly cargo protected by acceleration gel. Sunlight glinted on their indigo metal skins as they hovered briefly below the force field. Then they passed through and disappeared in seconds.

His lips pressed into a grim line, Aerodin looked down on Arlantis and turned the flyer toward the mainland. The island had been home to his people for thousands of years, a silent witness to their efforts and triumphs.

Helmion's hand descended on his shoulder from behind. "They're finally settled down." She took the other control couch next to him.

Aerodin nodded. His sons, Elodin and Khalin, wanted to stay in Arlantis. They have been lashing out at each other since the evacuation had begun.

The alarm cut through the gentle hum of the flyer as a large weapons platform emerged from the clouds, triangular and charcoal, bristling with turrets and weapons ports. His stomach clenched. Blue and white energy jazzed along the rounded edges with wicked speed.

"Arlan help us," Helmion said. "Where did that come from?"

Aerodin switched the image to the planetary grid and saw that countless orbital sensors had burnt out. He opened a channel to the AI. "GAI, you said the Theians had no ordnance stashed near Earth."

"My sensors showed nothing at the time," GAI said. "The platform must have been deactivated, perhaps cloaked. It came from the far side of the Moon."

Aerodin cursed the damaged AI. Built by Ganymede's faction of the Theians, GA-I was a self-aware orbiting utility mind. It was ancient, but after the Shatter Wars, his people needed all the resources they could find. His ancestors had awakened it and coaxed it into Earth orbit. GAI had obliged, because Ganymede was either dead or departed the Solar system. Aerodin knew GAI was lying, but he didn't know why, because it hated Ezeus and his cronies.

With shaking hands on the controls, he dropped lower and increased their speed. His stomach roiled with a sick feeling at the thought of his people. More than half of them were still on the island when his family had left.

His screen showed Doradus, above which hovered the weapons platform, spewing out a thick column of purple energy. The shield of the island was demolished, and automatic defenses fired pulse beams at the platform, which all slid off harmlessly.

"It's aiming at their core unit." Helmion's voice trembled.

"Destabilizing the magnetic field of the fusion plant," Aerodin said. His knuckles turned white as he gripped the controls.

Explosions sparked at the center of Doradus, and its towering walls rippled and fell inward. He glimpsed at a crimson fissure, followed by water and steam jetting to the surface. The energy pillar from the weapons platform dissipated and the enemy moved off.

Tears were coursing down Helmion's face. "It's heading for Arlantis."

Words of comfort fluttered agonizingly on the tip of his tongue, but he was unable to say them.

A giant, ruby plume belched from the island's center, shooting magma into the air. The atmosphere darkened and everything began to funnel inward.

The image flickered as more sensors burned out around Doradus.

As the shockwave hit them, Aerodin gripped the controls with two hands. The flyer floundered in hurricane-force winds for a few moments, then dropped. He gritted his teeth and wrestled them higher. The remaining sensors showed them a horrific scene. As if slammed by a giant fist, the ocean floor cracked, sending steam and rubble into the air. A low rumble filled his ears. Slowly, the water closed over the wound of the earth with a thunderous slap, erasing Doradus from its surface. Waves rippled outward and grew, heading toward the main continents.

"Let's go to the sanctuary," Helmion said. They had prepared a retreat on Adelphi where all their people could blend in with the normals.

Mount Theur might not be high enough to withstand the tidal waves caused by the sinking of three islands, but he didn't want to voice his fears. "Let us remain aboard the flyer for a bit longer."

Helmion turned away.

With shaking fingers, Aerodin switched on the fleet comgrid and wished he hadn't. As the green dots representing Arlantian ships winked out one by one, his heart turned to stone.

A glint of metal high up caught his attention, and from it a green, pencil-thin beam reached down to an Arlantian flyer.

The flyer exploded.

"GAI," he said, as the realization hit him. "It's not the Theians. GAI is attacking us."

Helmion looked at him, eyes wide. The flyer shuddered. Aerodin jerked at the controls and turned south. "We're heading for—"

As far as I know, Khalin and I are alone. After the sea has washed our lifepods to the shore, we have searched the coastline on foot, and searched again. We have not found Aerodin and Elodin's lifepod.

After five decades in Adelphi—the village where people both respect and fear me—I will go and search for survivors while our cell treatment hold and I still have some youth left in me. Khalin is a grown man now, with grandchildren, settled in the ways of the normals. He has nearly forgotten Arlantis. In such short time, even the name of Ezeus and that of his cronies have been changed by the normals. They call him Zeus, a god of thunder. Soon, we shall all slip into the realms of legend. But GAI is still up there, watching. I see it sometimes on a clear nigh, and I wonder why it did it. Perhaps GAI has used us to rid the world of the Theians, and in that, I cannot help but concur.

Alanna's Hair

ALANNA TAPPED HER FOOT IN IMPATIENCE and watched her suit's diagnostics run a final check. Data scrolled on her retinal screen. Before it showed every strand of hair covered by a nanolayer of the suit, she shut off the program and stepped out onto the balcony slab.

A mote flickered in her peripheral vision. She whirled and activated the pulser in her glove, scope vision scanning the plaz wall of the building.

Air stirred behind a patch of scrubnits. Her arm moved in a blur and, vision aligned on the hazy patch, she fired off a steady pulse. With a faint puff, the seeker program assembled a field around the object, then plasma reduced it to ash.

Damn, she was shaking. Omicron's spy filaments had nearly gotten her, attracted to a strand of her hair not yet covered by her suit.

She scanned the immediate area for spybots and seeker gnats, and when she was satisfied that none lurked nearby, she lunged off the balcony's edge. From the glove control, she guided her AG belt and flew around Sky sphere, crowded with hairless people arriving for the afternoon show. Several of her commandos patrolled the area, ready to defend the residents. She flew to the park and dropped to the ground.

The bloody rays of the waning sun leaked through the buckyglass dome and spectered into blades of light, carving the city into angles. High up, the sky etiolated and became one with the skin of the arcology.

It was a glass prison. She didn't remember when she had begun to regard it as such, but she blamed it on Omicron.

Steps echoed to her right. Weapon ready, she pivoted.

Zac stopped and raised his palms. "It's just me. I've been waiting for you by the trees." He laughed and extended his hand. "I'll never get used to your reflexes. But I love you, anyway."

Alanna relaxed and slid the pulser back into her gloves, then took his hand. A tingle began in her fingers and ran up her arm and through her body, settling in her heart as though it belonged there. Zac had told her it was love.

He touched her hair gently, as though it was precious, whispering, “So beautiful.”

She laughed in delight and shook the shoulder-length auburn hair that required so much care and the constant adjusting of her suit. “I’m glad you told me about hair.”

“Sometimes I almost regret it.” He swallowed. “You must be careful. So many breaches. I’m worried about you.”

He was concerned about her mindprint aboard the ship, a print Omicron had taken sixty-two years ago while she’d interfaced with it in a moment of youthful curiosity. It was stupid and impulsive, but she’d wanted to see. The experience had convinced her that her ancestors made the right decision resisting the AI. It had also given her nightmares, seeing the rows of sleepers in stasis capsules and the uploaded minds pretending they were living. Alanna shuddered at the memory.

She squeezed his hand. “Don’t worry. I can take care of myself.”

“Let’s go to the lake.”

She slipper her hand out of his and began to run, the grass swaying under her feet in silky ripples. Zac ran after her. People hurried in the other direction, as if leaving a scene.

Alanna stopped.

A Security mobile parked next to the trees. Commandos stood by with a decon bubble ready. The smell of the forest wafted to her nostrils, mingling with an undertone of decay.

Alanna walked over, flashing her Captain ID to the quad. A woman’s body lay under a tree. An autodoc in the shape of a squirrel squatted on her chest, its fur cilia bristling with unseen energies, paws enfolding the face of the woman, and its webs of nanocilia probing the hairless skull.

“Body is dead,” the autodoc said. “It has been copied recently. Mind is blank. Last visual record shows a real crow entering the glade.”

The quad leader looked at Alanna. “Captain, I’m Smith, quad seven.” He flashed his ID to her augment. “Looks like Omicron designed new sensors and more aggressive recording devices.”

"Has the shim wall been breached?"

"No, the sniffers found nothing."

Alanna bristled with frustration; the death of a citizen caused by their technological inadequacy was a blow to the Security Division. She exchanged a glance with Zac. He had predicted that they wouldn't be able to keep pace with Omicron indefinitely. The AI would get weary of humoring them. He had also cautioned the Council against further attempts at altering the Earth's biosphere, which the AI sabotaged anyway. But the Council had disregarded his advice and continued sending reclamation teams outside. Zac had given up hope of convincing them and changed careers. A few decades ago, he had begun to study ancient history and catalogued all the available records on file, hence his fount of knowledge on folklore about hair, flesh sex, and marriage.

"It could be a flesh spy," she said, looking at Zac. "Councilor Horowitz, please refresh our memory on the replacement incident."

Zac nodded. "It happened a little over three hundred years ago. Omicron sent in a data packet of one of our people's DNA, a person it has copied previously but didn't upload to the ship. The AI cloned a blank body, then used one of the already uploaded mindprints of a different person and created a spy. The data of both the body and the mind was already in the arcology's records. Eleven people were killed and uploaded to the ship before Security identified the flesh spy."

"But our sensors would report any mind-body incongruity," Smith said. "They were developed *after* the replacement incident."

"Omicron keeps upgrading its tools," Zac said. "It has mindprints of some of our people it never uploaded to the ship. A few cells from those people and Omicron could have perfect flesh spies inside the arcology. Same body, same mind would *not* alert your sensors."

Alanna's stomach lurched; her mindprint was in Omicron's databanks. Despite their filters, suits, fields, and new sensors, obtaining genetic sample was the easier of the two necessary steps for Omicron to upload them aboard the ship. A mindprint was more difficult to obtain.

"We need better sensors," Smith said. "But I don't know how. Our suits' memory storage is already overtaxed."

Alanna's chest tightened as she looked at the victim. *And my suit is even more overtaxed by the hair growth.*

Zac put an arm around her shoulder. She forced a smile, trying to dismiss the dreadful thoughts.

Her mind wandered to last night's virtual lovemaking with Zac, his love, and his delight in her hair, and she decided that having hair was worth the added risk.

The murder in the glade had caused panic among the residents, and so Alanna ordered extra commandos to patrol the streets. After a long day, Zac had waited for her at Defense Headquarters. Holding hands, they walked toward her residential complex. The wispy fronds of feather trees swayed in the artificial breeze, hypnotic and lovely, as she had never seen the park before.

"Tell me about the Hairy tales."

Zac laughed, his rich baritone playing along her skin, hair, and every fiber of her being. She savored the delicious shivers that ran down her body and waited for him to speak.

"Fairy tales were popular in ancient times. There's one about a goddess called Sif, whose golden hair was stolen by Loki, a minor deity of mischief making. In the end, the dwarves, people of short stature, managed to restore her hair. And Rapunzel, a princess of sorts, who had such long hair that it reached down fifty stories from her tower prison." Zac smiled, his eyes animated by his favorite subjects of ancient history and folklore. "I recorded them as the Wild Ones recounted them. You should come out with me and meet them. You can listen to their stories. They're wonderful people, and so . . . so free."

"I don't want to meet them." Alanna gave a dismissive gesture, afraid she would resent the Wild Ones even more. "Are the tales real accounts?"

Zac shrugged. "Omicron validated some of them. The ones in our own archives are sadly lacking details."

She wondered how much credence she could put into the tales of the Wild Ones. "How can they remember that far back?"

"Folklore, handed down verbally through thousands of generations. The Wild Ones want to preserve history, unlike us." His expression held admiration and respect, something akin to when he looked at her.

"But they live such harsh and uncivilized lives, short and brutal and pest-ridden."

"But they *live*, and we merely exist."

But we live, was exactly what Alanna had said to Omicron sixty-two years ago, *while the sleepers and the uploaded simpersons exist in storage.*

A storage not very different from your arcology. Omicron's answer echoed in her mind.

And Zac, he was going outside more and more with the reclamation teams. While the scientists released reclamation nanites to change the Earth back the way it had been, Zac visited the Wild Ones. Sometimes Alanna suspected he held the Wild Ones in higher esteem than he did his own people. Jealousy nibbled at her. Was she competing with primitives for his affection?

They passed under the Arches of Statues, gleaming figures carved of alabaster and over a hundred meters tall.

Zac stopped. "I love you, Alanna."

"And I love you." She held his gaze for long seconds, wondering whether their love was even real. Not once had they experienced a real touch skin to skin, a caress, or a kiss. Ever. Aside from their virtual lovemaking, they were practically strangers, isolated flesh encased in energy suits.

We're just mere suits.

They started walking again, and by the time they reached her residential complex, her mood had plummeted below nadir.

Facing each other, Zac reaching for her hair. "In the era of the fairy tales, possessing one lock of a maiden's hair ensured eternal love."

Alanna closed her eyes and imagined his naked fingers running through her tresses.

"Logon at nine?" he asked, voice caressing.

On a sudden impulse, she said, "No, I want to experience real love. Come over at nine and we'll do it. We'll do it like in ancient times. Like the Wild Ones."

His eyes widened in surprise. "You would unsuit for me?"

She nodded, suddenly apprehensive and not trusting her voice. No one in millennia had unsuited in the presence of another person, not even family members. People arranged for children by pre-selected sperm and ova stored in the Genetic House.

Zac brushed his lips over hers, and she tried to suppress her annoyance at the tingle of their suits, a warning of contact. He whispered, "I'll come, my love." Then he turned and left.

Alanna stared after him for a few moments before she rose up to her balcony. The field recognized her suit and formed a bubble that held her for three seconds before the inner layer parted and admitted her to her house. A white light from the ceiling bathed her in a warm glow for a few seconds. "Your suit is clear," said the house AI.

Through her augment, she made her suit deactivate and watched it collapse into a fist-sized energy ball.

She undressed and padded into her bathroom. First she switched on the disintegrator unit and then she stepped through the field into the shower stall. From the menu in her retinal screen, she selected the scent of lilacs. Fragrant water, preset to her preferred temperature, cascaded down her body, massaging away the fatigue of the past nights she had spent roaming virch environments with Zac. The slight resonation under her feet—generator for the molecular disintegrator to destroy cast off skin particles in the drains—irritated her now.

The ship should leave without us. But Omicron wouldn't; it claimed that its duty was to protect the Wild Ones from her people.

Angry with the Wild Ones for causing so much misery for her people, Alanna shut off the water and stood under the dryer for a few moments, staring at the water statues along her swimming bowl. She walked across her spacious bedroom to the form bed, enjoying the heated crystal floor under her feet.

"Wake me up at ten to nine," she said to the AI.

Consciousness unfolded like petals of a spring flower as the house system gently released her from sleep. Alanna stood and stretched, feeling invigorated by the three-hour sleep. She walked into the dayroom and faced the MA unit, then opened the recipe file of her wardrobe. A display of various gowns floated before her, some of them she had worn in a virch experienced with Zac. She selected a white dress of filmy fabric and clicked the execute icon.

While the unit assembled her dress, she stared out the window field, watching it distort moonlight into ripples of iridescence. How she yearned to walk under the moon barefoot, to hold Zac's hand and laugh, to sink her teeth into fruit picked from trees growing outside the arcology.

A faint swishing sound and the gown appeared in the dispenser slot of the MA unit. Her hands caressed the silky fabric for a moment before she donned it.

"Give me a three-way mirror." Alanna spun around, admiring the generous flow of the skirt and the way the low-cut bodice clung to her shape. She twirled, laughing, and saw the tangled mass of her hair.

The house AI gave a sputtering sound. "You . . . you have a visitor. Councilor Horowitz is requesting entry."

Alanna smiled. "Lower a bubble, scan his suit, and pass him through." She picked up a silver brush—a gift of Zac—from the table and ran it through her hair a few times.

"Into which environment?"

"Into the house, you moron."

"I advise against admitting him."

"Noted," she said with a touch of impatience. "Now, do as I said."

"I advise a health scan. Mental—"

"Let him in *now*!" Alanna placed her hands on her hips and glared around the room, then stomped her foot for good measure.

From her retinal view, Alanna watched a bubble forming outside the shimwall of the balcony. The bubble slid down and wrapped around Zac, then lifted him up. She rushed to the balcony, holding her breath. Zac cradled something in his arms, wrapped in silver tissue foil, and when the bubble placed him upon the balcony slab, he looked up, his eyes alight. After long seconds—she suspected the house AI checked his suit twice—the field parted.

Alanna found herself in his arms, crushing the thing he held so gingerly. She pulled back and looked down at the silver tissue cradling two pale yellow roses on long stems. "Beautiful," she said.

"Not as beautiful as you are." Zac's suit flowed off him and rolled into a ball of energy. He dropped the roses and kissed her, caressing her hair with one hand, and her neck and shoulder with the other.

Waves of pleasure coursed through her, invaded her every cell, and turned her body into an instrument of delight. She didn't remember how they had found the bed, tangled as they were; only the ecstasy of flesh love remained etched into her psyche.

Hours later, they lay on their backs, shoulders touching and hands entwined, sharing a long span of silence and watching the moon waltz across the star-speckled sky.

"I love you, Alanna."
"I love you, Zac."

She fell asleep in his arms and dreamed about running across a meadow strewn with wild flowers, breathing the fragrant air and not choking on carbon dioxide. Zac's hand grasped hers and they were laughing, the breeze caressing her skin and whipping her hair around. Birds of bright plumage clamored in the tree branches, singing and chirping and causing a delightful explosion of sounds and colors. Strange tree fronds swayed raced by her. Willow branches bowed over a burbling stream at the edge of the forest, from which Wild Ones peeked through, their greenish faces displaying a welter of emotions Alanna couldn't read.

A deep rumble drew her eyes to the sky. Bruised clouds rolled in, then split by lightning and released a deluge of icy rain.

Alanna woke and sat up suddenly. For an inexplicable reason, Zac's naked body next to her filled her with anxiety. What had she done? The dangers of her actions slammed into her with a brutal reality. She touched his arm gingerly. Zac turned and smiled in his sleep, his fingers folded into a tight fist, gripping something. Copper tresses glinted in the dawn light. Holding her breath, she leaned over him and gently pried his fingers open.

Alanna jerked back as if stung, staring at the lock of her hair nestling in Zac's curled fist. Was he Omicron's flesh spy? No, she shook her head in denial, not Zac.

Yes, she thought as the memory surfaced to the forefront of her mind: *"Omicron validated some of them,"* Zac had said this afternoon. She cursed herself for not catching on before that the only way to speak to Omicron was a direct link. The AI had printed Zac's mind. It was standard procedure; Omicron copied everyone that ever communicated with it.

"One lock of a maiden's hair ensures eternal love," she recalled Zac's words about the fairy tales. Eternal love, Alanna glanced at the lock of her hair in Zac's hand. Eternal life, or something close to it, was only possible by uploading.

Zac planned to upload them.

Betrayal, fear, pain, and a whole gamut of unknown emotions coursed through her. She sobbed, then caught herself and covered her mouth with her fist.

Alanna slid off the bed and tiptoed across the room, keeping her eyes on Zac as she called her pulser. The weapon slammed into her outstretched hand, came online, and she aimed. A moment before she pulled the trigger, Zac sat up and opened his eyes, his expression a mixture of horror and shock.

Alanna fired.

Illuminated from the inside, Zac's body turned a glowing red for a second, and then rippled once, like liquid fire. The charred residue bucked and slowly settled back to the bed as it turned to ash.

Tears ran down her face, and she stood there naked, staring at the remnants of Zac, the love of her life.

Her spirit crushed by her deeds and his intent, Alanna plunged herself into a drugged, dreamless sleep. Hours or days later, she suited up and decided to examine his clothes. *It can't be dangerous now.* Whatever weapon Omicron had sent in with him would be inactive without his augment. She rummaged through his tunic and trouser pockets but found nothing. As she stood up, a silver glint caught her attention. With shaking fingers, she picked up the silk cloth and unwrapped the roses. Tears blurred her vision, passing through her suit and falling on the pale yellow petals. Her body shook with sobs, fingers clutching Zac's last gift.

Hoarse from hours of crying, she finally decided to kill herself. But her teeth chattered and her hand shook, and the pulser slipped out of her fingers. She tried again, asking the MA unit to assemble a potent poison. After staring at the black pellet nestling in her palm for minutes, she couldn't bring herself to swallow it. She took a deep breath, gathered saliva in her mouth, and brought the pill to her lips. And gagged. Though horrified by her own cowardice, she admitted defeat after the third attempt. There was only one thing left for her to do. Come what may, she had to interface with Omicron.

"Save Zac," she said, her lips trembling.

"I cannot save him, his mind is gone and I have no imprint."

"But you must have his mindprint. He's been in contact with you."

"I have never imprinted him because he was planning to join the Wild Ones. Zac Horowitz was waiting to see if you would go with him."

"But he's your—"

"Spy?" asked Omicron. "No, he was not."

Her heart shattered into a thousand pieces. Alanna gasped, the sick paranoia of her society suffocating her. After a while, she mustered a tiny resistance and said, "It's your fault. Why can't you leave us alone?"

"I cannot allow your people to interfere. Aside from causing minor damages to the biosphere, your reclamation nanites won't work. Still, your attempts to remake the world must stop."

"It's our world. We want it the way it used to be."

"It is not your world any longer. Your ancestors have damaged the Earth. They fled in ark ships to other star systems. Others holed up inside the arcologies, but the bulk of the population has been left outside. Billions died during the Plague Years, but some survived and adapted to the new environment. The Earth is theirs now."

"Stop spewing history at me," she spat. "For all we know, you could've made it all up."

"You know I did not."

"Kill me, you sanctimonious collection of hardware," she sobbed. "I don't want to live without Zac."

"I cannot kill you."

"Liar, you've killed plenty of us."

"No, I uploaded thousands of you, and in the early days, I even managed to place some of you in stasis storage."

"I will never board the ship."

"There is another choice."

The other choice was equally abhorrent. Had Zac really planned to join the Wild Ones? He had asked her several times to accompany him on his visits, but she'd assumed that studying the Wild Ones was just something to satisfy his intellectual curiosity. The silence nibbled at her doubts. Fear had already corroded her humanity, for she had killed him in a fit of insanity, fed by her paranoia. *We're all sick, a society built on fear.* Zac must have known it for a long time.

Alanna moaned and buried her face in her hands.

She didn't belong, not aboard the starship and not in the arcology. The Wild Ones. Fear carved icy channels in her heart. She must let go of the fear. What would Zac want her to do? But she knew.

"I want a child, a boy," she said. "Zac and I made love, flesh love."

"If you want me to grow a child for you, you must come aboard."

"No, I want to do it like the Wild Ones."

Information flooded her mind, coded data packets containing instructions to alter her body on a molecular level. She stored them inside her augment to mull over later.

"Follow the directions implicitly and you may, and I emphasize, you *may* succeed. And since you will live outside, you may not survive it. But there you have it, I gave you the means to achieve one or both of your wishes, to die or to live and bear a child."

Five months later, Alanna took a cautious whiff of the air and stepped away from the shimwall. Colors exploded across her vision, cerulean sky dotted with fluffy clouds, trees in every shade of green, flowers of yellows, reds, and violets, and birds of great flocks in rainbow plumage. A gentle breeze lifted her olive green hair, the stiff shiny strands soaking up the sunlight and carbon dioxide and converting them to oxygen to fuel her body. She put a pale green hand to her bulging belly protectively and took a few more steps.

She didn't collapse, breathing the carbon dioxide rich atmosphere came naturally. Emboldened, she began to walk away from the arcology in long strides. The Wild Ones awaited her. Exhilarated by her body's harmony with the environment, she was eager to meet her new people.

The Head of Saint Mark

Death stalked him in alien guises, borne by the economy of Quardeen Station. But dying was not an option for him.

Plans of sabotaging one of the station's maintenance systems formed in his mind. If he could pull it off unseen, it might get him a repair job, something to tie him over for a day or two. But he'd have to disable the repair bots first, and that was risky.

"Reus Saint Mark, your gas and water consumption will exceed your account balance," the cubicle system informed him. "Your six galactic units will cover half the night cycle."

It occurred to him that he should regulate his breathing to conserve the air he had left. Spending time outside his cubicle wouldn't help much, as each sector scanned Sophonts that entered the common areas and tallied up their gas consumption. In a worst-case scenario, he could live inside his suit and roam the airless slums of the station once his funds ran out. Fuel cells cost less than keeping up an entire cubicle.

No, in a worst-case scenario, he'd be spaced.

Reus calculated how long he would last orbiting the station on suit power. Not very long out here beyond the edge of both Human Spheres.

"You have a call." The system projected an image above his head.

How rude, just to open the comlink without asking his permission. Perhaps the station system knew he'd take any calls.

The image of a Lertia wove her eyestalks in his face. His augment automatically selected a translator program. "There you are." The cluster of eyestalks rippled like a thatch of hair around the oval yellow head, mandibles clicking. "Something just came in that might interest you. But perhaps you may not want it because it's a rush preparation and we don't know much about the client. However, it pays well due to certain health hazards. The contract also contains a strict confidentiality clause."

Reus jumped off the web that served as his bed, and it retracted into the ceiling. The Lertia was employed by Flesh Flex, one of the agencies specializing in interspecies exotic services. They had given him only two stints, but he had earned enough to keep himself afloat for weeks. "Go on."

"A TualMot ship is arriving at 3600 station time. The message states: 'queen requires necessary bodily interaction.' She prefers bipeds of your general physique. Minor injuries are to be expected."

Duty meant more than life to Reus at this point, but to carry out his, he had to live. At Quardeen Nexus, the only wormhole that concatenated the worlds of the Thuurin Conglomerate and the Human Spheres, selling one's services, emotions, and soul for entertainment was a profession.

For Reus, it meant survival, *if* he survived the hazards of the profession. He'd been stuck here for nearly an earth-year, waiting for any spacecraft from the Inner League worlds to dock. Even an outdated Outworld Terrator ship would do. Unfortunately, ships from the Human Spheres seldom ventured this far into the Sagittarius arm of the galaxy. Reus was a damned good pilot, but that didn't count at Quardeen Station, as he'd been repeatedly told by the station system. There were species with two heads wired to interface with any systems, endowed with several manipulative appendages. They made him look like a slug in comparison.

Another day, another unsavory stint. Reus walked the Oxy Sector towards CCtavilon's Parlor, the designer of fetishes and the molder of flesh. A sneezing fit took him. Alien odors, sour, vegetal, citrussy, and moldy assailed his nostrils. A group of Roovils stepped out of a sensory lodge and stopped when they saw him, their snout glands tasting the air. Reus tensed but kept going and finally passed them. The faint swishing of their stiff robes and their nose-curdling stench of rotten meat reached him. Beady eyes followed his passage; he felt them on his back, their questing and quivering glands lusting after his emotions. They could suck a human mind dry in minutes.

Reus turned the corridor and stopped at the tube access. Lights blinked, and a centipede-shaped transport crawled in, its silver green segments shimmering with the energy field that powered it. Doors hissed, spilling air redolent with bodily exudations, followed by a flood of Sophonts small and large. Quardeen Central was busy during the nineteen-hour day cycle.

After the passengers exited, Reus entered the tube. Plopping into one of the variforms that didn't quite form to his buttocks, he closed his eyes. The particulars of his next stint worried him, which the agency had omitted as usual. This time though, his client was a TualMot. Station Net had little info on them: honorable, secretive, insectile, and large. Reus never liked bugs, least of all intelligent ones. *Form conforms to function. Or was it the other way around, function follows form?*

The tube passed through a murky brown water sector, then a divider field shimmered, followed by translucent green water.

The necessity to warn the Inner League Defense sizzled in his brain like the acid seas of Somor. Perhaps after this stint with the TualMot queen he could afford passage on one of the alien ships. Anything would do to get off this station; he would scrub alien decks or travel in a cargo hold. Visions of the massacre at Jewel flooded his mind. When the probe had sent data back on Jewel, a distant AA-class world that didn't require any terraforming, the opening of the remote Virgis wormhole and the colonization of Jewel had begun in earnest.

Jewel is a dead world now. By the time Inner League received the new colony's plea for help, they had all been massacred. Reus shut his eyes to the images of the brief battle, annihilation, rather. As soon as his squadron had emerged from the Virgis Nexus, enormous dumbbell-shaped ships attacked them. Inner League weapons slid off the silver and purple mosaic hulls, but the aliens' weapons cut his squadron to scrap metal in a few hours. As far as he knew, he was the only survivor. Who were the Dumbbells? They appeared out of nowhere and ignored all comm signals.

After he arrived here, the station AI had eaten a large chuck of his funds to run a search on the Dumbbells, but it came up with nothing. The Dumbbells were unknown to the Thuurin Conglomerate.

Reus stood up and queued behind a large alien. A vertical tube carried him to the next level up. His steps faltered for a second until he adjusted to the lower gravity, then hastened across a commercial plaza, hoping that CCtavilon could do him immediately. It wasn't the first time or the last, but he hated it when the agency sprung a last minute stint on him.

Holos of strange Sophonts with grafted parts marched by the entrance of the Cleave Parlor. Reus put his finger inside the pulsing purple flesh that looked like an alien sex orifice, and the door morphed open between two entwined Sakarans. He squeezed through the pulsing flesh gingerly and walked to the secretary unit. It was a mass of rippling purple tissues, above which perched the large head of a Sakaran secretary associate. It lifted a meter above its body, supported by a ribbed neck, and regarded him.

"Reus Saint Mark," it said in sibilant sounds but otherwise in perfect Human Galactic. "I believe you're here for a tail."

Reus nodded, not trusting his voice to speak. Drastic body alterations unnerved him. Having lived most of his sixty years on Inner League worlds where Purist tenets prevailed, he had a narrow view on body image: Reus Saint Mark, pure human and pilot, first Lieutenant aboard the *Providence.* Whose luck had run out in the Virgis Nexus. But his duty kept him going. The Inner League Defense must learn about the Dumbbells.

Reus recalled his Captain's words as she ejected him in a lifepod amidst enemy fire while the *Providence* was disintegrating. *"You must survive and warn Defense."* But it's been nearly a year, and all he had achieved thus far was obeying her first command. He had survived but just barely. The alien ship that had found his lifepod drifting had taken him aboard and transported him to Quardeen Nexus. Transport fee to the aliens, stasis reversal by the station, and his consumption of the essentials, air, water, food, had already put him in debt by then.

"Fortunate for you that CCtavilon is just finishing," the secretary unit said. "He will take you shortly." The head lowered onto the body and a small claw appeared, rooting inside the liquid screen lodged in its horizontal section, rearranging the scrawling data. "Ah, your credit is in the red." The unit's head whipped up, large mouth oozing saliva.

"Flesh Flex will advance CCtavilon's fee." Reus kept the annoyance out of his voice. It was disconcerting that everyone at this station was so mercenary. Though the Human Spheres were not much better, at least they didn't charge visiting Sophonts for air.

"I'm ready for you," CCtavilon said, his cluster of head tentacles fluttering. One of his flesh arms waved Reus towards the throbbing caul leading to the surgical theater.

Reus walked through the snug entrance and felt its cool, slimy caress as it dissolved his clothing and disinfected him. CCtavilon followed him inside, his four cyber arms clanking, blades and micro drills whirring. Reus shuddered and couldn't decide which he hated more, the four indigo tentacle arms or the glinting mechanical attachments.

"On your stomach," CCtavilon warbled through his speaking mouth and gestured to the surgical cradle.

Naked, Reus lowered himself onto the opaline pulsing surface and felt its micro and nano sensors sink into his body.

"Aware costs twenty units, anesthetized costs forty," CCtavilon said.

"Aware," Reus said, turning his head sideways to avoid the cradle's slimy surface touching his mouth.

Reus shuddered as CCtavilon's flesh arms descended on his buttocks, the silky tassels all the more vile for their sensuous touch. Metal arm flashed silver, and then a sharp pain stabbed his lowest vertebra, shooting up all the way to his head. Reus stifled a moan.

"The worst is almost over," CCtavilon said. His head shifted before the hovering diagnostic screen, purple beak clicking. "I will give you a mild relaxant, free of charge. You are a good test subject."

Reus felt a wet touch on his lower back. The surgical cradle surged up his sides and oozed over his body until it enfolded him, leaving only his head free. It throbbed and pulsed and tingled around his buttocks, but he couldn't muster enough energy to be repulsed.

He must have dozed and woke disoriented.

"Removal of the TualMot tail will not be painful, because I have grown it from synth-flesh."

Reus grabbed the glutinous sides of the cradle and heaved himself out of its alien flesh. It made a plopping sound as it released him. He tottered for a moment and almost fell backward, but one of CCtavilon's purple arms steadied him.

"Look," CCtavilon said and pointed to mirror. "A fully functioning TualMot tail, the first one I designed."

Reus gasped. A slim, pale-bodied human stood there, sporting a huge russet tail that quivered wetly. He took a few steps, bending forward to balance the massive weight. "What does it do?"

"She'll tell you. We're not here to dispense information. Besides, this commission has more confidentiality clauses than the station has Sophonts. Anything I say could be used against me. But don't worry, the TualMot is the most honorable species in the Thuurin Conglomerate."

Reus grunted and tried to disengage from CCtavilon's grasp.

"Hold still." CCtavilon supported him with two tentacle arms. "I inserted a power-assist into the base of the tail, but it will take a few seconds to integrate with your nervous system."

Reus swallowed and flexed the muscles around his coccyx. The tail jerked and pulled him sideways. He grabbed one of CCtavilon's cyber arms, cold and slick under his trembling fingers. His head spun, and he swayed.

CCtavilon loomed over him, his four orange eyes darting around in their bony sockets. He enwrapped Reus' head in his four flesh hands, all thirty-two fingers sprouting nano cilia and probing his brain.

Reus felt a sharp pain in both ears and then the alien fingers released him.

"That should do it. I adjusted your sense of balance."

"Thanks." The pain was gone and he took a few tentative steps. "It's better."

CCtavilon's speaking mouth warbled, "It will take a few more minutes for the compositor to reassemble your garb. Unless you want to leave wearing only your hide."

No one would bat an eyestalk or a sensor cluster if he left naked; many Sophonts eschewed clothing. Besides, few on this station knew human customs. But Reus felt better wearing his coverall, because he didn't relish alien flesh brushing against him on the public transports. He hoped that the compositor had the good sense to allow for the tail when it remade his coverall, otherwise he'd have to instruct the fabric to make one. That would suck power from station air, another expense added to his debt.

Gratified by the hole for the new tail, Reus pulled on his coverall and left.

*   *   *

Reus leaned back on the tail and trembled, trying to avoid her touch. Warmth smothered him, and he found the small chamber claustrophobic.

The TualMot queen stood three meters tall, her fine russet fur a rippling velvet in whorls of patterns. The body was roughly hourglass-shaped with the lower part larger and bulging at the front, stretched shiny and lacking fur. The top body—too large to call a head—had two rows of eyes, hard as onyx chips and running all the way around. Below them, three rubbery holes opened and closed rhythmically. Six ball-socket-jointed, short legs supported the large bulk. Several appendages grew out of both upper and lower parts of her body, like lengths of sausages pinched off at random places. All limbs ended in various manipulators, two of which reached for him.

Fear paralyzed him. To control it, his mind automatically searched for patterns that would put her species into a familiar category. She had fur and bones, not chitin or carapace, so perhaps her species didn't evolve from an insect. But she still looked like a nightmare.

"ReusSaintMark," the artificial voice issued from a translator she wore on one of her upper body appendages. The sound was overlaid by a trilling and chirping that came from an orifice on the upper body. "Must make haste before they emerge."

Reus stepped back and bumped into the rubbery wall of the chamber. It rippled, and he snatched his hands away, watched the queen advance. The rounded center of her tumescent lower body ended in a short umbilical and was open like a gun turret, oozing a viscous fluid. At close up, her velvety fur was actually a thin skin so tightly pleated that it appeared bristly.

She spun him around roughly. "Push your tail into the egg sack," the artificial voice demanded. The chirping sounds from her upper body were frantic, like a disturbed nest of birds.

It's not my tail. Reus stiffened, hesitating.

"Quick, do it or I'll crush you!" A strong stench of ammonia and decayed vegetation enveloped him.

Egg sack. He swallowed a rising gorge and closed his eyes, then lifted the tail and searched for her moist cloacae blindly. A smooth-skinned appendage grabbed the tail and shoved it halfway into the pulsing warm hole. It closed around the hard alien member like a sphincter. Although not truly a part of him, Reus almost fainted from the horror of it.

"Move the tail around to slay them all!"

Slay what? What have I gotten myself into? This must be infanticide. But he numbed his mind and obeyed, otherwise he would suck vacuum soon. Flexing his coccyx, he felt the tail gyrate inside her, as though doing it on its own accord.

"Release the venom. Quick!" Her body heaved and buckled, clutching his to hers as though she'd never let go.

How do I release the venom? He cursed CCtavilon for not telling him how to operate the graft. Reus moved the tail faster and faster, hoping that that would release the venom. Sweat drenched his body, mingling with the alien fluids of the queen. Finally, he felt the tail squirting acid inside her egg sack. A shout escaped his lips as her flailing appendages whipped him.

She shoved him away and shuddered a few times, her shiny lower body quaking. Ten she grabbed the cloacae with three appendages and ripped.

Reus flinched at the wet slurping sound as the tissues tore. A batch of fist-sized, pinkish ovoids surged onto the floor, accompanied by a nose-curdling stench. They twitched a few times, but then fizzled and popped loudly, releasing more fetor into the already saturated air.

He pinched his nose shut and breathed through his mouth.

But it was too late, his stomach heaved and he vomited onto the rubbery floor in great gushes. When he felt empty but still soiled, he staggered a few steps away from the foul liquids and wiped his mouth on the sleeve of his coverall.

"That was wonderful, a joint release. I did not realize that you were also in need of purging." The queen's lower body began to shrink, creasing into minute folds until it looked like velvet, matching her other parts.

"Just an automatic reaction—" He pointed to the mess on the floor.

"All the more remarkable. I never had that kind of pleasure reaction from an alien. Thank you, ReusSaintMark. I am sorry if I have spoken harshly to you, but haste was imperative. I truly appreciate your service, because I could not win the upcoming combat in a gravid state."

"I just helped you kill several of your offsprings."

"Those?" She gestured to the odorous puddle. "Those are parasite eggs. I lost my last male a while ago. With no male to purge me, the junior queens would have defeated me. That is why I had to avail myself to the station's services."

The rubbery deck folded over the remains of her eggs and his vomit, rippled once, and then smoothed out, swallowing the mess.

Reus wondered what losing a male meant in the context of the TualMot, dead, displaced, or perhaps eaten. Then he remembered that the TualMot were herbivores. The tail stunk and felt sticky. This nauseating act had nothing to do with reproduction or even sexual enjoyment; it was a simple purging. From Lieutenant to janitor to sometime art model, he had plunged to a lowly cathartic, a laxative to flush parasites from a constipated alien queen. He was thoroughly disgusted with himself and turned to leave.

"Wait," said the queen. A trilling sound and a smell of spring bouquet wafted from her. "I am now honor bound to you. Before the ship allows you to leave, I must grant you a wish, a service, or a favor."

"I trust you transferred payment to my account."

"Shipmind transferred your fee, but the pheromones of the honor vigilator inform me that I am honor bound. I must grant you anything within my spectrum of means."

A smile split his face. "Well, there is one thing you can do. Take me to the Orion Nexus." Hope welled up inside him. If he could return to Inner League space and give Defense the record of the massacre at the Virgis Nexus, it would save lives. Or not, the intel was almost a year outdated, but it was his duty.

"Orion Nexus is out of my way. I consulted the honor vigilator and found that your wish is too burdensome for me to grant. The ship is bursting with cargo and crew." A bitter citrus smell accompanied her decline. "A junior queen will show you off the ship."

Annoyance sparked, flaming into anger. Was she toying with him?

"Guard your emotions." The station AI had told him. *"Many species here communicate by pheromones."* Reus didn't care, he was sick of the profit-minded Sophonts of Quardeen Station. Honor, duty, and dignity, he had lost all during his stay here. Following a smaller

version of the queen along the ship decks, he allowed all his resentments and frustrations to spill over. *If you can sense that, choke on it.*

Once off the TualMot ship, he headed to CCtavilon's Parlor. At least his repugnant act had earned him enough units to stay alive for another month. That was better than being dead, and while he lived, he hoped to carry out his duty. The certainty that he would be shunned on the Inner League worlds didn't deter him, though it made him sad.

Reus kicked at a pile of rubbish the cleaning robots had missed. After the countless grafts and genetic manipulations during the past year, he was hopelessly contaminated by Purist standards. The more he thought about it, the more narrow-minded the Inner League seemed. It suddenly dawned on him that he was an Outworlder now. For the first time in his life, he found himself on the other side of Inner League snobbery. Shame flooded him for having served an elitist government for so long. He always knew that people of the Outworld Terrator couldn't afford terraforming the marginal worlds they had settled. That left forced mutation and genetic alterations of themselves, which sometimes resulted in unsightly appearance. Never mind that it was circumstances caused by Inner League economy and the fact that they controlled the wealthiest worlds, the majority of Humanity was considered un-Pure.

Reus stood before the TualMot queen again and steadied himself on the elastic wall of the chamber as it buckled once. Though she could have reached him through station link, she had requested his physical presence. Hope swelled in him again; perhaps his pheromone release had worked.

Since CCtavilon had removed the tail already, Reus was not equipped to provide the same service to her, not that he would. He was a wealthy Sophont now, heady on air, and he could even afford to swim in water. He had treated himself to real food meals instead of the nutrition paste he'd been eating.

"ReusSaintMark, my honor would not allow me to leave without you." She exuded the smell of exotic flowers.

Much improvement from the malodorous infanticide we committed. With an effort, he dismissed the nasty images and waited, daring to hope.

He could finally carry out his duty. Perhaps he was not too late to make a difference.

"The honor vigilator can be fickle at times. Alien chemicals confuse it, but it found, after all, that I was still honor bound to you. That means we were stuck at this station until I fulfilled the honor code. After much thinking, I found a way to transport you to Orion Nexus."

Relief flooded him. "Thank you. I'll pack and come back." He turned to leave quickly before the honor vigilator or the queen could change her mind.

"We are already on our way."

"What?"

"As soon as you boarded, my pheromones released the ship. It left the station. We are en route to the wormhole. We have lost much time with my purging and the following combat. Ship's holds are full of perishable merchandise. Further delay was not cost effective."

Reus shrugged. His suit could always be replaced. "Great, so where do I bunk?"

"Bunk?"

"Sleep, you know. Where do I spend the journey?"

"In here." Two of her upper body appendages plucked a green metal sphere out of the chamber wall.

Reus laughed, but it was tinged with apprehension. "I'm small but not that small."

"We can only transport your head, your body must be spaced."

His stomach plunged and he felt dizzy. A cold sweat broke out on his face. In seconds, his coverall was drenched faster than the fabric could convert it. "Fuck your honor. You can't do that."

"Yes, I can. This stasis unit will accommodate your braincase. It is designed especially for humanoids of your type." She twirled the green sphere around.

Suddenly, it looked menacing. His throat constricted and the curses he wanted to shower upon her were left unsaid.

"I looked up data on your species. Humans have establishments that can grow you a new lower body once they receive the upper part."

"You don't understand." His voice shook. "The Inner League Sphere doesn't approve that kind of treatment, only the Outworld

Terrator practices body grafting, cyber fusion, and radical genetic alterations."

"You are Human, are you not? What difference does it make which of your spheres does the grafting?"

She shamed him into silence. Even now, he considered himself an Inner League citizen.

"Honor bound does not mean extreme sacrifices. I cannot destroy cargo and merchandise to accommodate your whole body, because that would be an honor conflict." She took a step towards him.

Reus began to shake, unable to control his fear any longer. He took a swipe at her, but she swatted his arm away and filled his personal space with her body.

"I am sorry this is so distressing, but I promise you that I will deliver your head. I thank you again for your service, ReusSaintMark."

Held by her appendages, the green sphere hovered over his head, an opening forming in its lower hemisphere. It settled on his head with a cold finality.

Reus flailed his arms, fingers clawing at the stasis unit. Suddenly, he felt a sharp pain in his neck and his fingers fell away.

Both his arms fell away.

Reus couldn't feel his body, but he howled mutely as the darkness closed around him. He drifted in a limbo, clinging to the hope of arriving at Orion Nexus. *I must warn Defense, I must warn Defense,* he chanted to keep his sanity until a white fog smothered him.

Author's note: I have read four to five short stories within a couple of weeks, and each one featured a female protagonist who was forced to prostitute herself. It was annoying. So I thought up a situation for Saint Mark.

"The Head of Saint Mark" was also published in Greek translation in *Ennea*, in 2009.

Tomb

SILENT AND COLD, hidden beyond uncharted space and harboring dreadful secrets, Tomb danced between the uneasy concord of two stars.

Commander Tivor Corlin had argued against physical ground exploration after he'd seen the alien structures and the remains of bodies from orbit, but he was in the minority. He shook his head and turned off the shower. And stopped. Snatches of whispers drifted from their room. He plastered his ear to the prefab door and listened, dripping water on the plaz floor.

"Have you disabled it?" he heard Hanna's voice. "Purge the EI's memory and transmit only the data I left you."

What was she talking about? Hanna was his wife, also the senior xenobiologist of the ground crew. Why was she whispering? They shouldn't have secrets between them. Instead of switching on the dryer, he grabbed his skinsuit and pulled it on, waiting as the machines sandwiched between the bucky weaves soaked up the moisture.

"Be careful, we don't want the NP commandos down here." The tension he heard in Hanna's voice made him stiffen. One hand clumsily fumbled with his suit belt while the other one grabbed his wrist unit. The EI, a Human Neuron Enhanced Intelligence aboard the *Celestis* automatically sent down the Nano Police if the data transmitted contained even a hint of a biohazard.

Corlin pushed the door open and entered the room. Hanna turned and flicked off the 3D image, but he had seen enough.

"Tiv, I thought you already left." She reached for her suit, fingers trembling. As she slipped it on, the limp grayish skinsuit conformed to her body and turned flesh color.

She had been talking to Kate, a junior xenobiologist, but he asked anyway, "Who was that?"

"Tom. He was checking if we needed supplies."

Anger suffused him. Hanna had been acting strangely for the past few days, but he had never caught her lying to him before.

Corlin was tempted to remind her that the ground crew was cutoff from the starship; all the landers had returned two weeks ago, even before the construction robots finished erecting the base. But instead of starting an argument, he sealed the head flap of his suit and left her standing there.

Through his implant, he ran through the checks: air-handlers, visuals, interfacing nanites, suit integrity. All functions appeared in green on his visual field. He hurried through the long corridor of the residential complex and turned into the supply shack. A small float pallet detached from the rack. Corlin slaved its simple system to his wrist unit, then piled on a handheld analyzer, a vibraknife, and a queser gun.

He was about to leave when his wrist unit projected a flustered image of Zephan, the senior medic. "Commander Corlin, please come to the science complex. I'm in the sickbay."

"On my way," he said, swallowing his annoyance. Normally, each department functioned on its own, collected and analyzed specimens. Then every night they collated the pooled data, discussed it, and transmitted everything to the *Celestis.* But the archeological site on Tomb was far from normal; it stretched both their individual and collective expertise to the limit.

Before the ground crew landed, orbital surveys and surface probes had confirmed the remote probes' data: alien ruins and the remains of a humanoid species. Though the small settlement and its many oddities bothered him from the beginning, the most recent find undermined his faith in Coalition technology, because the probes should have shown the bones Mara had found in the central structure yesterday.

How did the probes miss them?

Tivor left the supply shack and hurried across the frozen ground. Tomb was slowly slipping into an ice age. Remote from Coalition space, it was in the region of the Mantus Nexus, the newest wormhole. The Mantus station was still in the process of assembly when they had passed through the nexus, and the Neumanns had just finished constructing the CoalNet sats. The *Celestis* was the nearest ship, just one wormhole away when the probes' data had reached the headquarters of Exploration and Survey Corps at Mars.

Corlin looked at the orange sun rising above the serrated mountains, limning the ice plains into an illusion of saffron warmth.

Through the containment field, the landscape shimmered slightly, lending it a sinister specter. He quickly entered the science complex. Portable lab units lined the central passage, each one with its own containment field. When he saw the shimmering field encasing the sick bay, his stomach lurched. The field detected his suit and allowed him to pass through.

"How's Sam?" he asked the medic.

"His spinal cord fell apart during the night," Zephan said. "Four of his vertebrae show spots like these." He stabbed a finger into the diagnostic screen that hovered above the autodoc containing Sam. It was a smooth buckyglass resembling a coffin, resting on a mobile sled and humming quietly.

The screen showed a dark, star-shaped smudge and four lacy vertebrae that seemed like delicate spider webs rather than solid bones. Sam had broken his back three days ago while eating dinner. With the medchines in his body working properly, there should be some improvement.

"The trouble is," Zephan continued. "The autodoc doesn't know what's causing this. According to the analyses, his immunites are working, so it's not viral or degenerative disease. The autodoc's disassemblers can't even crack that cloud surrounding the anomaly. Look at this."

The image changed, displaying the nucleus of a nerve cell. Chromosomes appeared, like chewed clumps of yarns amidst a silver cloud. The view panned and individual genes unfolded.

"See those shiny snowflake shapes? We can't get a larger image, but I'm guessing they're flywheels, though they look different from ours." Zephan pointed to tiny twirling machines that seemed to move with purpose. "They're generating the fog."

"So what's the fog?"

Zephan looked distressed. "Well, the fog, I don't know. You can barely see the flecks, the flywheels that manufacture them. But that's not important." He flicked a wrist in a dismissive motion. "I'll put Sam in stasis, because it's spreading."

Corlin nodded, stifling a stab of fear.

"We must get him up to the *Celestis.*"

"We can't."

"We must." Zephan grabbed his arm. "The medical bay aboard the ship could reassemble his spinal cord and vertebrae."

"Do you see any landers?" Tivor sneered, gesturing outside the building. He lifted a hand to forestall further arguments. "No lander would come. Nothing goes up until we're finished here and cleared by the Nano Pol."

"This is an emergency."

Corlin turned away, unable to meet the man's eyes. He felt like a monster as he said in passing, "Put Sam in a stasis unit, then activate an individual containment field around it."

The door slicked shut behind him. He kicked at the frozen ground, scattering ice chips around.

When he reached a designated port site at the edge of the base, the system reacted and formed a bubble in the shimmering side of the containment field. He slipped inside and stood patiently until an individual containment field built up around him. His implant informed him that he could step through.

He shivered but not from the cold. Zephan's anxiety was another indication that Tomb was getting to them. For a medic to risk breaking quarantine when a stasis unit would keep his patient stable indefinitely didn't bode well for morale.

Face set in hard lines, Corlin took long strides away from the base. As the senior xeno-archaeologist, he would be remiss in his duty if he didn't check the remains Mara had found yesterday, an important find that filled him with dread.

"Tiv, wait for me," Hanna said through his wrist unit, running after him. "I want to take tissue samples of the bones."

Her black eyes sparkled and held a devilish gleam, a slight reddish tint caused by her containment field. Rarely was such extreme caution necessary; the skinsuits ESC used were normally more than sufficient protection on alien worlds. Not on Tomb, though. Her small float pallet trailing behind her reminded Corlin that he had left his in the supply shed.

"Going to the center, aren't you?"

He nodded and took her hand reluctantly, still upset about her secret talk with Kate. "I didn't sleep much, kept thinking about Mara's find."

"I was actually tempted to sneak out last night."

"We better not start breaking rules." He gave her a severe look. "No night excursions on this world."

"Fine." As if dismissing the dangers, Hanna waved at the alien ruins. "Some of the crew still hope we could get Tomb approved for colonization. The planetary engineers could fix the ice age. Between the two suns, it wouldn't be such an awful place."

"It's not worth the resource expenditure. The red star is receding, Tomb will get colder and colder. Be content we're allowed to study the ruins. This place will never be another colony." The star system of Tomb was a physical binary of a K8 orange dwarf and an M10 red dwarf. Tomb was the second world of the orange component, and Tomb Guard, the large gas giant, the third.

"Dex has a viable plan to reengineer the deep core drillers. The Neumanns could incorporate his designs and in a year or two we'd have enough drillers to heat a continent," she said, but her voice sounded hollow.

"Tomb is at perihelion now. Let's just take one day at a time, Hanna. We're all desperate to find another world to colonize, but I'd rather err on the side of caution."

"And forgo an earthlike planet."

Corlin chose not to argue. He was glad they arrived at the edge of the alien site, a circular maze of streets and buildings constructed from a fused material that the analyzer registered as some form of carbon compound bonded by an unknown force. It was not buckyglass but perhaps something even more enduring. Considering the age of the settlement, over seven hundred millennia, it was in good shape.

He pushed aside the crumbling gate and walked along the curving street. Walls and stairs were streaked with hues of cinnamon and henna. Rubble stood in heaps here and there, collapsed roofs and fence-like structures moldering under the alien sun.

"Commander Corlin," he heard through his implant.

"Go ahead, Kate."

"Is Hanna with you? She's offline."

A flash of fear crossed Hanna's eyes before she said, "What's up Kate?"

"The EI is finished with the new analyses."

"About time," Hanna said, giving him a sidelong glance.

"Yeah, well, the EI got confused." Kate gave a nervous laugh. "The result is shocking. It could've addled its brains."

Corlin deduced by Kate's prattling that she must be perturbed, so was obviously the EI. The probes had already determined that the alien colonists had *not* originated on Tomb. The cellular structures of the local marine life differed considerably from the one tiny creature whose bones lay naked outside the settlement, which they had designated Site I. The other 407 bones inside the settlement, Site II, were humanoid, covered by a greenish glassy substance that the probes' disassemblers couldn't penetrate.

"Vex you, Kate," Hanna said. "Just tell me what the EI came up with."

"Fine, but you're not gonna like this. I ran it twice to be sure. There are three different types of genetic structures at Site II, even though the bones all look the same. All three types match the human genome to ninety-six percent."

"What?" Hanna stared at Kate's image, her expression full of disbelief.

Corlin felt his stomach knot. Even aboard the *Celestis,* before they landed, he had dreaded this. He had known when the shapes of large ribcages, femurs, and skulls first appeared on the probes' data. They were so obviously human bones. Despite its earthlike atmosphere, liquid water, and lack of killer microbes in the biosphere, he knew something dreadful had happened here.

"Yes," Kate said. "The EI can't even analyze the other four percent. Its main theory is that they could be super genes. The Chief Science Officers are in conference with the Captain."

Hanna swallowed. "Thanks, Kate. I'll get samples from the specimens at Site III. Finish collating data on the marine fauna."

Corlin flicked off the view and turned away. He didn't want to see Hanna's fear. But whatever frightened her didn't matter; what he had overheard this morning was treason, Hanna asking Kate to purge the EI's memory. He wondered what she wanted disabled.

"What do you make of this, Tiv?" Hanna hastened along the maze, following the curving structures.

He shrugged, disturbed by her behavior. Perhaps she had found something important she didn't want to share with the other departments. Professional jealousy was not unheard of among ESC crews. Exploration was clearly the playground of the xenobiologists, because most worlds didn't have ruins. ESC had found some derelict human settlements on marginal or hostile planets, abandoned by early colonists of the 'Ark Ships' era, but those were barely millennia old. He always felt that even the probes neglected xeno-archaeology, programmed to seek only earthlike planets. Regretfully, his chosen field was considered a minor branch of science.

Until Tomb.

Corlin found it hard to fathom that human bones had moldered on this world for over seven hundred millennia. Or nearly human, he reminded himself. Where did they come from? Parallel evolution was out of the equation; besides, nothing else on the world supported it. But he said nothing about his thoughts. "Let's see what info the other bones yield."

"Right," she said in a tone of contrition. "Too bad we can't use the gravbelts."

The alien field that partially covered the maze and its environs interfered with the mechanisms of the gravity belts. Instead of risking accidents, he had decided not to use them. "Be glad the float pallets also have wheels."

Most tenement walls were intact at places, laced with frost. Fluted columns adorned large gates. Balconies and tongues of slabs extended from the top stories.

Geo-imagers had shown a large chamber hundreds of meters below the ice, and the bots had started digging yesterday. A drilling bot churned inside a concave cavity, its upper chassis and shovel arms glinting orange with the rising sun as it threw out piles of ice. Analyzer units sifted through the sludge and recorded its composition.

As they neared the central complex, Corlin slowed imperceptibly, following the curving avenue and turning at the final junction. His heart pounded as he looked around, eyes searching for the growing webs that had started in this ring of the maze. Then he checked the grid image assembled by the flybots, slowly turning it, checking for any spread. Though he had run a quick surveillance at the base last night, he wanted to be certain. Some of the sensors they had placed inside the structure disappeared during the past few days.

"Wait up," he called after Hanna. She was already at the edge of the path that bled into the central plaza. In a quick bound, he was at her side. "Don't rush this, Hanna. I mean it."

She stopped. "Sure, Tiv."

He read tension in her rigid shoulders, and urgency in her voice. They crossed the frozen ground in silence and reached the least damaged section of the alien energy shield. It was the color of a brown dwarf star, and it ebbed and flowed. A little further, it fragmented into sharp ebony cracks, then thickened to murky brown corroded sections at the bottom.

Corlin turned away, his eyes smarting. They passed an amalgam of mechanical and biological jumble. Large pieces of machinery were fused together by filaments of barely seen webs, glinting with crystalline sheen at places, and then abruptly jerking into coarse black surfaces that seemed to suck light out of the surrounding area.

Hanna entered a grisly tunnel, corrugated and lumpy. It seemed to undulate at their passage, like an esophagus of a large beast struggling to swallow them. According to the experts, it was a trick of the senses, because none of their sensors had ever registered any movement. When the tunnel ended, they ducked under a shiny blue arc.

Corlin consulted the map grid again. "Below us to the left." He pointed across the large chamber. Hanna activated her light and it bobbed up in the air. She hurried after him.

Gossamer strands of crimson and violet fluttered at their passing. From his peripheral vision, they looked like they would touch him at any moment, but when he turned his head, they became still again. It was a nightmare scene, obscene and wrong. None of the disassemblers was able to analyze the samples they had taken thus far from the maze.

They stopped. Corlin felt his gorge rising. His skin flushed. Fortunately, the containment field was more than protection, it also concealed his fear.

"This is it." He stared at the wall. A mosaic of thick olive slime, wet fur, red pulsing sphincters, wrinkled yellow hide, and sharp spikes covered it. The entire tapestry looked like an experiment in biological outer coverings. Only the bodies were missing. They had passed it several times on previous visits, keeping well away from it, but Mara had stumbled and fell through yesterday.

"Come one." Corlin grabbed Hanna's hand, closed his eyes, and pulled her into the wall. He couldn't help shuddering at the sound of sucking noises and moist embrace as they passed through.

Large machines littered the chamber. His suit enhanced the images while he recorded everything for further study. The scene became even more disturbing, flowing into fractal patterns of chimerical shapes, playing havoc with his neural implants as his eyes strained to fit them into some perspective. Almost like a span of caterpillar thread, a ribbed wheel, and cranes with serrated mouths marched at the edge of his awareness. Sections of the machines had liquefied and then froze after the cold penetrated the settlement.

With a sigh, he moved his scanner in a wide sweep, downloading the data into his implant.

Glancing at the device, he said, "Background dating only, a little over seven hundred thousand years old."

He approached the crystallized bones timidly, aware of Hanna shuffling beside him. A sense of unreality gripped him at the sight. Preserved by whatever the glassy casing was, the white bones radiated an ancient warning. They were the partial remains of humanoid figures, giants of at least two and a half meters tall.

Corlin stood there and stared, palms slick with perspiration until his suit absorbed it. The bones were not just humanoid; they were human.

But the time, the time, the time, it echoed in his mind. The time factor was all wrong.

Some of the skeletons were nearly intact, others covered by purple mossy growths. A humerus lay detached from a shoulder bone, the green casing cracked. The skeletons were dotted with brown holes from which violet tubular structures burst out in clusters. A ribcage leaned sideways, poking curved bones skyward, as if imploring the heavens. Between the arcing bones, bundles of oyster masses protruded. Corlin moved closer and squatted, adjusting his vision.

He gasped and scooted back, landing on his rump.

"You all right, Tiv?"

"Fine," he said after his suit adjusted to his rapid breathing. He stood up and approached again.

From the glistening globs, tiny faces glared at him, mocking human faces. He blinked and shook his head, but the vile scene remained. Some of the glassy coverings showed fractures and the faces underneath those looked like shriveled prunes.

He stood up, legs shaking, and started recording each of the sixteen bodies by moving his scanner over them. Corlin didn't blame Mara for having neglected to take visual records last night;

she was a greenie. He was not, but this place touched something primordial in him.

"Let me." He reached over his shoulder and removed the specimen gun from Hanna's float pallet.

She stood in silence and stared, too paralyzed to protest the usurping of her work.

Corlin crouched next to the least damaged giant figure and pressed the specimen gun at the large femur. It punched through the pale green crystalline sheen that covered the bones and took a few grams of tissue sample. He checked the stasis window on the gun and saw it blink green, preserved and isolated. The question rose in his mind again: why were the probes unable to obtain tissue samples?

"Let's find the Hall of Statues now."

"Mara said that's even worse." Hanna walked before him but kept glancing over her shoulder. They carefully wove their way below the hanging mucus and gossamer threads, ducking to avoid contact.

Seven more skeletons lay at a short distance, barely recognizable through the layers of petrified organics and frozen crust that entombed them. Corlin ran his analyzer over them, and again, it didn't register what the material was. "We could've done this by using the remotes and we probably should have." He couldn't help the reproach in his tone, as Hanna was among the scientists that had argued for landing.

"Physical surveys yield more answers. There's always something the drone sensors miss. Besides, the probes couldn't take tissue samples."

"Don't you find that odd? We're using the same tissue guns the probes did." A chilling thought occurred to him, so ominous that it nearly paralyzed him.

"Maybe the probes got damaged."

Corlin nodded, but he couldn't suppress his gnawing suspicion. He routed the data to the *Celestis* in mechanical motions. The physical specimens would be analyzed by the portable EI at the Base.

They walked through another arch, then a short tunnel, and finally stepped into a chamber. *The Hall of Statues, where Mara saw the standing figures.*

Barely discernible fractal patterns played on his retinas. The hovering light seemed to dim a fraction. The figures were a variety of shapes, all exceeding three meters. Standing upright and nearly jet-black with a faint luster of viridian and wine, like oil on water, they presented a menagerie from hell. The shine skidded across the hard surfaces of long knobby appendages that had five joints and looked like gears. They were undamaged and seemed full-fleshed. No bones showed.

Misshapen large heads displayed deeply set ruby eyes that he could've sworn were animated by malice. All had long hair, but the way it hung in neatly coiled fleshy tassels gave the impression of slim tentacles. Two had four arms coiling around their torsos, and one sprouted clusters of pincers from a human-looking mouth.

The fourth had six legs, but two of those dangled in the air. Its head was only a protoplasmic blob, folded and creased like a swollen brain from which scarlet cilia sprouted. Some were connected to a round black disc.

Heart pounding, Corlin reached over and tried to pry away the disc. It didn't budge.

The grisly statues stood in a rough circle. Some had tails with metallic-looking spikes, and others were covered with round mirrors. Some sported tiny black clusters of eyes sprouting from shoulders, abdomens, and backs. Corlin tried to guess the function of the overlapping blue flat organs covering a triangular head, but gave up.

He took the tissue gun again and pressed it to a leg. And pressed it again. The tool emitted a shrill sound, but the covering of the statue remained unbroken. After he checked the stasis window, he tried another it another statue. Nothing. He circled around the chamber and repeated the procedure, but the hard casing didn't yield to his tool.

"Looks like we'll have to skip these specimens," he said. "Let's go, there's nothing more we can do here."

He guided Hanna across the hall and then through the slimy wall. They hurried toward the exit, taking long strides in doubled up positions. He could've sworn the filaments hung lower, fluttering at their passing and extending barely visible strands to reach them.

"So what do you think?" Hanna's voice trembled.

"Something from space attacked them."

"Or runaway replicators engineered by the colonists."

"No, it's more like a tailored swarm, a set of virulent replicators to kill the colonists." He wondered why she argued her point when the evidence was against it. "Perhaps they were refugees fleeing from an enemy. And the enemy found them."

None of the native life had suffered the same fate. The marine sediments and crust samples showed no great extinction in the timeframe when this happened. The ancient colonists were killed by a plague that had *not* originated on Tomb. Analyses showed that much, even if their instruments couldn't decode the structures of the pestilence.

Corlin called Dan at the base. "Allocate four robots to install sensors in the new chambers Mara found."

"Right away," Dan said.

Corlin ate dinner in the science complex, sitting by the portable bioanalyzer and munching a clish sandwich that Hanna had brought him from the mess hall. Impatience gnawed at him, and he silently cursed the strident protocols of quarantine that slowed the analyses by adding numerous safety features.

Disturbing scenarios crossed his mind: Maybe the central complex was a testing site, an ancient battleground where a molecular battle had been waged, subsuming foreign agents, decoding secrets, and forging alliances by wielding molecular armies within the silent tombs of each encased bodies.

The shrill sound of the alarm almost made him choke. He dropped the sandwich and jumped up, coughing, then blinking at the blurry image his implant generated.

The Nano Pol. A chill exploded in his stomach as the image cleared. Silvery red forms stormed the corridor of the residential complex, stunners and blasters glinting with cold intent. They shoved crewmembers out of the dorms. The seasoned crew fled instinctively, but some of the greenies milled around, staring, until one of the NP commandos barked at them. Another one of the commandos pointed a finger at a room, and a containment field formed instantly.

"Biohazard in room six," said the base system. "Residential section is presently—"

Another image popped up, showing Captain Norris aboard the *Celestis.* Distress lines marred her face. The curses and grunts emanating from the residential section nearly drowned out her voice. "Commander Corlin, the Nano Pol landed. Response to a biohazard."

He stood in numbed silence, looking stupid with his mouth hanging open. Finally, he said, "It's Rob's room."

"Yes," said the Captain. "From the images we've got, it looks like something's replicating in there. It started from the tissue gun he used at site II. He took one of the EI units into his room."

Corlin swallowed and felt his heart turning to stone. He didn't understand how this could have happened. The sealed systems were nanoimmune, hacker-proofed, and heuristic.

His earlier fear returned. The plague that infested the alien colony was beyond Coalition technology. He remembered Sam's bone cells and how those giant machines churned out millions of miniscule ones inside his genes.

He barely heard the Captain voice. "The NP will investigate if there might have been a human mistake. They'll examine the analyzer in—"

It happened silently. Rob's room buckled and turned vermilion, as if lit from within. Liquid fire oozed and burbled and consumed furniture, walls, and equipment, melting them rapidly. The NP commandos were backing out, their cyber arms spitting more thermnites into the residential building.

Corlin ran outside, yelling to people, "Get back! Clear the area." He frantically searched for Hanna, while he questioned the base system, "Where's Rob?"

Four commandos stood outside, pelting the residential complex with thermnite pallets.

"Is everyone out?" Tivor yelled. "Hanna!" Then he saw her angling toward him, whispering urgently to Kate. "Where's Robert?"

"Rob was in his quarters," said the base system.

Corlin felt like a punch in the gut.

He ran to the confused crowd and herded them toward the science complex, wondering who else might have remained inside. They were halfway across the open field when the residential building began to glow. The plaz walls swelled, bubbled and frothed, emitting a deep rumble until the entire structure began to collapse. The crimson goo kissed the ice with a loud slap, oozed and sizzled for a few seconds, then slowly crackled into pewter ash.

Four NP commandos stood in a ready stance around the inactive thermnites, cyber arms running analyzers over the ash. The sun stood high in the sky, etching their shapes into caustic shadows.

* * *

No one talked about Rob's death the following day, but some people looked cowed, others stoic, and the majority seemed neurotic, eyes shifting left and right. Hanna and Kate looked guilty.

A small crowd gathered behind Dimitri in the science complex. He wore an interface design cap, its glistening convoluted surface like an extra brain, flickering with blue sparks. Corlin walked over and glanced at Dimitri's slowly turning 3D image. It showed a tubular, yellow object with blue spikes and barbs arranged around its outer surface like a cylindrical brush.

"It's a new disassembler he designed," Eli whispered. "He's running a final check, then we'll test it."

Dimitri had developed the disassemblers that traced some of the plague's structures. But his machines had halted at a certain stage.

"All right," Dimitri said and snatched off the interface cap. His black hair was matted but his eyes sparkled with enthusiasm. "These might do the trick. I just routed them to the sealed specimen container that has the bone tissue from site II."

The image showed Dimitri's large yellow machines swimming to the site of chaos. Silver flywheels spun in a blur, spewing out snowflakes. Or things that looked like snowflakes. The crew watched in silence as Dimitri's machines started rotating also, snagging some of the silvery flakes.

People began to cheer halfheartedly.

The yellow nanomachines attenuated some of their spikes, but they seemed to be quivering. Clogs built up rapidly, and the tool arms stiffened. After about thirty minutes of painful struggle, they just circled the alien particles in a vague disorder, quickly losing their functioning abilities.

Dimitri zoomed in on one of his machines. It was covered by millions of snowflakes, busily winding filaments around it. When the snowflakes stopped spinning, his machine looked like a moth cocoon, the greenish substance similar to the casing of the bones.

"God, we're all going to die!" Carrie screamed. She began to cry, covering her face.

Corlin rushed over and led her away from the group. "Calm down, Carrie, we'll be fine," he whispered. "We have the best suits, plus the containment fields." Her body shook with great sobs, and she tried to shake off his arm. He felt sympathy for the greenie scientists. Tomb was a cruel blow to their illusion of grandeur, that Humanity could do anything.

Mark, one of the medics appeared at their side. "I'll get her a tranq." He led Carrie away. Corlin shot him a grateful glance and returned to the group, gauging the reaction of the others. They milled around nervously, glancing covertly at the cocooned machines.

"Blast it," cursed Dimitri, as if unaware of the commotion. "I know the plague corrupts protein, carbon, and even necronites." He looked down at his boots.

"But not Tomb life," Ryan said. He was with the marine biology section. "We've tested them on tissues and bones of several sea fauna."

Dimitri looked up. "Hey, you've just given me an idea."

"It's been a long day." Corlin slapped Dimitri on the back. "You can start fresh tomorrow."

Dimitri snorted. "A twenty-one-hour day is not long enough to wear me out. I couldn't sleep anyway. Maybe I can give my disassemblers an edge by incorporating some characteristics of Tomb life into them. A hybrid."

Corlin left and walked to the supply shack, their quarters since the destruction of the residential complex, and hoped that Dimitri's hybrid disassemblers would work.

Hanna lay on the airbed the robots had installed, wearing only a white shift. Though not as comfortable as the variforms that conformed to bodies, an airbed was better than the bare floor. Ground crews weren't too fastidious. She looked up from the image she was scrutinizing, then turned it off and gave him a careworn smile. "You look as tired as I feel."

While he removed his clothes and suit, his conclusions kept running through his mind. He lay down next to her. "Our probes activated the plague."

"What?" Hanna looked away. She fiddled with the cover, hands shaking.

"The interstellar probes ESC sent through the Mantus Nexus activated the plague."

"Oh," she said, and still didn't look at him.

"The probes couldn't take tissue samples from the bones, because they've been sealed by that greenish substance, but they reactivated something dormant that reacted to our own disassemblers. Whether it's a lure to get us here physically or just an automatic recognition subroutine I don't know."

"You're saying it was premeditated, but I can't believe that." Her voice sounded false, and when she finally looked at him, her expression held fear.

"If someone wanted to infect us with the plague machines, they couldn't have gone through the probes, because the probes only transmit *data* to the Coalition. They had to get us here. Our curiosity did the rest."

"Tiv, if what you're saying is true. . ." She looked sheepish and buried her face into his chest. "I'm so sorry." She began to sob. "We knew, Kate and I, from the initial samples. I ordered her to falsify the data sent to the *Celestis,* because—"

—you were afraid of the Nano Pol. He pulled her shaking body closer.

"I, I suspected since the Site II samples that, that we were dealing with plague replicators, something beyond our scale." She pulled away and wiped her eyes with the blanket.

"Dimitri may design something useful." Corlin embraced her, feeling his body responding to the warmth of hers. He didn't want to talk anymore, so he covered her mouth with his own.

They made love, then without the aid of their implants, they fell into a natural sleep.

Corlin woke up rested. After they ate a couple of cold ration bars, they went to see Dimitri.

A bustle of activity greeted them at the science complex, visual fields flickering with data loops, portable analyzers humming. A few stasis capsules passed them on floating sleds. Corlin wondered why they were being moved when he saw Dimitri sitting alone and staring at a holoscreen.

Hanna shook her head slightly, and he gazed at the images, trying to swallow his disappointment. Dimitri's hybrid disassemblers didn't work either; they just sat at the edge of the sub cellular structures of the ancient colonists.

"Commander," he heard from behind them. Eugene Thomas, the geophysicist waved at him, his voice filled with trepidation. "Please step over here."

He dashed to the other end of the room, Hanna behind him.

"Something's tunneling through the ice." Thomas pointed to his visual field.

The base with its flickering containment field and the alien site above ground was rendered in color. The images below the ice looked a ghostly monochrome, but he could clearly see a bullet-shaped object heading in their direction.

"What is it?"

Thomas shook his head. "It's coming from here." He pointed to the central construction in the alien maze. A convoluted passage began below the ice, moving even as they were watching, not fast but relentlessly.

"Site III," Corlin whispered. He contacted the base EI. "Track the object's progress and work out the location of its emergence."

"I am tracking and prepared to isolate the intruder," said the EI.

"Keep an eye on it," he said to Thomas and left.

The containment fields had been borne out of the Plague Years centuries ago, a brutal span of eighty years during which billions of people died and thousands of ecosystems were ruined. Everyone had worn them outside their communes and enclaves back then. As the plagues had reorganized themselves and adapted, people invested more and more in field developments. But would the fields protect them now?

He sighed and opened the general com. "This is Commander Corlin. Everyone suit up and activate a personal containment field. This is an order."

Then he transmitted his report and recommendation to the *Celestis.*

The eye symbol, a classified reply to his report, appeared on Corlin's retinal screen at 1400 shiptime. In a cold dread, he blinked away the icon and left the science complex. Walking behind an ice rover, he activated the security program through his implant. For a moment, he closed his eyes, hoping the scientists aboard the *Celestis* disagreed with his assessment. When he opened them, he gasped. DATA RECEIVED NECESSITATES A LEVEL FIVE BURN. BETWEEN 2000 AND 2400 HOURS. PREPARE CREW.

Tomb lingered in the wan sunlight of its orange primary before slipping into the long night. Corlin gazed out the plaz window of the science complex, between the jagged mountain peaks at the mauve sky, and dreaded the sparks that would soon appear on the horizon.

Hanna was awake somewhere, but the rest of the ground crew slept. By regulation, he and Hanna should be as well, perhaps dreaming about the future and a tomorrow. But he couldn't bring himself to sleep through the coming Burn.

A guardian of dreams now rather than a Commander, he grimaced and stood up, heading to perform his last duty. The prefab plaz door moved aside at his approach, and he stepped into the makeshift corridor. Robots had turned sections of the science complex into a dorm, partitioned them into tiny cubicles after the contamination of the residential building. A futile gesture to keep up morale, for they could have slept anywhere or nowhere for the short time, but ESC Quarantine Law was specific.

He stopped at the first door and interfaced with the base system. The occupant was in deep sleep. Nora Stanley, planetary geologist, the image of the woman appeared on the holoscreen before him. She was young, thirty-six, and this was her third ground exploration. Corlin felt the guilt eating at him, but he had to remind himself that they had all signed the ESC contract.

I'm sorry I ordered your death, Nora. He left the sleeping woman's cubicle, his boots making loud clangs on the floor.

At the next cubicle, he closed his eyes to blot out the images of Dimitri, working until Corlin had released the sleepnites into the compound. Interface cap on his head, Dimitri slouched in the chair in front of his data streams, face lax in sleep like a child's. The scene twisted Corlin's heart. Dimitri was the youngest crewmember, barely out of Space Force Academy, on his very first exploration of an alien world.

Corlin hung his head and left Dimitri's door, then proceeded to check the next one. From here on, he did them automatically, just making sure they were in deep sleep, then onto the next crewmember. By the time he finished, he was exhausted and emotionally drained.

Hanna waited for him by the door of the supply shack. He walked slowly, trying not to think about what was coming. The Burn was a rarely mentioned topic among the crews of ESC, but it always hovered below the surface of their consciousness. A subliminal monster, it was the ultimate cure for a plague.

The low hum of the field generator barely penetrated his awareness when he passed the compact machine. They could even turn the force field off now. But then again, they had more power than they could ever use. A bitter laughter escaped his lips.

"You all right?" Hanna held their suits.

Corlin shook his head and didn't take his suit. "No, I want to go outside and see this world with my naked eyes."

Her full lips tightened into thin lines, but she nodded. "I suppose it doesn't matter—"

He looked down, unable to face the despair in her eyes. He was grateful she didn't state the time; he didn't want to know, needed to pretend for a while yet that these were not their last hours. They had agreed after he recommended the Burn—which he shouldn't have told her—that they wouldn't act, speak, and think morbidly. It's over, it doesn't matter now, we're dead, wouldn't enter the remainder of their lives. But they crept in more and more as the hour neared.

Hanna shoved the suits into the supply shed and took his arm. He avoided looking at the two contained alien substance, baleful red domes protruding a meter above the ice, glimmering faintly. The containment field was fighting a losing battle, visibly dimming as the alien disassemblers rendered it useless.

When they reached the edge of the main field, Corlin asked the base system to form an aperture. Alarms rang through his implant, informing him that he needed a suit. The 3D schematic of the base was stitched with red blinking lights. Then all the pre-designated exit sites fused, and a biohazard sign hovered before him.

"Damn," he cursed. The stupid system thought there was still something worth protecting. He consulted the main program and found the override algorithm. From there, he shut down the field generator.

Beginning at the top of the coruscating dome, the containment field slowly etiolated and flickered once. In the next instant, the field shimmered up again, making a sizzling sound as its energies singed the atmosphere of the world. It wavered above their heads for a moment and then righted itself.

"Shit," Corlin cursed again. "I forgot about the backup generator."

Hanna's hand slid up his arm. Her eyes filmed over as she sent the command through her implant. "Fixed."

The field shuddered. Its rainbow colors rippled and lost coherence, turned red, and the field bled into the bruised sunset of Tomb.

Corlin hesitated, glancing back at the building that housed the sleeping crew. For both Hanna and him, the next landing would have been their hundredth on an alien world. Neither of them would achieve that now, not in this body.

A level five Burn. He visualized the planet bombarded by thermnite missiles, consuming the atmosphere, the ice, and the ocean, liquid fire circling around. Dirty missiles would follow, exterminating whatever remained and thoroughly wiping away any chance for life for the unforeseeable future. A pang of sympathy stabbed through him at the thought of the native life, but then the full horror of *their* predicament hit him.

He gritted his teeth and led Hanna from the base, lacing her arm through his. They walked in silence. The clouds had parted before the spilled ink of the sky, bejeweled with stars. The wind tugged at them with icy claws. Tomb had no moons, but Tomb Guard the gas giant shone bright, its light flickering above the jagged teeth of the frosty mountains. Corlin sought calm by counting their steps.

Slowly, reason started nibbling chunks out of his fear and the tapestry of his life appeared in his mind's eye. He had woven that tapestry by threads of hard work, ambition, accomplishments, love, and even courage. How would all that reside in a new body?

As if reading his mind, Hanna said, "I wonder how the reppers feel. You know, when they first realize . . ."

"Maybe they don't know they're reppers." *Or maybe they're not allowed to know.*

"We won't remember any of this." Her voice sounded small.

Corlin agreed, but couldn't stand voicing that their new bodies would be robbed of the events on Tomb. He felt cheated. He dug his nails into his palms as a silent rage swelled inside him. He blamed ESC, but mostly Defense and Intelligence, because they had enacted the Quarantine Laws and carried out the, the . . . What was he thinking?

Murder.

Except they had all signed the consent forms and left tissue samples in stasis and memory records on file at ESC headquarters. Murder with consent, then.

"It's the price we pay for traveling between the stars," he said finally.

"The universe is exacting a steep price for expansion." Hanna sounded resigned, her voice inflectionless, words falling on the darkness like stones.

Corlin wondered if he'd be happy being a cocoa farmer, or a corporate executive, or a virch designer, or a historian.

"What if we'd gone through a Burn before?"

"We could have." The possibility had occurred to him recently, because he had never seen or talked to a repper before. There were ways that ESC could alter individual records and keep the identities of replicated persons classified.

"You think the Johannists are right?" Hanna sidled closer to him.

"About what?"

"Our souls, that they're embedded in quantum packets of the universe."

He didn't put much credence in the Johannists' claims that some of them tapped into the inter-dimensional cracks and read the soul-memories. He wasn't even certain he believed that souls went into another dimension. But for Hanna's sake, he said, "They've published enough *True Human History*, so it's quite likely."

"Our souls will wander around for some time before the *Celestis* can reach Coalition space. It'll take time to grow the clones even with the accelerators, then more time to imprint them. I wonder if our souls will recognize our new bodies." Her voice sounded distant, as if she was preparing for a long journey.

They stopped by the rise of a low hill and sank down on the ice. Their thermal clothing would protect them long enough not to freeze.

"I would've liked more time to study the sites since—" Hanna shuddered. "Perhaps not, because we don't know how long it would take to end up like the bones."

Corlin knew it was worse than that, that whatever killed the colony could still be out there among the stars. He regretted that they would never know why a species of super humans died on Tomb seven hundred millennia ago. Fear clawed at him again. How could the Coalition defend Humanity against a threat like that?

Corlin was glad that he had slipped a small dose of tranq into Hanna's coffee at dinner. She seemed calmer than was possible under the circumstances. He pulled her closer, and she leaned into him. Her even breathing calmed him eventually.

The wind stopped tugging. There was stillness in the air, as if Tomb held its breath. Abruptly the sky lit up with tiny red sparks, growing into fireballs, and then after a while into a sheet of plasma.

A feeling of déjà vu gripped him as he stared, mesmerized. The next instant, pain seared through him as the heat slammed into them. Corlin held Hanna in a melding embrace and felt their bodies blistering.

Captain Norris watched through the viewport of her cabin, blinking to stem the flow of tears, useless moisture that didn't wash away the pain. Crimson worms crawled over the world as the thermnite missiles landed, expanding into blankets of fire. The oceans boiled as the nuke-tipped missiles ruptured Tomb's crust, throwing up steams of cloud and dust.

She turned away, wiped her face, and prompted her implant to file her report, "Celestis Log, Inner League date March 8, 3821, 2310 shiptime. Successful Burn at Coordinates: MNX-006485979. Interdiction filed, see data attached."

Number nineteen on the list of interdicted systems, she thought. But the scourge must be contained. During her long career in Defense and Intelligence, Captain Claire Norris had watched four other worlds going through a Burn, though not in this replica of a body. Despite the enormous expense invested into opening the Mantus Nexus, the wormhole would be dismantled.

Tomb, a world that should never have been named, has been named. A plague that should never have been awakened, has been awakened.

Author's note: Another story set in *The Dhyany* universe, this one in Book 2. In the book, Tomb is visited by the main protagonist, but he gets to leave. I wanted to write a story from the landing crew's point of view.

Mirage

VIRIDA DIPPED BELOW THE HORIZON in a celery haze, pursued by Mobe the faint orange star. Seija blinked and activated her far vision to record the double sunset when the sky fell. Wispy clouds rippled in rainbow colors, followed by a jewel-studded veil tumbling to the earth. The sudden jolt snatched her out of the spell.

Sounds jazzed up the rocks like a drum roll. Her heart pounding, Seija looked down the mountainside, into billowing dust clouds. *Did the Angylnet fall?* The way she was cut off from the spell suggested the worst.

She reached out with a healer spell, searching for the familiar fractal patterns and straining to pull the threads together. Ragged holes glared back at her, and like an injured animal, the Net recoiled from her touch. More gently now, she tried again. Frayed edges of lacy loops quivered, chrom-nodes unfurled into a tessellated double helix, from which filaments extenuated to weave the gaps together, writhing like silver snakes. The Net was repairing itself, but the damage was extensive. Hoping to aid the repair efforts, Seija guided the severed strands to the chrom-nodes, then another and another, until her head seemed to burst. When she released the loops, they snapped back and hit her like a slingshot. She grabbed her head and moaned.

Seija uncoiled from a sitting position and ran down the decline, weaving around copses and blue-gray boulders. Gravel rolled under her boots, propelling her feet faster than her body could follow. She fell on her rear-end. Panic flooded her as she slid down the mountainside, rocks poking into her shoulders and hips.

She reached out and grabbed a bush. It stopped her descent, but her bones and muscles ached, and blood trickled from her palm where the thorns had slashed it. Gritting her teeth, Seija tightened her grip while she reached up with her other hand and seized a leafy cluster.

Dust covered her. The pain in her shoulder almost made her release her hold, but she gathered her strength and held on while pebbles bounced off her head. For an eternity, she lay there like a splattered bug. Panting from pain and exhaustion, she moved her feet from side to side to find a stable spot.

Her stomach clenched when she finally looked down. A silvery cobweb covered the valley floor, hyaline threads woven into sheets and supported by metal struts. The contraption rested on top of the trees in a tangled mess, twisted rods poking into the sky like broken fingers. Wan lights flickered yellow and green.

With a groan, she turned and stood up. Keeping her body slightly bent forward for balance, she started down, careful not to disturb the gravel underfoot.

Seija stared at the dying lights, hoping this piece was only a small part of the Angylnet. Bile rose in her throat, and her eyes filled with unshed tears. *We were right all along.*

With her far vision in recording mode, she swept her gaze around the destruction. They would incorporate it into the play her rebel group was planning to release, but this kind of proof she would rather do without.

The Angylnet was indestructible, or so they had been told. But worst of all, her people couldn't survive without Net support. During the past few ten-days, Seija had noticed the Angylnet developing coughs and hiccups, shutting down some of its functions and blocking spells that had worked perfectly well before. Other Mages complained. Seija had been watching the sky for days, fully prepared for something terrible. She was not prepared, however, for the end of her world. Magic was dying.

She had studied the ancient history texts and the stolen tech journals for decades and knew that the Net was ailing. Her warnings, however, had found deaf ears among the mage communities. But now—what would they do now?

A bellow shook the valley. She looked around in the deepening gloom and quickly conjured a glow globe. The roar approached. She stood still, thinking about the predators of Mirage. For thousands of years, her people had relied on the suppression spells that kept the predators away from cities and villages.

As the roars came closer, Seija readied her spells. A blast of nose-curdling stench hit her from behind. She whirled and faced a huge ksopir, its black crest framing a narrow head, dagger teeth bared. And it was real, not one from a play.

For a moment, she stood frozen, but instinct quickly took over and she assumed her dragon avatar. Relief flooded her when green sparkle sprang up around her; at least that part of the Net was still functioning. Eyes on the ksopir, she threw the glow globe at it and backed away. Blinded for a moment, the creature shook its head and hissed, exhaling a blast of humid breath smelling of rotten meat. A blue tongue whipped out and swiped her arm. Seija yelped and dodged behind a fat bush. The ksopir advanced, black claws cleaving furrows in the rock. Seija turned and scrambled up a narrow path between thick-boled trees that would hinder the ksopir's passage. A roar followed her, but mercifully, the beast had given up.

Idiots, she fumed as anger replaced fear. Her people have been deluding themselves for thousands of years. When she had first announced that their magic was a network of invisible intelligent machines, albeit self-repairing ones—as the tech books described—the Mage Council had given her a warning. Fortunately, she had used her Divina Draco persona because the second time she'd published the nature of the Angylnet on the Net, most mage communities turned downright hostile toward her and her friends. After that, the collection of questionable books and tech journals had been deleted out of the Angylnet. She had not realized that the Mage Council's power extended to destroying parts of the Net. Fortunately, Cliff had saved copies of those books on his data crystal.

The techno crash over two thousand years ago, followed by the death of the specialists, had stolen much of their knowledge. What little remained had been pilfered by perfidy and enforced ignorance throughout the centuries by the Mage Council. But the Net was failing, and the mage community couldn't afford to live in its comfortable ignorance. Everything hinged on the play, designed to open the eyes of the mage community and to expose the Council's deception.

Seija conjured another glow globe and hurried home.

Seija rubber her tired eyes and paced along the wood floor of her salon.

"Southern Yorn had a phase-out today," Cliff said to the group. "Nine people were killed by wild animals."

"We can't rely on the play alone," Seija said. "It's time to confront Carver."

Her friends sat, sipping tea. None of them met her eyes squarely except Cliff, an artificer Mage who wasn't afraid to use his considerable skills for illegal purposes.

"Carver again?" Cliff leaned back into the settee and stretched out his long legs.

"Just checked before you came," Seija said. "He did something which used so much power that it drained even his island." Carver was the oldest Mage, older than it was humanly possible. Most people feared him for a good reason. Vague rumors circulated about his unholy activities, nothing specific and nothing recorded, but the rumormongers had always disappeared. For several years, Seija had been flinging her spynets wide to observe Carver from a distance. She had also found on the Net the genetic files and, despite her limited knowledge as a Healer, she discerned the changes made to her people in the distant past: augmented minds to interface with the Net, genes conjured to breed through the next generations.

Lorwen nodded. As a biotist, she spent most of her time studying microscopic critters. With her help, Seija had discovered that the chrom-nodes, parts of the Angylnet, were modeled after human chromosomes. Word had spread slowly, but Seija had acquired a group of followers, looking to her for solving the problems with the Net. Their years of digging and sleuthing had convinced her that Cy Carver was the cause of it.

Seija handed a data cube to Aram. "Hard copy of the full record. You have proof now that the Net is not magic. Incorporate it into the play."

Aram fingered the data cube thoughtfully. "I gather you want me to edit your face out."

"Yes, make it shocking and bloody, that's what the mage community likes."

Aram was a playcraft of the Entertainment Guild. His eyes twinkled with excitement. "When I'm done, this play will show the ksopir taking bites out of you."

Seija smiled. "Very good, the Annual Play Quest is this Freeday."

Cliff stood. "All right, so what are we doing about Carver?"

"I'll pay him a visit." Prepared for an argument, Seija pulled herself up to her full height. "After I hear back from Captain Dremil, I'm all set to go."

Cliff stepped into her personal space, scowling. "You're not going to Smog Island alone. I'm coming with you."

Seija nodded, relieved that he was not dashing her idea as too dangerous.

"An invitation would've been nice," he added in an injured tone.

Dear Cliff, he was always ready to protect her.

Seija exited the tunnel train and followed Cliff toward the access tubes. She glanced back over her shoulder and saw the iridescent door sliding shut. The train rippled once—truly like an exotic snake from Arth—and took off with a hissing sound.

"No one followed us," Cliff said.

"I know, but Carver could've stationed Horcs here, to watch who gets off."

They picked a large access tube and stepped on the float rug. Seija held her breath until the rug stiffened and started moving upward. They should locate the stairs just in case the rugs got damaged, which were also Net controlled.

Cliff encircled her shoulders. "So what if Carver knows we're after him? He's old."

"I wouldn't underestimate him."

"He's no match for you."

"Us," she said as Cliff gently pushed her toward the moving walkway after the float rug had deposited them at street level. They stepped off at the main intersection and exited the terminal.

Seija took a deep breath of the chill air. At two in the morning, there were few people out. The street was lined on both sides with warehouses and office buildings, their doors and windows shuttered against the night wind that sometimes reared up from the south sea. She pulled her cloak tight and walked toward the pier, boots clicking on the moist pavement. The smell of raw fish and brine lingered, and the stale sweat of the ocean was overlaid with the faint mechanical exudations of ships and boats.

"We're early," Cliff said.

"The boat will be here."

"I can't believe Dremil agreed to take us. Few dare to approach Smog Island."

Seija smiled. "The Captain needed a bit of a nudge. I started listing some of his cargo on the Net and—"

Cliff laughed. "You're a scoundrel."

"Look who's talking."

Cliff had broken into the old archives more times than any of them, even Seija. As they reached the pier, the city sounds diminished, muted by the blanket of moist air. Water lapped against the rocks.

"Here, put two drops in each eye." Cliff halted and handed her a tiny pen-like object.

Tilting her head slightly, Seija put the drops in her eyes and blinked. When she opened them, she was able to pick out distant landmarks clearly.

At the end of the pier, a wide boat swayed on the dark water, tied up to one of the metal bollards lining the pier. A man appeared in a doorway on the port side, muscles bulging in his chest and arms. His blue-haired head was too small, rooted to his body by a neck that looked like a tree trunk.

Seija swallowed. "Captain Dremil?"

"Who's asking?" The voice was high pitched and didn't match the burly physique but still managed to sound pugnacious.

"Divina Draco," Seija said, using her fake identity. She pulled herself up to her full height and looked down on Captain Dremil. Cliff remained silent, but his posture showed he was ready for a fight.

"Step aboard," Dremil said and disappeared through the door.

Seija grabbed the rope and stepped over the fender, carefully placing her boots on the silvered boards. Cliff landed next to her, their boarding rocking the vessel slightly. She looked into the pilothouse. Dremil smiled without involving his eyes in the act, one hand dancing on the controls and the other gripping the wheel.

The engine purred and the boat drifted away from the pier.

Seija walked along the keel. When she felt they were far enough from the pilothouse, she leaned against the gunwale.

"I don't trust him," Cliff said from the side of his mouth.

"Nor do I, but we can't be choosy."

"True."

If Dremil decided to renege on the deal, they'd be stranded on Carver's island. Neither of them could swim to Yorn.

The water exploded next to Seija, and two flycrabs landed on the deck. Seija screamed as one rushed toward her, its segmented legs clicking on the deck. Cliff aimed his fire wand and the thing turned sideways, severed mandibles snapping the air. The other one jumped for his knees, nearly biting his legs off before he burned it. Seija was shaking and not just from the cold. She brushed off the water from her cloak as best she could, wondering how much of the suppression spell, or rather the field that discouraged native life forms to approach the city, was damaged.

Watching the water for danger, the twenty-minute trip seemed longer. When they arrived, Dremil came out of the pilothouse and tied up the boat to a mooring buoy. He looked at the mess on the deck and smiled. "Half of my fee," he said and extended his hand.

Seija shook her head. "When we return."

Dremil looked at her, the muscles in his neck tensing. His hands curled into fists, but Seija stood her ground. From her trouser pocket, she pulled out the crystal chip worth a thousand silvers and opened her palm. Dremil's eyes crinkled with avarice, and he reached for it in a quick swiping motion.

Cliff blocked his way. "We don't wish to stay overnight, so I'm sure you appreciate our predicament."

Dremil nodded reluctantly. "Two hours."

"You'll wait until sunup." Seija lifted her hand as Dremil opened his mouth to speak. "Pray that it won't take that long." She turned and stepped over the fender. Cliff followed silently.

Water lapped at her boots, soaking through in seconds. She shivered and hastened to reach dry ground. They stumbled along wet sand and finally reached a copse of trees. Cliff stopped so suddenly that she bumped into his back.

"Traps," he whispered.

Seija squinted into the distance. "We can't go around, they extend to the house."

A nacreous web, barely visible even with the vision enhancer, laced the tree branches above. She followed the convoluted threads to the largest trees and saw a black, fist-sized hole in the purple landscape. "Spinner," she said. They were ancient guard spells not mage-forged, but of the originals that no one used anymore, conjured in the images of Arth creatures. She had found them in the old tech archives and spent days learning how to cancel them.

Seija pushed her hand in her pocket and closed it around the sage stone, smooth and warm. She conjured up her mouse avatar, and using the stone's power, opened up old channels in the netscape. A large sphere coalesced out of haze, across which ancient symbols moved. An image of a dark fort appeared next. With its nose twitching, her mouse ran up the heavy gate, which flew open. Inside was filled with dreadful animals and chimeric shapes hovering in the air and crawling on walls and pictures and stairways, a mass of colored lights in constant motion. Seija's gaze slid over the fearsome menagerie, searching.

There, a black, many-legged creature squatted high up in the corner of the hall, spinning. Careful to avoid the other guard spells, Seija guided the mouse to the spinner, using its tiny paws to tap the obsidian carapace in the learned sequence.

The hall disappeared from view and was replaced by lines of sigils. Seija sent the mouse through pages of the menus until she found what she was looking for. Carefully, she issued instructions, not to disable but to pause the guard field for two hours.

She withdrew her mouse avatar from the matrix and watched the spinner relax its jointed legs, shudder once, and curl up into a ball, its threads slowly falling around it.

Cliff showed a flash of white teeth. "I don't know anyone else who could've done that."

Seija moved aside so he could lead, and if necessary, use his fire wand that he had assembled secretly, a short rod that spat out modulated queser beams, whatever they were. She hoped that between the two of them they equaled Carver, because if they were caught. . .

As they wove through scraggly trees, she felt the sound before she heard it: a low-pitched resonance in her facial bones. A metallic taste filled her mouth, and a sudden hunger gnawed at her middle. "Reed singers," she said and grabbed Cliff's cloak.

"What?" He stopped.

"Can't you hear them?"

Cliff cocked his head. "No, but I'm starving." He gritted his teeth and grabbed a tree branch.

Seija stood next to him and heard her stomach growl, followed by a hunger pain. She bit her lips to stop herself from crying out and concentrated on moving away from the cluster of reed singers. The cold breeze carried the stench of death.

"The bastard planted them here," Cliff said.

As they got further away, the pain subsided. "Of course he did. Reed singers are not native to Yorn." *How did I miss that?* Smog Island still held surprises for her, despite her spynet.

"We'll go around these shacks and approach the main house from the rear."

Seija nodded, fingering the sage stone in her pocket. As the sea receded behind them, her unease increased. Silence and darkness embraced them. Something stirred inside the shack they had passed. She grabbed Cliff's arm and whispered, "More traps."

Using the sage stone, Seija looked inside the shack. In the center stood a huge glass jar filled with live icons that squirmed and clawed over each other, trying to climb out. She directed her vision to the shadowy corners, where a beast coiled on the floor, enwrapped in its own fetid air. It yawned and lifted a yellow head, exposing dagger-sized bicuspids of black crystal. Then it slowly slithered to the center, sinuous body covered by scales of yellow and black. A chimera, Seija thought. These guardians had multi sensors that probed the surrounding area, and some extended to hundreds of meters. She stood still and held her breath, hoping that the sage stone offered enough protection to hide them from the beast's senses. She opened the gate to the castle and sent in her mouse avatar again. In a few seconds she disabled the guard spell and the chimera slumped to the floor.

"We can continue now, but let's be alert."

They passed the shacks without further delay, slinking between the blue willows. Under shadows of the building, they stopped. Seija looked up and searched for an entrance along the obsidian stonewalls. Arches, buttresses, carved beasts, and columns hid more than they revealed, and the shadows of the willows danced along the house like dark wraiths seeking entry.

Cliff walked along the wall, stopping at every column and looking around carefully, hand gripping his fire wand. They came to a low cylindrical stone structure about two meters around. Seija put her hand above the opening. "It's a heat vent."

"Why would Carver need a heat vent?" Cliff peered down and shook his head. "Can't use this to get inside. Too hot."

"Heat," she said as the realization hit her, "is what makes the fog around the island, coming from these wells and mixing with the cold air."

Cliff nodded. "What generates the heat?"

Seija shrugged, worried about the time. It seemed the sky had lightened. They walked around the entire edifice twice and passed several more heat vents and a massive metal gate.

Seija stood before the gate and released all her probes. The netscape showed creatures crawling over the metal gate, not touching it. After a while, an image of a skull and crossbones appeared.

"We won't get through here alive." Disappointment filled her. Carver was a powerful Mage, but she had been so sure her collection of spells would gain them entry.

"What now?" Cliff walked over to a stone beast.

"It's time to try the tracer."

"It could trip all his alarm spells."

"We're running out of time." Determined to learn what Carver was up to, Seija removed the small metal worm from her belt pouch and stuck it to the stonewall. It flickered once and turned a pale blue. She covered its light with her palm and moved it up and down, then sideways along the wall, searching for the secret spell Carver must have used. Alert and muscles tensed ready to run, she felt a slight tug under her palm. She released the tracer, and it scuttled away, metallic legs clicking too loudly for her liking. They followed it to a carved effigy. The tracer stopped and stiffened; its segments lit up in different colors and rippled in a psychedelic fashion. One eye of the stone effigy began to glow red. The tracer slithered up to the eye and buzzed once.

A creaking sound issued from the ground as a large square rose up from among the pavement.

"Isn't magic sweet?" Cliff said in a sarcastic tone and hugged her.

Seija laughed and pocketed the tracer.

They stepped on the stone square and descended into darkness. Cliff pulled her close, one arm around her shoulder. His male musk made her head spin, and she was tempted to yield to love, his and hers. But she couldn't allow romance to distract her until they solved Mirage's enigma. Still, for a few moments, she leaned into the comfort of his body.

"It's getting too hot." His breath fluttered the hair on top of her head.

"Like hell described in the books from Arth," Seija said and gave a nervous laugh. She owned a couple of books from the home world, held in stasis fields so they wouldn't disintegrate, of which she had read copies only. Her knowledge of history came from the Net, secret texts about exotic matter, dark matter, Dyson spheres, Matrioshka brains, and Clarketech.

The slab stopped in a large, irregular cavern. Cliff looked around, his knuckles white over his fire wand. With a nod, he led her to stand behind some stacked crates. "I hear machinery." He pointed to the gloom across the chamber. "Stay behind me."

They took the meandering corridor, following a distant red glow. Moisture glinted on the rough stone. Cliff sidled close to the wall, and Seija followed, heart thudding in her chest. Something slithered across her feet and she almost screamed. Just before the dark tunnel bled into another large chamber, they stopped, huddling in the shadows. Sweat trickled down Seija's back. She wanted to shed her cloak.

Carver's voice echoed from the chamber ahead. There was a rhythm to it, sharp and soft, which sounded like ominous incantations. Seija watched in silence, stiff with fear. Carver stood in front of a panel lit up in tiny lights. His seamed face looked nervous, small mouth twitching and eyes darting left and right. Seija stepped back a pace, plastering herself to the wall. Her hand sought Cliff's, and he squeezed gently. She knew Carver couldn't see them, but the black eyes seemed to bore into her.

The incantations suddenly stopped. Carver's black cloak slid off his bony shoulders, revealing desiccated arms and stick legs. His body rippled once, then the shriveled flesh began to slough off. Like soiled attire, it pooled around his feet, a pale quivering mass revealing a silver metal man.

It's a construct, Seija gasped. What stood before them was beautiful. And deadly.

She frantically searched her memories of illegal archives, one after another, anything relating to constructs. Robots, they were called robots and there had been some among the original crew of the starship that had brought her people to Mirage. She scanned a tech book: *Nano-engineering of Advanced Interactive Planetary Networks,* which wasn't found on the Net anymore, not even passed off as fiction like the other technological books. The book described the ANGYLNET, Artificial Neuron Ganglial Y-Loops Network, designed by people and built by AIs to reside in the sky. It was some sort of . . . Clarketech. And there was also a master command to control all facets of the mission, the robots and the AIs and the entire Net. She had seen it; it was the name of an important Mage, made into a command that hadn't been uttered in over two millennia. With her eyebrows notched, Seija concentrated. No, the master command was a law of physics, or maybe a quote of a famous man from Arth. Arth, Arthur.

Arthur C. Clarke, her memory clicked.

"'Any sufficiently advanced technology is indistinguishable from magic,'" she quoted aloud.

Carver the robot nodded, crystal eyes lit up in the silver face. "Precisely," he said and took a few steps toward them, "what the Mage Council has been using to establish its reign."

"Stop," Cliff said, lifting his fire wand, "or I'll make scrap metal out of you." He pushed Seija behind him.

"Hardly a wise decision," Carver said.

Seija heard the faint humming of Cliff's fire wand. She touched his arm and stepped out from behind him, glaring at Carver. "Your meddling with the Net is killing people."

"My meddling with the Net is the *only* thing that keeps people alive."

"Indeed?" Seija said to cover her confusion. "Explain." She crossed her arms over her chest and waited.

"Mirage is the second world of Virida, one component of a physical binary system. Mirage has a stable orbit, and it's nearly a perfect world that needed little terraforming. But its ionosphere had to be enhanced to filter out the excess sunlight. The Ionoscreen is a layer of engineered clouds high up, invisible machines that filter and convert the radiation that would rain down on Mirage. Unfortunately, 2178 years ago during the alien attack, their weapons have damaged some of the nanomachines. If I didn't divert machines to the repair effort, you would start dying by increments."

"The techno crash," Seija said. "What, what?—"

"We'd never learned why those alien ships attacked us, but they have destroyed the starship and hundreds of landers, crews, scientists, and AIs, everything and everyone that was not on Mirage. Few scientists remained alive. Soon after, the administrators took control of the populations."

"Who's we?" Seija asked.

"Cy Carver, the human engineer. He was the only man who didn't scramble to gain power for himself. Cy Carver was one of the designers of the Net and the Ionoscreen, and I used to be his personal robot. When we lost the AIs, he upgraded my memory. He established a control center here." The robot spread out his gleaming arms. "To repair and adjust the machines of the Ionoscreen."

"And the Ionoscreen is part of the Net." Seija stated.

"Which I've been repairing for centuries," Carver said.

Cliff stirred. "What about the people you killed?"

"I haven't killed anyone. I have transported trespassers and trouble makers to other continents."

"I don't believe you." Cliff glared at the robot. "Some of them should've returned or contacted relatives through the Net."

"The uncomfortable side effect of belligerent curiosity—and some were downright destructive—is that I've been forced to disable their interfacing augment."

"You bastard—"

"No, wait," Seija said, giving Cliff a pleading look. "We need to learn what's happening." She turned back to the robot. "So what's draining the Net? Your repairs?"

"Yes, and I'm sad to report that I'm losing ground."

"But—" She recalled the incident of the falling component of the Angylnet. She had knit some of the severed chrom-nodes together. "Patterns, chrom-nodes, and fractals," Seija said, notching her eyebrows. "You need help, Carver."

The robot snorted, crystal eyes rolling in a disconcerting way. "From the mage community? They're users. They don't want to learn. After Carver died, I tried recruiting some humans."

"*We* want to learn," Seija said. "What's more, we can already help. Pattern recognition is wired into the human brain, that's why I was able to guide the machine wisps to reform." Excitement filled her. "We can repair the Ionoscreen." She was looking from Cliff to the robot.

Cliff nodded. "We could. We already have a tech group. They're skilled."

"And after we let the truth out, we can train more people openly," Seija added.

"You don't need training," Carver said. "There are programs you can download into your augment."

Seija grinned. "That's great. And you," she said, stabbing a finger at the robot, "are under my command."

"I am under your command."

"Really?" Cliff looked at her with a puzzled expression.

How did he miss it? "The spell is a master command, 'Any sufficiently advanced technology is indistinguishable from magic.'"

The robot nodded his metal head. "Why on Earth they chose that I don't know, but yes, that is the master command."

"It's Arth," Seija corrected.

"No, it's Earth," Carver said. "If you want to start letting out the truth—I doubt you can change the establishment overnight—you'd better start by knowing the correct name of Humanity's home world."

"Fine, Earth then," she said. "And I never said we'll do it overnight. We'll do it like the Mage Council did, slowly, wrapping the truth in plays. And in the first play, you'll get a starring role." She grinned at Carver and tapped her retinal recorder. "All on record and ready to roll."

"Is that a good idea?"

"Don't worry, Aram will alter Smog Island, your bastion, and your appearance. It'll be a jolly good play." *If I can get the Hills to show it.*

Seija ran her palm over the surface of the wall and, through her augment, commanded the door to turn visible. She flashed her invitation before the eye set in the black metal and stepped through the opening.

"This is a private party," the Horcs guard said. He pulled himself up to his one meter height and glared out from a furry face, trying to block her way to the float rugs.

"Seija Langdon," she said. "Guest of Ginger."

He consulted his list. Like all natives of Mirage, Horcs lacked the augment to allow them Net access. "Right, Langdon," he said. Brilliant golden eyes looked up at her.

Seija walked to the float rugs and kicked one under the tube, then stepped on it, careful so the mud wouldn't touch her shiny black boots. The gravity repulsor machines woven into the rug turned on in shimmering colors. She said a silent prayer before she directed the rug to rise. Their play, crafted under the guidance of Divina Draco the rebel Mage, must be shown. But she had to be careful because the Council could have spies here.

As the rug reached the top level of the mage house, laughter and music drifted toward the lift tube. Seija breathed in and out. The Hills were one of the most influential couples in the play industry. They approved the release of hundreds each year. Playcrafts jostled, charmed, and conjured up ways to impress the Hills so they would look at their work. Now Seija had to entice the Hills to view their play, even if it was crafted by an unknown. Lives on Mirage depended on it. She cringed from the task ahead, but if the Hills agreed to release it, millions would experience it. In time, some people would make the connection. With the help of her friends to disseminate the truth, a lasting change could be forged. In the meantime, her rebel group would start fixing the damages of the Ionoscreen. It was simple in theory but difficult in execution.

She sashayed off the float rug and pulled out the wrapped box from her cloak pocket, looking for the gift table. The shimmering wrapper caught the light of the crystal chandelier as she placed it on top of the other presents. She felt a twinge of regret at parting with the ancient family heirloom. It was a book held in a stasis field, which she had never deactivated for fear of the thing falling apart—it was that ancient, dating back to Earth.

An Anzy server passed her, his brown-furred, muscular arms balancing a tray laden with drinks. In a slurry tone he said, "Bubbly beer, musk wine, or fruit twirl, Mage?"

"Thank you," Seija said and took a glass of fruit twirl.

"Seija!" Ginger detached from a group of people and ran to her. "I was beginning to fear you wouldn't come." She laughed, large eyes gleaming with mischief. She gave Seija a hug and whispered, "Do you have it?"

Seija squeezed Ginger's arm.

Ginger nodded. Her powder-blue leggings and tunic, worn over a ruffled white shirt, gave her a boyish look, but there was long hair underneath the cap, with a quill sticking out the side.

"A Scribe?" Seija asked, eyeing the costume.

"Oh, you're the best." Ginger giggled. "No one else guessed right. And you? No, let me guess." She tilted her head and put a finger to her mouth.

Seija smiled, knowing Ginger couldn't guess, simply because she was not wearing a costume but one of her green dresses with a matching cloak.

"Hm, a Forest Nymph?"

"Right out of history," Seija said. *Fairy tales, rather.* A silk dress assembled of tiny leaves resembling the foliage of Hail Willow might as well be a Nymph costume, she thought.

Ginger clapped. "Come, I'll introduce you to Mother and Father."

Her young friend led her to the nearest group and pulled her into the center. The crowd parted like soil under a hoe. Curious gazes followed them until they stopped at the host and hostess.

"Mother, Father, this is my friend, Seija Langdon. I'm so glad she accepted my invitation," Ginger said with a big smile and stood slightly behind Seija.

Seija inclined her head. "It's a pleasure to meet you both."

Beth Hill was short and slender, and Paul Hill had inquisitive black eyes. They both wore costumes; Beth a flowing red gown, and Paul a black ruffled shirt and black trousers tucked into his boots.

"Welcome to the Annual Play Quest," said Beth, her eyebrows arcing toward her hairline.

"Seija taught me the technique of color-tasting while reading poems," Ginger said.

"How wonderful," Beth said, looking at a group of women standing nearby. "Excuse me, Seija, but please enjoy yourself." She turned and walked to the women.

Music drifted from the band, and Seija watched people dancing, angry with herself that she hadn't acted quickly. Ginger must have seen her disappointment because she squeezed her arm. Seija turned away and bumped into Paul Hill.

He held a plate of food for her and smiled. "Ginger told me about you."

"She'll be a great Mage one day," Seija said, accepting the food. She smiled at Ginger affectionately. The youngster clung to her elbow, for which Seija was grateful, because a nervous tick was developing in her left eyelid. So much depended on the play that she was horrified to discover that meekness lurked inside her. But she couldn't have that; she must act confident.

"I heard you're a healer," Paul Hill said.

"And she's the best," Ginger said. "But today she's here to sell a play."

Seija reached into the folds of her dress and withdrew the data cube. "Yes, indeed, a historical play." She handed it to Paul. "Whether you decide to broadcast it or not, please treat it as reality. All our lives depend on this play." She handed him the plate and glass, and then turned to Ginger. "This is a wonderful party, but I have a speech to make at the Healers Guild. Thank you for inviting me." Seija leaned down and kissed Ginger's cheek.

With head held high, she turned and walked toward the lift. She almost reached it, when she tripped on a float rug. *Pow dung,* she cursed silently. *I just had to ruin a grand exit.*

Virida crept over the horizon, bathing the mountainside in pale green light. Seija sat next to Cliff and watched the double sunrise.

"I'm looking forward to the play," Cliff said. Several artificers were helping Carver with the Net repairs nowadays, and Cliff was in charge. One of his arms encircled her, and with his free hand, he took a beerberry from the picnic basket and put it in her mouth.

"It'll be released before Winter Fest." Seija snuggled closer to him and bit down on the fruit, savoring its subtle flavor. A sense of accomplishment filled her, even if most people would never know the full extent of her involvement.

Beneath the Alien Shield

A SCARAB SCUTTLED BY ON THE WALL of Habitat A, a purple streak of alien menace. Kestra stiffened, ready to defend herself, but the creature disappeared around the corner.

"Speak waves, meaning," said the head, eyes darting left and right. The lips quivered, and bloody saliva drooled on the chin.

Kestra suppressed a shudder. There was something infinitely obscene about a human head connected to alien nerve ganglia and mounted on a green sphere. Grateful she didn't know the person the head belonged to before the Hermits murdered him, she examined the face, trying to search for the human in there. But only blank eyes stared back. The young man had been a Belter, like most people caught on the asteroid.

The head telescoped higher from its spherical base, the slack face inches from her own. "Speak waves, meaning," it said again. Trace molecules of confusion wafted to Kestra's hair sensors, but as she further analyzed the biochemicals from the nerve ganglia, the dense alien proteins and ancient lipids didn't yield understanding.

"What are you?" Kestra Lockwood, Special Ops agent of Defense and Intelligence, hated the aliens. *Whatever you are, I came to kill you.*

The coil of green nerve ganglia fused to the neck stump lit up at places, flickering intermittently. Translucent gummy flesh throbbed, encasing tubes like veins and arteries. "Match, join," the head said. A trace of chemicals that implied puzzlement or curiosity reached Kestra's hair sensors.

"Match what?" Anger made her reckless, but she also wanted to test the aliens' understanding. "Analyze this," she said through gritted teeth. "You will *join* the denizens in Hell when I *match* my templates to the power grid."

The head cocked to the side. "Hell . . . hello?"

She nodded, unable to speak. It was so human a mannerism that Kestra held her breath and waited for the darting of the eyes that signified Hermit confusion. But it didn't come.

"Do," whispered the head. Face muscles contorted, then turned slack, but the expression in the eyes was pleading.

Kestra closed her eyes. This was the first indication that a remnant of human awareness still existed within a head. And he had understood what it meant to release hell on the asteroid. That he wished for it filled her with dread. But maybe this one could help bridge the gulf between alien and human, and bring about the beginning of a negotiation.

To achieve just that, she addressed the Hermit. "Perhaps we can come to a peaceful understanding. In our corner of the universe, what you're doing is wrong. Killing sentient beings is a crime. You must stop—"

"Sound stop," said the head, eyes darting from side to side. It telescoped down to its base, the long fleshy tube wrinkled like a soggy hose. The head rolled away from her, nerve ganglia sliding into the rubbery sphere, but the visible ones flickered in several colors.

Two human hands rolled by; the alien eyes implanted into the palms regarded her with animosity before they escorted the head along the corridor of Habitat A, toward the control center.

Shoulders slumped, Kestra turned and headed for the commons where the eighty-one survivors holed up. Jason stepped out from the doorway of a vacant living quarter and joined her. His awkward movements caused by his missing left arm tore at Kestra's heart. Jason was only sixteen, a grandson she never had. Victor's deep laughter rang in her mind—memories forty years in the past, still fresh—the smell of salt in his hair, and their long walks on the beaches of Mafia Island. They had toyed with the idea of settling down and raising a family, but in the end she returned to Defense and Intelligence. She sighed and swallowed the bitter taste of regret.

"Don't antagonize them, Kestra," Jason said. "I saw the hands watching you at the turn of the corridor."

"I know." The hands also served as guards for the Hermits. Kestra wondered if Jason had ever recognized *his* hand among the hundreds roaming the corridors of Ursa. And the heads, so jittery, speech confused them and sound irritated them. Yet, the Hermits kept sending human heads to communicate with the Belters.

She had arrived at the asteroid four days ago, on the exact trajectory of a previous DI ship that had been drawn in through the caul-like energy membrane. But unlike her predecessor who had tried to plant a bomb on the alien ship and died for it, Kestra carried no ordnance.

A few hours after the alien ship had landed, they closed off Ursa by the caul, hence the name Hermits. During the past seven months, the Hermits had atomized several DI ships equipped with dirty missiles and Resonating Pulse Beams, and their energy caul deflected all the missiles fired from distant platforms. In retaliation or as a warning to stay away, the Hermits had vaporized five small asteroids, all inhabited. With the four thousand Belters on Ursa, the Hermits had killed over thirty thousand people.

As soon as they entered the commons, Kestra shook her head. "I'm sorry. I was unable to communicate with the Hermit part that controls the head."

A sense of failure filled her as the others surrounded her. Most had already suffered the Hermits' maiming, minus an arm or a leg. Mark and Helga were missing both legs, dragging their torsos along by their arms. The Hermits had spun the asteroid to .36 gravities, but for the disabled ones the miniscule gees of Ursa would have been kinder.

"The head, that was Tom," said Gordon, his brown face a landscape of sorrow. Gordon was an older Belter, in possession of all his limbs. "Tom went to check out Habitat B and never came back. He insisted because he was intact and knew the air shafts."

"Tom . . . is aware," Kestra said. *But for how long?* None of the heads retained function for long, which was a blessing, as it cut short needless suffering, and a curse because the aliens took more humans to replace them, though fewer lately, as they converted more of the Belters' robots to their use.

"God help him," Helga said. Tears ran down her face.

"God won't help him, or us," John said. His face was pale, and his one remaining hand was shaking.

Mira leaned on her makeshift crutch of a plaz pipe and put an arm around John as she addressed Kestra. "Can Tom help us communicate with the Hermits?"

"I don't think so." Kestra deactivated her hair sensors through her augment. She didn't want to read these people's pheromones. Having spent days with them, their despair was already taking root in her; trapped under an alien shield with no way out, with the certain fate of being dismembered was not something she had imagined before this mission. She shoved her hands into her pockets to hide their trembling. "Maybe the Hermits managed to subvert part of his speech center, but I doubt they understand the meanings behind most words, let alone sentences and concepts like moral."

Terry nodded, face muscles twitching. "They understand human anatomy and biochemistry, but not the mind. That's what Petrov said. He was a psycho analyst, before he volunteered for the Acid Squad."

"Acid Squad?" Kestra raised her eyebrows.

Jason swallowed and explained, "Six of them, they scrounged up acid from various assemblers and went into the control center. The first squirts made the Hermit mound smoke, the second squirts just sizzled on its hide, and the third one it neutralized. The acid just slid off the creature. Then the scarabs attacked and cut them to shreds."

Terry blinked and looked off into a distance. She was one of the two survivors that had visited the main cluster of the Hermit in the control center. "The Hermit, the main mound, is an extremely robust organism. It adapts to adverse situations quickly. I can't imagine the world it's evolved on, but it must be vicious."

"But we're clever little monkeys." Kestra forced a smile. "We'll find a way to defeat them." Thought she believed it—after all, DI had made the right decision to equip her with organic weaponry, detectable only if one knew what to look for—she too found their situation bleak. And she could do it. Her hand stole to her right hip, a regrown pelvic bone, femur, one lung, and one kidney, crushed during the Arctic mission when the dome had collapsed.

Since the Hermits had sealed off the research sector by their energy caul and taken over the main computer, the survivors lost their equipment to study the aliens. Only visual observation remained, but by piecing together the sketchy data, Kestra suspected they were facing a single Hermit with its helpers.

David came in and sealed the door behind him. "None of the pods left yet. They're still under the shield, and that's good. But there are sixty-three now."

"Two more since yesterday," Jason said, gazing at the food storage bins that contained the dry nutrient bars. After the alien ship had landed, the Hermit and its helpers consumed the contents of the hydroponics chambers, both crops and nutrient tanks sucked dry within a few weeks.

"I'm going to the control center." Kestra turned and walked toward the door.

"Kestra, please don't go." Jason ran after her. "What if they'll—"

"I have to."

"Here, take it then." Jason removed his cap and gave it to her.

"Thanks." Kestra looked down at her boots, suddenly embarrassed by the boy's concern. She put the cap on her head and left.

Walking along the deserted corridor, she activated her T-cam in her upper left molar. Water-based micro lenses held in electrostatic fields and the sonar imagers responded to her subvocalized command. They interfaced with her visual nerves and augment, and began recording.

Two hands fell in beside her at the next bend, rolling along on their gummy spheres. They turned at the wrists this way and that, fingers splayed and ready to squirt poison through the nails. The turquoise eyes embedded through the palms and the back of the hands glared malevolently. Human robots rolled by, creepers and uprights, their logic centers ripped out and replaced with Hermit nerve ganglia. They all carried large pieces of the greenish alloy, sections of the pods the aliens were assembling from local material.

A human leg unit with Hermit manipulators mounted on the hip pushed a cart, the bruised legs uncoordinated, stumbling on purple feet. A faint smell of decay wafted from the thing.

The indignity of it clawed at her sanity. Rage threatened to spill forth, and she wanted to smash them with her bare hands. But that would accomplish nothing; the thousands of dead Belters that had attacked the Hermits attested to that. Energy weapons, projectiles, and flechettes didn't work, the Hermit cluster absorbed all.

A blast of cold air greeted her at the door. The acrid smell of the alien sent a burst of data to her augment: superconducting proteins folding in alien ways, strange lipids and microtubule production, metallic and crystalline molecules, and several unknown compounds.

Around the frame of the open door, clusters of Hermit nerve ganglia clung in various colors and shapes. They pulsed inside transparent casings, extending ropy appendages down into the doorway. One brushed over her face. Kestra passed through quickly, grateful for the Jason's cap covering her hair sensors. What would the Hermit make of those? Her hair sensors were composed of super skin cells, perfectly natural if a bit enhanced. Still, one of the reasons she had postponed visiting the control center was that she couldn't afford close scrutiny, or losing her head or arms. She had to remain intact to carry out her orders.

She stopped and stared at the main bulk of the Hermit squatting near the asteroid's hexagonal control column, a pale green, teal, and pink mass of pulsing muscles, spikes, and ridges. Extended portions of it filled most of the open spaces. According to the Belters, it had grown thrice to its original size during the seven months it's been on Ursa.

On its top perched a giant translucent organ, vaguely flower-shaped, fleshy petals quivering wetly around the cluster of purple nerve tendrils, which extenuated into hair-thin jell-like strands wrapping around and reaching inside the twenty-meter wide hexagon that housed the main computer. Sections of the Hermit mound were covered with blue and green oval and star-shaped creatures. At one section through a pulsing hole, the dog-sized purple scarabs emerged.

Kestra stiffened, ready to bolt or defend herself, but they ignored her. They landed with a metallic clatter, shook themselves, and scuttled out of the control center. One of the hands that had accompanied her rolled inside another hole held open by a silver frame.

A biochemical factory, she thought, following the convoluted bulges and recording everything. With a quick motion of her hands, she touched the rippling flesh at several places, imprinting it for the ThermNites. Her fingers tingled from its coldness, or from its strangeness, but she managed to snag a few alien cells. For her report, *if* she could send it.

In a hollow place on the Hermit mound, upright racks made of muscular ropes caught her attention. The blue trellises undulated, each one holding a human body held tight by Hermit cilia. Her heart skipped a beat when she realized they were alive. Some were partially flayed, and others displayed slashed abdomens with the organs inside missing and replaced with alien tissues. Organic tubes carrying blue ichor were connected to each human. One of the victims was headless, the body twitching under the ministrations. She glimpsed of woman whose eyes followed her, her mouth wide open but no sound issued forth as a rope from the trellis wrapped around her arm. The rope tightened and exuded a sour stench, then pinched off the arm, which dropped onto the mound. Two star-shaped creatures shoved it into a hole.

Kestra looked away, blinking. It was her job to end this, no matter what the price.

No matter what the price, echoed in her mind. She wiped her eyes and continued studying the alien.

Below the trellises, four hands not of human flesh but green Hermit tissues held ready, rubbery fingers fluttering. She walked around them and looked. An irregular opening pulsed once, twice, and then spat out a miniature Hermit. The hands caught it and carried it to a transparent tube, then pushed the thing inside. Her eyes followed the tube into one of the corridors that led topside.

To the waiting pods near the alien ship. The Hermits could release the pods any day. She quickly calculated the heat her ThermNites would yield if she were to activate them here. No, the minute spark her body's mass would provide was not enough to consume this monstrosity. And the pods might escape through the shield. She couldn't allow that; to insure that the Hermit and its pods were destroyed, she needed Ursa's power source plus the mass of the asteroid to generate plasma heat.

Ursa was a Main Belt asteroid, roughly in the shape of a bear's head with a diameter of sixty-two kilometers at its widest, but it was of low mass, hollowed out by the Belters over the years.

Kestra squatted and peered underneath the alien to see if it had fused parts of it to the floor. Hundreds of short legs?—various stumps, appendages, metallic and bony spikes supported the giant bulk. And some penetrated the floor.

From her meager arsenal, she selected the packet of pricor, insidious prion corrupter molecules designed to mimic the host's proteins and coax them to fold wrong, then turn the surrounding proteins into necronites. *It just might work; it has to work.* Her augment activated the dormant pricor packet, and another subroutine sent an impulse to the inside of her cheek. A tiny slit opened and squirted the mucus encased microscopic lipid capsules into her mouth. Kestra collected saliva around it, straightened and, angling toward one of the openings of the Hermit, she spat the pricor inside.

One arm accidentally swiped a passing hand. Whose hand? For a split second, nightmare images of Jason's severed arm flashed in her mind. The hand smacked to the foamsteel floor, its arm section rippling with the blue ganglia inside, one side of the eye flattening. The other side of the liquid crystal eye rolled a few times and then stopped, leaking a clear fluid.

Damn. Kestra dashed to the door. From her peripheral vision, she saw that two blue lozenges detached from the Hermit mound and dragged the injured hand through the open hole. She ducked under the undulating appendages and hurried through the corridor, heart pounding. She dared not glance at the hands that appeared next to her but kept her enhanced senses alert for attack. They escorted her to the commons, and Kestra entered.

At least she had done something, because the past two days spent topside checking out the remains of the Belter ships was a waste of time. Her plan was to repair them and evacuate the survivors, but all had been scrapped by the Hermits, like her own ship disassembled right after her arrival. Jason had told her about the six Belters as they had attempted to steal back spaceship engines, and how the scarabs sliced them up, armor and all. But she had to try, because evacuating the survivors was the first phase of her mission.

Her failure thus far began to erode her confidence. Kestra had never failed during her five decades of service in Defense and Intelligence. She had defused the Moon colony uprising with minimum loss of life, rooted out the bio hackers hiding in the old Martian domes, and led the team that unraveled the insidious plan of the Arctic Enclave, which would have killed millions had she failed. She had nearly died and spent months in regeneration tanks and rehab, but she had succeeded in her mission. Failure was never an option for her; Kestra knew she could pull off any mission. Was it true what other agents said about her? Was it really her arrogance? But here on Ursa, she had accomplished nothing in four days. Evacuate the civilians, gather intelligence on the aliens, but most importantly, destroy the Hermits, she recalled her orders given by General Haines. But destroy them at what cost?

* * *

Two hours later, just as she was preparing to descend to the lower levels, eight of the scarabs accompanied by two hands appeared in the opening doorway. The survivors shrank back and stared at the lump of Hermit tissue one of the hands threw on the floor. Scabs on it leaked blue ichor, then it shriveled up and turned into powder.

Kestra's stomach lurched; the pricor hadn't worked. Worse, the Hermit had discovered it and managed to excise the infected tissues.

The scarabs moved suddenly and in unison, one group of four toward Terry and another group toward David. Metallic carapaces shifted with grating sounds, as purple glassy antennae stung each human along the lower spine. Terry cried out and David stiffened, their faces carved in pain.

Kestra started toward them, but Jason, Gordon, and John grabbed her. "Don't," Jason said.

She struggled with the men, but they held her tight, and she watched with horror as the hands led Terry and David away, surrounded by the scarabs. Someone closed the door and the rest of them sank into variforms or on the bare floor.

"You shouldn't have restrained me," she said to the three men.

"The scarabs would've killed you," Jason said. "And you're our only hope."

A few Belters glanced in her direction, then away, their expressions full of bitterness and accusation. Helga burst into tears. Mark dragged himself to her on his arms and embraced her. The sight of them clinging to each other tore at her heart.

"I'm sorry." Kestra turned away. Not only she had failed to mount a rescue mission, she had made their plight worse. But Jason was right; commando training or not, she was no match for eight scarabs, even if with a bit more effort, she could have overpowered the three men. Instinctively, she hadn't, because her mission was more important then saving the lives of a couple of people.

Gordon put a hand on her shoulder. "The Hermits don't assign blame to individuals. To them, we represent one organism."

"I think," Jason said and moistened his lips. "We're all going to die slowly and painfully. I can't tell you how much that frightens me." He looked at her and continued, "But we have a chance now to prevent that. Right, Kestra?"

She nodded reluctantly. Kestra was suddenly uncertain whether she would be able to complete the mission, because this time she would have to give her all. Subconsciously she had known that soon after her arrival, but she'd been hoping to prove herself wrong, so she'd tried all her options, limited as they were. But the Hermits were too alien. Extreme as her final solution was, the alternative . . . dismemberment, was infinitely worse. She shuddered, stiffened her spine, and faced Jason. "Absolutely, I can prevent that."

"I think Space Force has given up." Helga said, her voice bordering on hysterics. "You the best they can do?" She gestured at Kestra. "Don't repeat our mistakes, we tried everything possible. You should be working on disabling their shield."

Kestra swallowed and refrained from telling her that the Hermits' shield was beyond Humanity's technological wherewithal. Her own ship's sensors had confirmed it when she had passed through. She remembered holding her breath while the alien caul was probing for obvious weapons, afraid her higher body temperature full of ThermNites might be noted. But the arrogant creature had allowed her to pass, so confident in its own abilities that Kestra almost found it an affront. As to Space Force? SF had lost several ships trying to penetrate the shield, so they *had* given up on the Belter settlement. But DI had sent its best commando. A bitter laughter escaped her lips.

Jason scowled at Helga. "Go tend your garden." The Belter insult used to chastise brats who were too immature for serious responsibilities seemed to quiet her. Then he turned to Kestra, his blue eyes steely. "If you need help, I'm at your disposal. Anything, just name it."

Kestra held the boy's gaze and knew she met her equal, and at that moment she realized that she was terrified, not of dying but of the mutilation she had seen.

"Count me in," said Gordon.

John hit a variform with his one remaining fist. "Nothing would give me greater pleasure than to hurt those fuckers."

Several Belters offered to help her.

Kestra shook her head, partly to clear her mind of the fuzzy thoughts and partly to restore self-discipline. "What I must do is best done alone. Less chance the Hermits catch on. But I could use a good representation of the lower levels, specifically the location of the power grid and the shortest route there."

Since they couldn't interface with the computer to call up schematics, and the scarabs had consumed all the smart papers, Jason took off his shirt, spread it on the dining table, and began to outline the details with ketchup.

Kestra studied the sketch for a while, then nodded. "I'll find it," she said and headed for the door.

Gordon stood up and extended his hand. "Good luck."

Kestra shook the hand and left.

Jason was right behind her. "I'll walk you to the dropplate."

Along their passage in every corner lurked a cold living fear. Whether human parts or Hermit tissues, they were watching passively. Ursa hummed with a controlled fervor of alien biomachines bent on production. Reproduction rather, Kestra thought as she recalled the miniature Hermits birthed by the monster and installed into the waiting pods, secluded under the shield and ready to spring forth.

"I have a sister at Clarke Station," Jason said quietly. "Her name is Katy, and she's brilliant. She's only twelve and already passed the fourth level of robotics." He smiled, face lit up with pride. "I see her when we dock at Clarke; she lives there with her mother. Katy's not a Belter brat, but we shared a father. She adores him, and doesn't know he's dead. He . . . Dad died trying to kill the Hermit mound after my arm was taken. I . . . I want my sister to survive."

The words cut through her heart, and Kestra almost stopped but thought better of it, no need to attract the attention of the hands. She took a deep breath and exhaled, then said in a low voice, "She'll survive, Jason."

"I know. I knew when I first saw you getting out of your ship."

Jason was on watch duty at topside when Kestra had arrived. He had quickly filled her in on the situation without losing his composure. His quiet strength and sharp intelligence impressed her then, but this vignette of his life struck a chord in her.

They reached the dropplates and chose a small one that wasn't in use by scarabs and robots manhandling pod sections and tubes. A lump filled her throat, and Kestra didn't know what to say. She forced a smile and extended her hand. "Thanks for all your help."

Jason shook her hand. "It was nice knowing you. Make it good, Kestra." Then he turned abruptly and left.

She stepped onto the dropplate and started to descend, blinking from the haze that suddenly obscured her vision. She sighed with an uncharacteristic sadness. Evacuate the survivors, she thought about her orders. Failed. The disabled Belter ships and the alien energy shield negated that. But with a little luck she could still accomplish two out of three of her mission imperatives: get data to DI, and annihilate the Hermits.

When the dropplate stopped at the lowest level, Kestra stepped off. Bent on destruction, she rounded the winding corridor in the belly of the asteroid, following the memorized path. Her augmented vision traced the conduits of the power distribution grid, a faint green glow under the thin plazoy walls.

She glanced at the hands rolling behind her and, to confuse them, started singing a song to which she had danced with Victor all those years ago, while she activated the routers embedded in her palms. She slapped her hands at the walls, marking the strongest nodes of the grid by leaving behind a few cells. Thermonanites would read her DNA and suck power from the grid nodes, speeding up the process of reaching the main Hermit mound, the pods, and the ship. Kestra sang louder, uttering screeches and bellows at the top of her lungs, hoping the hands would leave her before she reached the chamber of the plutonium pile.

Before the Hermit takeover, Ursa had an efficient production setup, the Von Neumanns chewing small asteroids and converting them into alloys, then into ship hulls, bulkheads, engine housings, and life support machinery. Engineering specialists and technicians assembled parts of the life support systems and engines, overseeing the testing and analyses. Everything now was reconfigured to produce Hermit pods, to spread throughout the Solar system.

She passed large pieces of alien equipment and translucent bubbles before she entered another down-sloping tunnel. Her IR vision drove back the shadows in front of her face as she proceeded, but the darkness swallowed her.

She reached the door and began to turn the mechanical lock of the power chamber when a metallic clatter caught her attention. Kestra pivoted, and dodged as a glassy proboscis stabbed at her.

A scarab streaked by. It turned sharply, careened into the wall, then came at her again. She jumped aside but the wall was in her way, and the creature's razor claws swiped the back of her wrist. Pain flowered in her, and blood squirted. She swayed and, through her augment, released a dose of painkillers and medchines to stem the blood flow. Her wrist hung by a few tendons, bones protruding, as Kestra watched the scarab getting ready for another assault. When the creature ran at her again, she jumped high, twisted in the air, and landed on its carapace. It cracked with a satisfying crunch. For good measures, she stomped on the head with her boots until it was just a purple stain on the floor.

Panting from blood loss, she turned back to the door and opened it one-handed, then quickly stepped through and locked it from the inside. She ripped off the sleeve of her coverall and wrapped it around her wrist. As the lights came on, her eyes followed a green rubbery conduit snaking out of the ceiling and connecting to the power source's housing.

The Hermit was sucking power for its reproduction and pod assembly. No one had told her the alien was so completely entrenched in the asteroid, but she was glad.

Placing her uninjured hand on the shielded housing, Kestra initiated the release through her augment. Following strict protocols, thermonanites scattered throughout her body began to rush toward her hand. Using her body's carbon, potassium, phosphor, and the implanted nanoscopic plasma elements, fast burning structures assembled into microscopic gossamer webs. She swayed, and felt her blood pulsing from the accelerated metabolism. Perspiration drenched her and she shivered, but her palm felt hot as the skin sloughed off and curled into a lump of programmed death. The lump turned cherry-red and began to burrow into the housing of the power source.

Lightheaded, she leaned against the wall and pulled out a dry nutrition bar from her pocket. She bit into it and washed it down with water from a bulb, remembering the last dinner she had shared with Victor on Mafia Island, real steak and champagne. She shook away the memories and glanced at the energy-mass ratio on her retinal screen; fourteen minutes until the ThermNites converted enough mass to critical heat.

After she finished her lonely meal, she returned to the hub by the tube access, a giant cable that provided inside transportation to the assembly platform. Work units of the Hermit seldom used it, for their caul-encased bodies were perfect for vacuum work, and their power provided faster traveling between sections of the shipyard.

Kestra exited the tube access and headed toward a giant girder near the alien shield. She had selected it two days ago, as the farthest from the control center, because she needed time to launch the message capsule. During the short walk, she subvocalized a personal addendum and attached to it Jason's recorded words. It was a message to Katy Newman of Clarke Station, informing her that Jason and her father died bravely.

Though she would rather return to the commons and spend the final minutes of her life among the Belters, it was imperative that DI received her data on the Hermits. They would use her data to develop weapons, but more importantly, engineers would program them into the already built sensor buoys scattered throughout the Solar system. Should there ever be another Hermit spacecraft, Defense and Intelligence would be prepared.

Her wrist stopped bleeding but it throbbed with a dull ache. Kestra grabbed a strut one-handed and climbed up as far as she could on the angling metal. She stopped a meter from the shield and felt a minute vibration through her boots.

It's getting close. She attached a line to the strut so she wouldn't be thrown off prematurely. Activating her T-cam, she recorded the energy shield. Close up the caul looked pearly, turning pinkish in the distance. No stars showed through, and it contained the thin air the Hermit had generated at some sections of the asteroid.

She felt a tremor, and the shield rippled, then righted itself. Below her was a heaving lump of crimson lava, but the ThermNites didn't reach critical heat yet. When they did, she knew they would destroy the control center with the main Hermit mound, the pods that contained the miniature Hermits, and the alien spacecraft. The shield would then buckle.

Kestra dislodged the T-cam from her molar and pushed it into a forming air tube. She checked the compressed air and waited, ready to shoot it as soon as the shield collapsed, as soon as the ThermNites reached the alien ship. She must shoot the capsule far enough to escape the immediate heat, then the micropile inside the T-cam would power the nanorockets and carry it out of harms way. DI would home in on it.

Perspiration drenched her face and body. Leaning against the support strut, she brushed her hand over her rebuilt side. She had courted death long enough, and she had extracted much from the courtship by ways of countless successful missions. And now, at the end of her most important mission, death had become her ally.

Another tremor shook her perch and she almost lost her footing.

A white worm of plasma surged below, growing rapidly. The shield rippled and began to turn dark, sections showing black space. *The Hermits are dying now, the pods have melted.* Kestra smiled, and felt a jolt, followed by a sharp pain in her back. She threw herself toward the collapsing shield with all her might and shot the message capsule outward.

Mission accomplished, Jason, she thought as her mind faded.

Mirror of My Mind

CORA STEPPED OUT OF THE DROPTUBE and found Sean standing in the hallway.

He ran over and embraced her thighs. "Mommy, you're home early. Emef lost track of time cause we played the Fringe Pirates."

She picked him up and planted a kiss on his face. "Emef?" she asked and looked at her Mother Fragment, her own face except for the short black hair, hovering close to her son. It seemed that the MF displayed a protective stance. But that was normal, she chided herself.

People had warned her not to have a Fragment cloned, but between motherhood, her work at the Alien Research Center, and her concert music, she had been on the verge of collapse. Since the drone ship had returned from Alpha Serenity, her work at the ARC doubled. She had finally come to accept that one person could only do so much.

"I named her Emef." Sean gestured to the Mother Fragment. "Put me down." He wriggled in her arms. "I can't keep calling her Mother Fragment. And she likes it, don't you, Emef?" He gave Cora a gap-toothed smile that included the MF too.

"It's a beautiful name, Sean." The Fragment returned the smile, her expression full of love and pride.

Cora grimaced and set him down, suddenly feeling jealous. Sean looked up at her, puzzled. She turned away, face hot with embarrassment, and instantly regretted her stupid reaction. Changing the subject, she asked, "So what are the Fringe Pirates up to?"

"We conquered the insect AIs in the Lentil Nebula. I'll tell you after we get back. We must go now cause Rudy's at the park and we're late. Come on, Emef," Sean said and reached for the Fragment's hand.

Cora stared at their receding backs until the droptube's door slid shut, wondering whether she was upset because Sean had named the Fragment or because he already seemed so attached to her. That smile, which Cora had always treasured, would be shared now with Emef. With a reluctance she had never felt before, she sat down by the grand piano and began to practice for next week's performance. Music flowed through her as she caressed the ivory keys, and Beethoven's Sonata No. 23 in F minor filled the room. Though the concerts had paid for the luxuries Cora coveted, playing was also an endless source of pleasure.

After his outing with Emef, Sean was exhausted and fell asleep within seconds after Cora put had him to bed. She brushed his curly hair away from his eyes and tucked him in.

Yawning, she walked to her bathroom and undressed. Coalition Network News came on in the shower, the screen showing a gutted orbital assembly near Mars. "None of the terrorist groups claimed responsibility yet," said a blue-haired commentator. The view panned to a debris-strewn space in the asteroid belt. "Several Belter ships are searching for survivors among the rubbish of Hygiena, the largest shipyard in Coalition until yesterday, when a mysterious explosion destroyed the asteroid and its manufactories."

"Dear God." Cora shot off the shower and switched on the dryer. The Belter Society was out of the race now. They wouldn't get a colony ship to Alpha Serenity. And Zach was out there somewhere, plying the Belt. She sent a quick message to him, annoyed that it would take hours for the response.

By the time she walked into her room, it was late. The opaque plaz door slid aside at her touch and Cora entered the Fragment repository. The silence always disconcerted her, not a snore, machine humming, or breathing could be heard. Lights flickered on the biomonitor of the neural interface equipment, showing the Fragment in deep sleep. Cora avoided looking at the translucent plaz capsule. Curved above it at the head like a question mark, was a neural imager with a gel cap containing billions of nanosensors.

Cora sat into the formchair, picked up the Fragment's senso recording, and inserted it into the slot of the interface computer. The gel cap flowed over her head from temple to nape with an intimate familiarity and the neurosensors connected to her brain.

After she experienced Sean's day through Emef's memories, her mind drifted, became distant, as though she had loaned it to someone. A thought burst into her mind, *Mirror Project. Host is behaving normally.*

Was that her Fragment's thought? Cora waited, but nothing else happened.

And then—

—Voices whispered in Emef's head, *Don't resist or you'll be eliminated. Follow instructions.*

Sometimes the voice was commanding and other times cajoling. Images of vast chambers intruded upon her, filled with containers from which nascent thoughts seeped through. A smaller chamber contained translucent capsules standing upright in rows, each holding a naked body.

Sister, sister, help me. Kill me, said a hoarse voice. *Please, kill me.*

Emef groaned at the mental voice of whining rhyming, *Mirror, mirror of my mind, Earth Government stole my life.* She was the most irritating of all the voices.

Emef saw a short man walk through pythonic corridors to a vault. He spoke to someone she could not see, angry words, *You must work out a way to control them before the ship is built.* Then he disappeared, but his voice cut through her soul.

Did she have a soul?

Pondering that, Emef lifted the translucent top of the capsule with trembling fingers and climbed out. Dark motes danced behind her lids, and with an effort, she pressed her eyes shut, hoping to drive out the voices. Her legs trembled as she stood up, but the familiar accoutrements comforted her. It was a relief to be home.

At the beginning, it had been easy to resist the compulsion of slipping into that otherness, until each rest period chipped away at her strength. Cora would know after this recording. Split Personality Syndrome was an insanity of Fragments, she knew that much. But she didn't want to be terminated; Sean needed her.

When she heard Cora leaving, she collected herself and went to Sean. None of the voices and images mattered. Sean gave meaning to her life, and he alone represented reality for her.

"Did you sleep well?" She walked through the monsters of his holo show.

"Yes, but please don't do that, Emef." He made a shooing motion, a mischievous glint in his eyes. "Odukar might get you, and then I'd have to rescue you." He then patted the couch beside him. "Watch this with me."

"All right, but after this show is over, we'll do your studies and then visit the Museum of Natural History." Emef smiled and sat down. As he snuggled close, the chill of the voices were thawed by a warm feeling.

Love—

Anger—

—"Damn," Cora cursed and removed the interface cap. That was yesterday's recording.

She bit her lower lip and sat up. Was this the beginning of Split Personality Syndrome? Delusions, paranoia, they were some of the symptoms. Yet, something didn't quite add up. *Host is behaving normally,* she recalled her Fragment's thought. Or was it someone else's thought? But how did someone's thought get into the recording? Who was the host, and what was the Mirror Project? These delusions might be SPS or, something else.

A dark suspicion reared up in her mind. Host and clone, host and Fragment, the thought reverberated in her mind. Perhaps her Fragment was spying on her, subverted by Earth Government, or she was developing a Split Personality Syndrome. Neither was good. She should report this to the Bio Regulation Agency. Failure to do so was a crime punishable by personality adjustment. The thought made her break out in sweat.

Cora didn't want to report the incident. The MF was her property, and even if flawed, she needed her.

"Rice wants to see you," Arthur said as he entered the lab.

Cora made a dismissive gesture. "He'll have to wait."

Paul Rice was the director of the Alien Research Center, and though she had seen his message, she was too busy with the specimens from Alpha Serenity.

"I just came from his office. He was furious," Arthur said.

"If he wants results faster, he should hire more scientists."

Arthur snorted. "He's paranoid."

A sophisticated torpid spy program might slip through even the ARC scans, but the resident CyMvecs would catch it. There were secrets within secrets. The Xeno-Biology department had the most crucial task of determining the bio rating of the flora and fauna, but even her people weren't privy to some classified aspects of the colonization plans. Cora, however, planned to secure a place for herself and Sean on one of the colony ships. Alpha Serenity was a cold world with long winters, but it had room to raise children. And to teach them what freedom tasted like. She was fairly certain that Zach would join them.

"I sent him the report on the wart tree. That should mollify him."

"Good." Cora retrieved the organ samples from the auto dissect and placed them into the bioanalyzer. "Full analysis."

"Disassembly commenced," said the machine

Robo arms lifted the remains of the two-foot long animal, nocturnal eyes slanted upward in a narrow face. She gazed at it with admiration. A predator from an alien world, and she had the privilege to study it.

She pulled her hand out of the senso glove, and the laser scalpels slid back into their niches. The buckyglass chamber was bathed in intense heat, followed by chemicals injected from the decon tubes.

Arthur watched her, his expression somber. "I think it's all starting out wrong, this race to get there first."

"A lot of people want to get away from Earth Government." It's been barely six months since Rice had lifted the quarantine, but the vicious race had started even before the drone returned.

"But to blow up Hygiena . . ." Arthur shook his head.

Zach hadn't responded to Cora's message yet, and that scared her. Through her augment, she sent the security code to access another alien specimen. "This one's yours. I'm going home."

"Thanks," Arthur said, eyes lit up.

"See you tomorrow." She closed the door and hurried along the corridor.

Before she reached R&D, she sensed movement behind her. She pivoted, and froze. Two CyMvec commandos passed her, silently, as if they were gliding on air. One turned back and looked at her, and though she couldn't see his eyes through the military augments and armor, she felt his scrutiny.

A quad of CyMvec commandos was a permanent fixture in any facility using an assembler-disassembler unit, but she had never seen them sauntering around; they didn't need to, because the sealed system was self-monitoring. Why were they watching her department?

The car was landing when a message told her that Zach would arrive shortly.

Her heart raced as she ran across the roof of her penthouse, face caressed by a breeze redolent of brine, fish farms, and the decay of nearby slums. Robo-security rolled around the perimeters, ignoring her when she passed them.

She took the droptube down and entered the hallway. A glance at the house monitor told her that Sean was still out with Emef. Normally, she would want him here when Zach arrived, but his absence now made it less awkward to tell Zach about the Fragment. Only Sean and Katie knew so far.

Cora felt a weight settle on her shoulders. Zach would understand. He knew it was difficult on Earth. It had taken her years of education to earn her degrees in biology, then to specialize in alien bio and get a professional rating, and more years until a position opened at the ARC. During her career climb, she wanted to have a child and never had the time, until six years ago. Once she had Sean, she didn't want him raised by household robots. A Fragment was much preferable. Her reasoning sounded solid, yet she felt nervous.

Cora hurried to her room, undressed, and stepped into the sonic stall. A few minutes later, she selected an indigo silk gown and donned it. With a last check in the mirror, she returned to the dayroom.

Her house monitor chimed. "Cora, it's Zach," said a deep voice.

"Come on up, Zach."

The door opened and he stood there; tall and dark, closely cropped hair and chiseled face. She tried to be collected as she ran to him.

Zach pulled her into an embrace and tilted her face up, caressing her long hair. "You look radiant." Then he kissed her.

Cora melted in his arms like dirty clothes in a matter disassembler. But she quenched her desire and moved out of his embrace.

Zach released her reluctantly and glanced around the dayroom, no doubt looking for Sean.

"He'll be back shortly. You arrived on a short notice. I couldn't arrange for him to be here. I just barely got home." She stopped blabbering and looked at him, suddenly afraid to mention the Fragment.

Zach nodded and walked to the robobar. He got a gloworm and sat down on the semicircular formcouch facing the large window. "You look fidgety. What's wrong?"

"Nothing," Cora said, biting her lower lip. "In fact, things couldn't be better."

Zach gave her a penetrating look. "So who's looking after Sean?"

"You'll see," she said. "Have you had any luck lately?" Of course, she knew that he must have, for he always stopped on Earth after an asteroid haul, to see Sean and her.

"Nothing big." He sipped his drink and crunched on the tiny green worms. "A small load of nickel iron. It blew up with Hygiena."

A shiver ran through her. She put her hand on his arm in a silent comfort. How many friends had he lost?

He covered her hand with his. "I don't suppose you heard anything. Some Belters swear it was EarthGov."

"Take their word for it then. I hear that Belters don't swear needlessly," Cora said in a meaningful tone, trying to convey around her security block that she suspected the same.

"Thought so," Zach said, looking at his spacer boots. "The Belter Society is building a new shipyard, so I can't stay long. I'm sorry, they need transport to haul—"

They both turned at the sound of the opening door. Sean ran inside, followed by her Fragment.

"Dad! I didn't know you were on Earth." Sean dropped his specimen collector kit and ran to him, embracing him around the knees.

Zach reached down and picked him up, threw him in the air, and then hugged him, pressing his face to Sean's.

"Dad, I decided I'm going to be a Belter when I grow up," Sean said with a gap-toothed smile.

Zach laughed. "Whatever happened to our space drive engineer?"

"Nah, it's too boring. I'm going to explore." Sean wriggled out of his embrace and slid to the floor, looking up at him. "Maybe even an Oort miner." He gave Cora a sidelong glance, then looked back at Zach. "You'll teach me, right? Cause Mommy says you won't cause it's dangerous."

"I'll teach you when you're old enough. But I'm sure you'll change your mind at least a dozen times before that." Zach sat down.

"No, I won't. This is final," Sean declared in a serious tone that belied his six years of age. He climbed onto the couch and sat beside Zach, admiration shining in his blue eyes.

Zach ruffled his hair and there was tenderness in his voice when he said, "You have grown, Sean." His expression turned stern as he looked at Cora, then at the Fragment.

Cora felt a lump in her throat and wished that this conflict between them were over. His disapproval struck a note of failure in her.

Sean broke the silence. "How long you're staying?"

"Leaving tomorrow night," Zach said and looked at Cora. "After I speak with your mom, we'll do something together. Run along now and think up where you want to go." Zach gently guided his son toward the hallway.

The Mother Fragment picked up the dropped collector kit and followed Sean, closing the door of the dayroom behind her.

There was waiting in the silence between them, a tense hesitancy that preceded a confrontation. Cora squared her shoulders and waited.

Zach took a deep breath. "So you had to do it," he said gently, but his voice belied the disapproval in his eyes.

"You knew I would when I told you I applied for the permit."

"I knew. But I was hoping you could work things out differently. You're taking a big risk, Cora."

Cora began to pace the smart carpet of the dayroom. "Look who's talking about risks? You're plying the Belt for chunks of asteroids that could very well kill you."

Zach stood up and embraced her. "I'm concerned about you. I've never heard of a Fragment that didn't develop a Split Personality Syndrome after a while. Why do you think permits are so hard to get?"

"But I got the permit, and that means mine won't end up with SPS."

"You wouldn't report it even if she did become insane."

"Don't be absurd." Cora snorted and looked away. It was disconcerting how well Zach knew her.

He gave her a doubtful look. "You're skirting disaster, my love."

She stole a quick glance at him. The grim set of his mouth told her how much this unsettled him. And he didn't even know that Emef already showed symptoms of SPS. But damn it, the Fragment was hers, and she wouldn't let the Bio Regulation Agency terminate her.

"Zach, please don't worry about me. Remember five years ago when you made me promise I wouldn't worry about you? I kept my promise and it wasn't always easy. Now I'm asking you to do the same for me."

"Fair enough," he said. "I'll try." But his eyes showed uncertainty. Cora didn't realize she was holding her breath until she heard him say, "I love you." He kissed her, arms tight around her. Then he released her and went to fetch Sean.

Before reaching the door, he turned back with a lopsided grin. "Now that you have the Fragment, you could spend more time with me. It's been a long time the three of us did something together. Why don't you come with us?"

"Hey, that's a great idea."

Cora was silent, walking next to Katie along the rows of trees, enjoying the ocean breeze and the pungent smell of growing things. Lowell Commune was one of the biggest moving islands, and they visited every Sunday when it was nearby.

"Come on," Katie said and pulled her along by the hand. "I'll show you my new creations. They won't be back for hours."

"They" were Katie's mate Dimitri, their two children, and Sean, gone to see the dolphins that swam with the island.

Cora and Katie turned the corner and entered one of the hydroponics domes, a humid, brightly lit chamber.

"Finally the Bio Regulation approved the patent and my first babies are growing." Katie spread her arms to indicate the rows upon rows of short trees. "Behold the sausage trees."

Cora sucked in her breath as she regarded the mauve sausages dangling in thick clumps from bright green stems.

Katie smiled. "I know they look repulsive, but they taste heavenly."

"So what have you spliced?"

"There will be a variety of flavors, but this first crop is the combination of pork genes, soy, a touch of cayenne, garlic, black pepper, and onion."

"You're quite a mixtress."

"I am indeed." Katie laughed, but then she turned serious. "Enough about me. Tell me what's wrong."

Cora swallowed.

Katie narrowed her eyes. "It's the Fragment."

"Yes, but I don't think she has SPS. It's something else."

"What?"

"Not sure, but I have a bad feeling about it." Then she told Katie about her Fragment's dreams.

Katie caressed the fleshy leaf of a sausage tree absently. "Heard some rumors, you know."

Cora nodded—Lowell Island, with its satellite and hackers and encryption specialist, picked up things.

"EarthGov wants to control the colonization." Katie looked up. "Some of the private investors disappeared. I would be scared . . . working for EarthGov. But you were always brave."

Cora began to walk toward the doors. "I am scared."

"Listen," Katie said and grabbed her arm, pulling her around to face her. "This would be a good time to move here."

Cora shook her head. "My work is at the ARC. When Lowell is up north—for how long, four months, five?—I can't travel three hours each day."

Katie sighed and stepped through the door of the hydroponics dome. "You're scared but you won't part with your Fragment. Other people either live in a Commune or use household robots."

"I'm not going to have my son raised by robots."

"I know. I wouldn't want my kids to be raised by them, either. But I'm worried about you. You pulled me out of trouble more times than I care to count." She grinned, eyes twinkling with the old mischief. "Literally pulled me out of the muck."

Cora laughed, recalling Katie's spying on a local recycling plant she suspected of dumping illegal chemicals into the waste system. She had tripped the alarm, and in her haste to vacate the premises, she'd fallen into one of the sludge tanks. Because of her suspicious behavior, Cora had followed her and pulled her out; otherwise, Katie would've drowned before she found the narrow opening.

She hugged Katie "You always make me laugh. But I have to admit, it wasn't funny back then."

"Let's get something to eat. We have home-grown coffee and baked buns in the commons."

Another conference at work, which had robbed hours of her time and failed to solve any problems, made Cora rather cross. But Rice had insisted that she attend.

Glad to be home now, she tiptoed to Sean's bed and kissed him. She had promised to take him diving, but Sean had to spend the whole day with Emef. With a sigh, she tucked him in and straightened. And caught sight of a lumpy shape across the room, illuminated by the screen of Sean's teaching robot. "It's you."

Emef was sitting in the dark, knees folded up to her chest, head buried in her arms. She looked up, pale face ghostly in the screen's light, blue eyes framed by dark circles. "I spend the night here. Sometimes," she whispered.

"You're not allowed to sleep in Sean's room."

"I don't sleep." The Fragment stood up and looked at the robot's screen pointedly before she left.

Cora glanced at the display of two figures, childish rendering of women with their heads connected by wavy lines. It was odd; Sean never liked drawing.

She sat down by the piano and began to play Chopin's Twelve Etudes in G flat minor. Sounds flowed from her long fingers and a sense of wonder filled her. Through the music she played, a connection formed between her mind and that of a long dead genius; Cora knew Chopin, and savored the wonder he had created.

After two hours of practice, she went to the Fragment repository. Cora lay down the recliner and pulled the gel cap over her head.

Joy of experiencing her Fragment's daily activities filled her, taking care of Sean, building quasi-life animals with him, and helping with his lessons. The experience flowed into the fuzzy realm of dreams.

A scream ripped through Cora's mind, followed by a formless terror.

Terror—

—the terror took the form of CyMvec commandos and rows of rester capsules. Defiance filled Emef. *I won't participate* . . . Strange faces swam before her, punctuated by the rhyme in a screeching voice, *Mirror mirror of my mind, Earth Government stole my life.* Emef was drifting in anguish—

Anguish—

—Cora snatched off the interface cap with a violent motion, heaving and gagging. The ceiling of the Fragment repository whirled above her, replaying the images from Emef's dreams. But maybe they were not dreams.

Perspiration drenched her body, and the inside of her head seemed like a battle zone. Arms shaking, she pushed herself up from the variform and staggered a few steps.

A wave of vertigo hit her and she grabbed the doorframe. Swaying, she wove her way to the bathroom and stumbled to the autodoc, unsealed it, and slumped inside. She vaguely felt the cool biosensors attaching to her temples, wrists, and ankles. It seemed like an eternity, but finally the headache and nausea subsided and the autodoc released her.

Fear replaced the throbbing in her head. Cora stood in her bathroom and tried to compose herself.

A pattern began to form in her mind: her Fragment's dreams, the difficulty of obtaining permit for a Fragment, the colonization plans, the Alien Research Center, nanotechnology, they were all controlled by EarthGov through agencies and security protocols. EarthGov was largely unseen, partly because the assassination attempts against its executives and mostly because governments kept secrets. Secrets and clandestine research. Where would they do that? At a high security place, like the Alien Research Center. Cora shivered; there was a place she would have to check out tomorrow.

Cora looked at the floating screen before her, flipping through the research text with a feigned nonchalance as she hurried to the droptube. She hadn't been to level six since the cursory tour Rice had given her after she was accepted as Chief of Department. "Old archives, unused equipment," Rice had said and steered her away from certain areas.

The droptube descended and stopped. Cora stepped out and looked around. There was no one in sight, but her heartbeats echoed in her ears. This was ridiculous, sneaking around. She had every right to be on this level.

She squared her shoulders and marched toward the branching of the long corridor, her projected screen preceding her. Closed metal doors lined both sides of the charcoal plazcrete walls. She turned at the first bend and froze.

"No, the host has not developed it," she heard a woman say from a distance. "Her security mind block prevents it."

Cora retreated around the corner, gauging the distance to the droptube and contemplating whether to flee or listen.

"All right," said a man. "You can start growing two more bodies. But keep monitoring her Fragment."

What were they talking about? Cora held her breath and closed the data screen.

"The Fragment thinks she's experiencing symptoms of SPS," the woman said. "She doesn't suspect anything."

"Regardless of that, keep monitoring. The ships will be leaving within a year and we don't have enough quantel pairs to keep us abreast of the situation aboard. With the clones going mad and dying, I don't know what we'll do."

"Then don't implant the military augs. That's what kills them."

"Don't be stupid," the man said. "Without the augs, we can't control either the clones or the colonists. And we can't have them forming their own government."

"You'll have the CyMvecs—"

As the voices receded, Cora leaned against the wall, mind whirling with the implications. Quantel pairs, Cora had heard rumors about Quantum Telecom, where experiments were done with augmented humans for long distance communication, communication without a time lag. EarthGov was planning to use cloned sets of quantels for communication, one on the ark ship and one to remain on Earth. And they were implanting them with military augs. No wonder the clones were going mad; most minds couldn't tolerate a military aug.

Determined to learn more, she started toward the next intersection and took the left branch, the one Rice didn't want her to see. The steel doors were equipped with unfamiliar sensors. She put her palm to one. The door remained shut. Urgently now, she tried all in her path, disregarding the nagging fear of tripping some alarm.

Her breath was ragged, upper lip covered with beads of perspiration when one of the doors parted.

Cora stepped inside and gasped.

Behind a plaz wall, scores of vertical, translucent capsules held bodies of men and women. And one of them was hers.

Her heart lurched, and she grabbed the doorframe. Their hairless heads were encased in gel caps, and some seemed to be conscious, lips moving and eyes rolling. Three of them down the row writhed in agony, enhanced muscles contorted and limbs jerked, their gel caps pulsing with odd nodules. Military augs. Blood seeped from the eyes of one man. Cora turned her head aside. In a cloud of disbelief, she walked along the row and stopped by her own Fragment, or maybe it was a full replica, to communicate with Earth Government or to control the colonists. But that meant her Fragment was a quantel. How, if Cora wasn't—Then she recalled what the woman had said, "The host has not developed it, her security mind block prevents it."

Cora had once read about a government experiment—over a century old—using identical twins. They had abandoned the project for lack of results. Or because they had switched to clones. The Mirror Project; clones had identical brains.

"No."

Yes, she realized, recalling her Fragment's distress. And the sketch of two stick figures on Sean's computer. He hadn't drawn them. Emef had, trying to tell her. Poor Emef, she thought she suffered from SPS when the reality was something far worse. And the voices of the others, the despair of whining rhyming, *Mirror mirror of my mind, Earth Government stole my life.* And another voice, *Sister, sister, kill me.* The clones knew that EarthGov planned to use them to communicate between Earth and the ark ship, and that might have been acceptable to some, but to force clones onto the ark ship while the original person remained captive on Earth was monstrous. How on Alpha Serenity they planned to control the colonists through the clones Cora didn't even want to think about, but she knew that only one in a million person could withstand a military aug.

How dare they? Cora breathed in and out, frozen to the spot. With a quick sweep of her eyes, she surveyed the lab. There was a Bioanalyzer ran by a quantum processor. The floor to ceiling hexahedron contained the stasis units and cell storage. Somewhere in the base of it was a heavily shielded atomic pile that would irradiate specimens if it became necessary.

Cora wanted to run. Why should she care if these non-entities suffered? *They're fragments and replicas. There's nothing I can do.* She started toward the door, stopped, and started walking again.

The feeling of eyes boring into her back made her turn. She faced one of the women, number 17. Face lit by blue light, her expression held such a pleading that Cora's heart broke into pieces.

"Kill us," the woman mouthed silently.

Cora stiffened and looked away. Plans of freeing them bounced in her head. But where could they go? Even the dole system would reject them and they would starve. Or the CyMvecs would bring them back.

"Please, end this," the plea was a whisper this time.

She shook her head. *I can't do it, I can't do it, I can't do it.*

"Please . . ." The sound ended in a choking sob.

Cora stood there for long seconds, unable to leave. Mussorgsky's "Night on Bald Mountain" filled her mind, the music generating images of evil. She loved to play it, reveled in it, but only when reality didn't match the evil that the sounds evoke. Her fingers twitched now, and a shudder ran up her arms.

Finally, she nodded. Cold, yet flavored with compassion, a decision crystallized. She walked to the variform and sat down. "EI, turn on the Sealed Bioanalyzer System."

She read the warning on the holoscreen: TAMPERING WITH THE SYSTEM WILL RESULT IN THE DESTRUCTION OF ALL LAB CONTENTS. PLACE YOUR PALM ON THE ID SENSOR.

Cora did. From the ceiling, a light flickered for a moment, and then the brain scan shut off.

"You are logged in."

"Acknowledged," she choked out. Not wanting to speak, she used the touchboard and placed all the cell samples in the test vats, then gave several commands to commence illegal assembly. That would activate the NanoPol program, irradiating all cells in the stasis storage. That wasn't too hard; they were just cells. But the next step . . . Tears ran down her face as she sent false data to all the clone capsules, biohazard readings that would destroy the clones. If the final command was given.

"Sledgehammer," she said, naming the file. She gene-typed it to number 17, and routed it to her capsule. Wiping the tears off her face, Cora stood and walked to the woman. "On your command."

The sledgehammer file opened inside capsule 17, displaying the biohazard sign. "Thank you," the woman said and pressed the sign.

A humming began.

Rooted to the spot, Cora watched as one by one the clones died.

A loud beep jolted her. She dashed to the door and bolted out of the vault. Heart pounding, she ran along the corridors to the droptube. As the door closed, scenarios of a mindprobe trawling for snippets of her memories, murder charges by Earth Government, and her quick disappearance went through her mind.

Her legs shook, and she closed her eyes, not wanting to see the waiting CyMvec commandos.

Silence registered in her awareness. She cringed and opened her eyes. And swayed with relief, as she stepped into the deserted main lobby.

They must be at the park, Cora thought as the building system showed that Emef's car was not in the garage.

She exited her car and ran to the droptube, pressing her palm to the sensor. As soon as the door opened, she shouldered her way through. She must pack, get Sean and Emef, and leave.

"What time did Sean and Emef leave?" she asked the house AI rather than calling the Fragment. Earth Government had probably tapped their com.

Silence.

Stupid system, she should've replaced it with a newer one. Cora looked behind and felt her skin prickle. A fallen statue caught her eyes on the floor, its pedestal knocked against the wall.

Running into Sean's room, she pulled a travel bag from the closet and stuffed his clothes and games in. Pushing past the mess in the hallway, she went to her room.

The bathroom door was ajar, the autodoc blinking red with no one inside. Heart pounding in her ears, she dashed to the Fragment repository.

She screamed. Her Fragment lay halfway inside the capsule that showed her vital signs inactive.

"Emef?"

Dead. Cora froze.

"Sean!" Where was her son? She began to shake as an indescribable fear gripped her. Feeling faint, she grabbed the edge of the capsule and noticed the red blinking light on the interface computer. An emergency message, coded to her. She quickly typed in the code and saw PARTIAL SENSORY RECORD on the small screen.

"Oh God, where's Sean?"

Cora removed the senso cube with shaking hands. Leaning over the capsule to look at the time, she saw a large open wound in Emef's midsection. Blood covered everything.

CyMvecs. Had they taken Sean? She grabbed the gel cap and pulled it over her head, then plopped down on the couch.

An excruciating pain clawed at her stomach and chest, and the room drifted in giddy circles around her. Faint sensations came to her, incoherent thoughts sliced by pain. Cora almost fainted from the sensory overload and reached up to tone down the output of the cap. The pain became bearable, but fear washed over her in waves.

Fear—

—"They're coming! Quick." Emef grabbed Sean, and they ran to the back door. She pressed the sensor. The door hesitated. Emef hit it hard and it finally budged.

From her pocket she pulled out the car remote and set the destination to Lowell Commune, pushing Sean toward the staircase. She gave him the remote. "Hurry, go to Katie!" Then she slammed the door and prayed that they wouldn't check the other side of the building.

She longed to go with him, but she knew they would follow her. Somehow. It had been stupid to assume the couple of days respite from the mental ordeals meant it was over, that they had tired of her resistance.

She must warn Cora. Emef pressed her wristcom, then stopped. They might listen to the call. Through the interface then, she'd leave a message. She ran to the Fragment repository and was almost in the capsule when she saw them.

Three figures towered over her, armor-like body plates glistening with an oily sheen.

She screamed, recognizing the mechanical men she'd seen in the corridors of the building where the clones were kept. They circled her in slow motion, inescapable images from a nightmare. Her teeth rattled, and perspiration drenched her body. Something flashed, blinding, and an excruciating pain tore into her chest and stomach. She fell onto the capsule, vaguely aware of a loud crash. Gradually, a dark fog smothered her.

When Emef regained consciousness, the pain was unbearable. The mech men were gone. She tried sitting up and fell back, bumping her head in the capsule's edge. She panted, gathering her strength.

I must pull myself together and position my head under the helmet for recording the message. Pushing herself backward with her toes, she felt a warm gush from her stomach. She ignored it and wriggled her body upward inch by inch, and finally felt the cap ooze over her head. *Cora . . . flee, take Sean . . . Government . . . experiment . . . tels . . . communicate arkship.*

Emef felt—

Sorrow—

—Cora squirmed on the variform couch, suffering another flood of sensuals: pain, fear, warning, and love for her son. The pain lessened, but she couldn't breathe. She was suffocating. She sensed Emef slipping into unconsciousness. No, into death!

Cora screamed and tore off the gel cap, wiping her eyes with a trembling hand. Tears coursed down her cheeks and ran into her mouth, giving her a bitter taste of Emef's horrible struggles. She felt numb with the loss, and sat there empty. Into that emptiness, love poured and filled her heart toward the dead woman.

Herself? No, Cora was sobbing aloud now. This fragment of her own personality was a better human being than she could ever be. She recalled Emef pondering whether she had a soul.

I may not be the best judge of that, but I'd say you have a soul. She leaned over the body and gently closed the staring blue eyes. For a moment, she stood there. *Forgive me, Emef, I treated you badly.*

After a few minutes, she went to her closet and started throwing a few necessities into the travel bag. She sealed it, and it shrunk into a fat rectangle the size of thick book. This she shouldered and pressed the car call.

Chill air greeted her outside. Cora shivered and hastened toward her car, pressing her palm to the lock. Tension tightened her stomach as she climbed in. "Lowell Island," she said.

The car rose and headed toward the moving islands. As Cora leaned back into the variform, it conformed to her body and began to soothe. Through her augment, she activated her Net link and called Katie on a secure Lowell line, grateful that the islands had their own satellites.

"Thank God you're all right. I was so worried after Sean arrived alone and your com wasn't answering."

"I'm all right, Katie. How's Sean?"

"He's fine," Katie said, giving her a searching look. "Says that Emef rushed him out of the house and—"

"Katie, please don't ask questions. I need a biohacker waiting. And call the Belter Headquarters at Ceres and send a coded, priority message to Zach: WE'RE COMING. MEET ME AT THE SAPPHIRE HOTEL ON CLARKE STATION. I'm coming to get Sean."

"Sure," Katie said and cut the connection.

Bright light shone through the polarized plaz of the car, followed by a sonic boom. Cora blinked and jerked forward. The car buffeted and began to spiral downward. She took the controls and felt a resistance.

"Losing altitude," the car said.

"I know." Cora fought to gain height, asking through clenched teeth, "What happened?"

"A guidance feed was knocked loose by the explosion. Repairing now."

A few tense minutes later the car rose again and she wiped perspiration from her face.

"What kind of explosion?"

"Insufficient data. The building we left is gone."

Her hands began to shake. "Increase our speed to the maximum." She scrutinized the dash console. "Any cars following?"

"Negative."

Cora was impatient to leave. A full day spent on Lowell Island might be enough for Earth Government to trace her here. She looked over at Dimitri and Sean, walking along the pier and laughing.

Katie shook her head. "So the Split Personality Syndrome of Fragments is just a smoke screen."

"I'm pretty sure it is, to discourage people from owning Fragments."

"Stay here, Cora."

"No, you would all be in danger. But I'm grateful for your help."

Sniffing, she touched her nose. It was still sore after the biohacker removed her augment, along with the security mind block the ARC had installed in her mind. Dimitri had taken it out by flyer and discarded it somewhere over Asia. He had also arranged seats on a Lowell shuttle that would take them to Clarke Station, where Zach was waiting.

Katie sighed. "I just want you to be safe."

Cora hugged Katie. "Maybe we'll get political asylum at the Moon Colony." She had lost everything she had worked for, her home, her work at the ARC, and her music. The mournful melody of Liszt's "Hungarian Rhapsody" filled her mind, the staccato sounds of a happy folk dance alternating with somber tones of oppression and revolutions.

"If you insist on leaving Earth, one of the Belter settlements should be safer. But wherever you go, keep in touch," Katie said as they disengaged.

Cora blinked her tears away and pushed Sean ahead to board the flyer. Without turning, she waved. *I'll miss you, Katie.*

Author's note: The story is from *Fragments*, Book 1 in *The Covert Files* series.

Fortune's Rule

MIG SLOAN BIT HIS TONGUE to keep from crying out as the whip cracked over his naked back. The electric barbs rode his flesh like a dark beast, gouging out chunks of flesh. Sweat trickled down his face and body, and he fought to remain conscious, silently cursing his stupidity. He should've waited with hiding the pilfered supplies.

After an eternity, the metal clamps around his wrists opened and he slid to the damp floor.

Rene crept closer and helped him sit up, keeping one eye on the receding guard. She unscrewed her water bottle and handed it to him. Mig stilled his shaking hand and took the bottle, spilling some of the water. "Thank you."

Rene nodded. Mig didn't know what she had done that landed her on Grombar, but she'd been a good team mate. She brushed a grimy hand over her white hair and looked at Barton, the other member of the team, then pointed to the sole ctepped they had caught in the past six days. Stunned and held by a net, its buff hide was covered in slime. Rene looked at the animal with distaste. "Unless we catch a few more, we'll get a beating for not meeting our quota."

Barton looked up and blinked rapidly, then nodded and blinked again. "Sloan will sneak off again and search the side tunnels." He snorted. "For ctepeds, of course."

That's where they hide when they sense a quake coming, Mig thought and glared at the other man, a prisoner for less than a year. He didn't trust Barton, who watched everything and everyone. Without a word, he stood up and walked to his hammock.

As Mig lay awake, he listened to the grumbling of the mountain and planned his escape. He could look for Gheet Riff, the pirate that had betrayed him. After years of piloting for a merchant fleet, ferrying luxuries and pharmaceuticals between the fringe worlds, Riff had approached him with an offer Mig couldn't refuse.

For a fifty percent split of his cargo, he had tight-beamed his coordinates to the pirates. He could have bought his own ship within another year, but four cargos later, he had been arrested and charged with grand theft. Mig's sentence of fourteen years forced labor was to work in the caves of Grombar.

Blink thirty-four, stare into space, blink thirty-five, Mig counted the times Barton was blinking. It could mean that Barton was in possession of his augment, spying on the other prisoners, maybe for the merchant fleet. Mig's augment had been removed, as had those of the other prisoners, so Barton must be working for someone higher up than the guards.

"Rest is over," one of the guards said.

Mig clambered to his feet and reached for their new catch. "I'll tow the cteped."

"I'll take over in while," Barton said.

"We should start planning for an escape," Rene whispered.

Mig looked at her in alarm, then at Barton. Their gazes met and Barton held his. At that moment, Mig knew that Barton was a snitch. He couldn't mention the hidden cache of supplies, his years of planning. Instead, he shook his head. "We could never overpower all the guards with our puny stun rods. They wear the neutralizer vests even in their sleep."

Rene shrugged, dejected.

The trio took up their places behind the line of prisoners that formed behind the guards.

A deep rumble filled the caves. Mig felt the vibration in his feet and pelvic bones first, and then it resonated upward into his torso. Mig looked at Rene; her eyes were wide, glancing at the guards. She fingered her stun rod. Mig shook his head, afraid she might attack.

"Lava flow in tunnel thirty-one!" one of the guards yelled. "Head for higher—"

"Come on." Mig ran towards his cache, adrenaline spurring him on. He stumbled when the floor cracked but quickly regained his balance and barely jumped over the rift when the tunnel behind spat gobs of molten stone. Smoke swirled around them, and the tunnel was barely visible from the dust billowing from cracks in the ceiling and walls. Mig coughed from the fumes of melting rock, but tried to keep an ear out for Rene's panting as the lava sputtered around him.

There should have been advanced warning from the platform in orbit, Mig thought, as he tore off pieces of his soiled tunic, poured a bit of water on each from his bottle, and handed one to Rene. "Tie them around your face." He fastened a cloth to cover his mouth and nose. Barton could do as he pleased, for all Mig cared.

"Thanks." Rene shot him a grateful glance.

They reached the branch leading to his cache and found the walls collapsed, with rock slabs blocking the entrance. Smoke curled out from the narrow gaps. Mig's stomach knotted at the thought of losing his supplies. He retraced his steps, recalling a long, narrow tunnel above and around his hiding place. The others followed silently.

When he finally saw the low entrance, Mig dared to hope. He bent over to avoid hitting his head and broke into an awkward run, pulling ahead of Rene. His breath escaped in a relieved sigh when he found the fissure in the wall. He reached in carefully, avoiding the jagged edges of the crevice, and pulled out a large net.

Rene and Barton caught up to him. Barton rested his hands on his thighs, glaring up from a bent position. Rene smiled, her sweat-soaked face and bright teeth shining in the nearby light of lava streams. She pointed to the net. "I'm glad you thought of that."

Mig nodded and turned away, then took off in the opposite direction from which they had come, without a word to either of the others. A lull descended, followed by a subsonic throb. Only the faint sizzle of distant fires reached them. They were going upslope, breathing in ragged gasps, but Mig didn't dare to stop yet, not while he still felt the tremors in the soles of his boots. He kept glancing back over his shoulder, hoping he was wrong, but the sizzling lava had finally burned through the corridor walls, chasing them with a renewed vengeance. Slow as it was, it would fill up this level soon enough.

Light flickered at the end of the passage.

"I think we're close," Barton said.

"Yes," Mig said. "But we must cross to the other side. A narrow tunnel leads up to the surface."

Barton broke into a run. Mig and Rene had to follow.

When they reached an immense cavern, Mig slowed down. Light crackled with static, illuminating the impossibly high ceiling. Mig stopped abruptly, and Rene bumped into him from behind.

"Stop, Barton." Mig took a few steps in Barton's direction when a loud clap split the ceiling and knocked him off his feet. Tons of rocks crashed like thunder. Mig crawled back into the tunnel from which they had come. Cracks in the stone floor extended outward from the center, widening and pushing the vertical walls. The floor shifted beneath him.

Mig heard Barton calling and turned to see him standing on a large slab, one side attached to the main wall but the others hung over an abyss like an obscene tongue. Barton looked up, his movements jerky. It was a miracle he hadn't been crushed by the falling rocks. He shaded his eyes and darted to the side when a black columnar stone pitched over. It had barely missed him but cut his perch in half.

"This way!" Mig yelled as the floor tilted with him. He grabbed a rock and groaned as it sliced into his palm, but he held on. Crevices appeared in front of him. The noise was deafening, and he doubted Barton had heard him, so he began to crawl in his direction, glancing at the walls and ceiling. "Rene, follow me but keep some distance."

He stayed close to the wall, hoping that the right angle would give it the tensile strength to keep it intact for long enough to reach Barton.

"Barton, follow my voice." Mig kept moving and avoided thinking about the chasm below from where a sulphurous stench wafted up on heat waves. "We're to your left. Take a small step and start walking."

Barton turned and took a few steps towards them, as the mountain grumbled and shook. Mig crawled faster on elbows and knees, low to the ground. He was ten meters from Barton when the remainder of the floor tilted. Barton fell face down and didn't move.

"Damn. Stay back, Rene. I'll get him."

The rock avalanche started just as he reached Barton's prone figure. Mig covered his head, cursing as pieces of debris struck his arms and back. He extended one arm, the other still over his head, and reached for the other man blindly. "I got you, Barton. We're out of here." He panted and began to pull, backtracking like a crab. Mig felt relieved that Barton was so light. Too light.

Barton gurgled, face contorted with pain. He coughed up gouts of blood.

"Conserve your strength, Barton." Smoke and dust swirled around them, obscuring the other man as Mig crabbed their way along the narrow tongue of cave floor.

A gust of cooler air current brushed past them and afforded a precious few breaths of clean air. Ad then he saw. Mig's heart lurched; Barton's body below the waist was gone.

"Take my augment, Sloan." Barton licked the blood off his lips. "It can . . . to the platform."

"What are you talking about?" But he knew, Barton was a snitch, just as he had suspected. Right now though, he hated to be right. "Hold on a little longer. Use your augment to slow the blood flow."

An avalanche of pulverized rocks and dust pelted them. Mig covered Barton with his own body. The primitive medkit he had stolen from the guards didn't have enough features to save Barton's life; they needed a full-body autodoc for such serious injuries.

Rene gasped when she saw Barton. "God help us. What are we going to do?"

"We'll climb upward. It's only about a meter high here, so don't stand up." As far as Mig remembered, it wasn't long, but they were already half asphyxiated. "Here, haul the cache if you want to help." He shoved the net full of supplies at her. It slid on the bloody floor like a well-oiled mechanism. He didn't want Rene to think about how much blood Barton had lost. He had to get them out of the collapsing tunnels or they would all die.

Mig pulled Barton the rest of the way. Cooler air greeted them. He looked up at the narrow opening, his breath wheezing as his lungs labored in the thin air. "Give me the medkit, Rene." With a sheer force of will, he made himself look at the truncated body. Barton's legs and pelvis were missing. Organs were covered in congealed blood, pulsing through the diagonal cut. It was a miracle he was still alive, no doubt his augment working overdrive. Mig swayed, then shuddered. Snitch or not, he felt a stab of sympathy.

Removing one of the water bottles from the net, he put it to Barton's lips. "Drink." His other hand lifted the injured man's head and held it at an angle. How long could his augment forestall shock and death?

Barton's eyes opened.

Mig reached for the medkit and grabbed the medpump. He touched it to Barton's neck and pressed. The smartgel attached to him, flooding his system with restorative fluids and medchines. Mig hoped it would be enough until they could get to the platform.

Barton lifted an arm covered in blood, trying to push the medpump off. "No use," he whispered. His eyes clouded, breath wheezing. "My augment . . . can't keep up."

"Don't talk. Rest and let the medchines work."

Barton shook his head, coughing up blood again. Mig wiped his chin and neck with the remnants of his shirt, hands shaking.

". . .take my augment, Sloan. Get the info to Defense . . . aliens." Barton's hand encircled his wrist and gripped more tightly than a man about to die should be able to.

Mig compressed his lips and shook his head.

Barton' fingers fluttered and a gurgling sound issued from his throat. ". . .take augment—" He shuddered and was still.

Mig turned his head.

Rene laid a shaking hand on his arm, her throat working but no sound came out. Sometime later, she fell asleep.

Mig sat there, staring up at the hole in the cave. He knew that they had a chance of getting off Grombar with Barton's augment but shuddered at the idea of digging it out of his head. Inaction would take the decision out of his hands soon, because augments shut down a few minutes after the host's death. Then it would be back to the lower caves, serving out his prison sentence of eleven more years. He sighed and pulled out the stolen v-knife, pressing the stud in the handle. The buckyglass blade vibrated, and he shut his eyes for a moment, remembering the expression in Barton's eyes. *He asked me to do it, for whatever reason.*

Jaws clenched, he held Barton's head with one hand and touched the knife to the forehead, then pulled it across in a quick motion. Dark blood beaded the white bone of the cranium, and the dura cracked with a sound like the whip of the guards. Mig swallowed the gorge rising in his throat and stilled his hands. Heart thumping, he lifted the head under the neck and cut around, like taking the top off a coconut. His glance slid down to Barton's face, as if seeking forgiveness. Perspiration dripped into his eyes. He sensed Rene moving behind him and heard the intake of a sharp breath. Then she retreated to the dark passage.

Mig gritted his teeth and lifted off the severed skull. He set it aside on the warm floor, and then pressed the knife into the brain.

It parted easily, and the augment, a nacreous worm equipped with thousands of silver hair-thin cilia, wriggled free. He shuddered as it crawled over his hand. His butchery and the anxious movements of the biotech almost made him vomit. The augment seemed to want to connect with someone, quivering with anticipation as it moved up his arm.

Mig sat down, closed his eyes and gave himself up to the inevitable. He wasn't about to waste the opportunity just by being squeamish. The augment reached his neck and kept crawling, its cilia brushing over his sweaty skin. When it found his nostrils, it slithered inside.

A sharp pain pierced Mig's forehead, followed by dizziness and nausea. He leaned his head against the stone and tried not to think about what he had done.

Mig woke to the rumbling of his stomach. A dull headache throbbed behind his eyes; his body was drenched, his lips parched. How long had he slept? Too long, he thought as the odor of decay cloyed into his nostrils. He avoided looking at Barton's corpse.

"You all right, Mig?" Rene asked.

He reached for the last water bottle and lifted it to his lips, but it was empty. He looked at Rene.

"I was thirsty," she said sheepishly.

He nodded, wondering how she had finished four bottles while he'd slept. "We're getting off Grombar."

Mig concentrated and found that the augment had connected with his synapses, branching out its hyaline threads. It was in the final stages of fusing itself to his brain, but he sensed data pulsing just for the mere asking.

"Is it working?"

"Yes, and it's an Alphega Expert system."

Left-recursive algorithms unfurled, integrating within his mind. Icy wind whipped his skin, then hot coals singed his hair. The smell of rot alternated with scents of flowers, and his mouth felt full of thick syrup. His senses spun in a sickening vertigo as his mind perceived a blur of sensory load. The synthesis congealed into some normalcy and the sensorium cleared gradually.

A closed file jumped at his awareness. Mig tugged at it slowly, not certain if he wanted to know what it contained. He tapped the protein icon and it unfurled, bearing the logo of Inner League Defense and Intelligence. He gave a cursory inspection to the data packets—gene-locked. That meant—his heart pounded as he realized why Barton had gripped his wrist so hard. Kevir Barton, agent of Defense and Intelligence, had genetically imprinted him just before he died, so that the augment would obey a new host.

Barton had been sent to Grombar to learn if the cteped eggs had any connection to a hitherto unknown alien species. An image of a charcoal creature appeared. Mig's eyes smarted from looking at the shifting skin of the alien as it rippled and moved in a gruesome manner.

He saw Larana Station and blurry images of the same alien on the station's main deck, tearing through security guards. The view panned to a ship owned by Cravits Pharmacorps, its cargo bays wide open. Then chaos: images of the alien wrapped in black fluid, a malfunctioning station AI, terse commands issued in a frantic voice to quarantine the station, scorched human bodies, melted bulkheads, the arrival of a Patrol ship, and finally the explosion of the station.

Mig shook his head and closed the file, then rooted among the data and found a priority command code that superseded that of a Space Force General. He was stunned. As he searched more, he also found Barton's ship, a Cobia class orbiting the moon of Grombar. He checked the pilot interface of the augment, satisfied that he could link with the ship's AI.

Their ticket to freedom.

"What?" Rene asked.

Mig lifted his hand. "Give me a minute to sort this out." He turned away to hide his shame. Barton was an agent all right, but not a snitch as he had assumed. And that alien . . . He had never seen anything like it, and he had ranged far and wide during his piloting between the fringe worlds. Mig scanned through Barton's files on the cteped and found his conclusions: the cteped were *not* the source of the Larana Station contamination. That was a relief, because the cteped eggs had been exported to countless worlds. Mig groped for the tech nodes among the xenobio data packs and asked for the platform's schematics. A wedge-shaped construction appeared before his retinas, showing four shuttles docking around the rim.

He opened a comlink to the platform, transmitted Barton's priority code to the platform's AI, and waited. A few seconds later a question formed in his mind, *"What do you need?"*

"I want three landers to this location." he said aloud, and then sent the coordinates to the AI. "And send a search team, autodocs, and med sleds." He closed the connection, wondering how many people had survived the quake.

"Why ask for a search team?" Rene reached for his knife, glared at the blood on it, then stuck it in her belt anyway. "I doubt anyone survived the quake."

Mig shrugged, too tired to argue. "Barton was not here to spy on us."

"He wasn't?"

"No. He was a xenobiologist with Defense and Intelligence, sent here to learn if the ctepeds are the source of some alien contamination responsible for the destruction of Larana Station."

"What kind of contamination?" Rene sighed. "And if the ctepeds are the source, why are we still harvesting their eggs?"

"According to Barton's assessment, the ctepeds *aren't* the source."

"What's going on?"

"I wish I knew. Anyway, there's a ship orbiting the moon."

They both looked up at the whirring sound coming from outside the cave. "The transport's here." Mig grabbed the edges and pulled himself up, then helped Rene out. A dust storm obscured everything. He blinked to adjust his vision, then grabbed Rene's hand and ran towards the lander, praying that the platform AI wouldn't challenge his authority, or rather, Barton's authority.

As soon as they boarded, they took the seats up front. Mig pulled the crashweb over his body and reached for the controls when the airlock closed and the craft lifted. "What the hell? And where's the rescue party?" he addressed the onboard system. "We need a search team down here. And medical help."

A crackle came through the comlink. Something was wrong. A glance at the instrument panel showed the destination preset to the platform and the controls code-locked. Probing it through his augment, he found it was an emergency lock-down. He tried to override it with the DI priority code, but the controls remained unresponsive.

"Damn, I didn't want to dock at the platform, but we have no choice. The lander can't go directly to Barton's ship."

"Can you do something?"

"Maybe when we get to the platform."

Mig looked out the viewport. Wind-driven dust and smoke swirled around the craft, charcoal gray. It reminded him of the alien with its rippling hide. He squirmed in the formseat and glanced over his shoulder, but couldn't shake the uneasy feeling.

Cone-shaped mountains came into view, and the one they had escaped from belched smoke into the atmosphere. Scarlet ribbons of high-velocity air screamed outside and licked the lander. It shuddered, armor plates heaving as it rose higher, leaving behind the monstrous clouds to devour the sky. Black space was a welcome sight. The wedge-shaped platform grew on the screen. Then finally, the lander docked with much clanging.

They walked through the umbilical. As soon as Mig stepped out of the airlock, the stench hit him. It stuck to the back of his throat, sweetly cloying with a trace of vegetal rot. Heat wrapped around him like a blanket. Rene gagged and covered her nose.

Mig took a few steps. There was some gravity, so the platform's gravity plates were functioning. Dim light from a strip on the ceiling barely illuminated the large storage area. Float pallets clung to wall tacks, and racks piled with plaz crates lined one wall.

Rene walked to the equipment and kicked a crate.

Mig linked with the platform AI and encountered a hazy field blocking his access. By accessing a status icon, he was able to determine that the power source to the drives was disconnected, and the flow alloy inner bulkheads were inert, their machinery in a disunited state, unable to extrude furniture at demand. Another attempt at linking with the AI resulted in a subsonic buzz in his head that grew rapidly into a headache. Evidenced by the stench and heat, the air scrubbers seemed overtaxed, but he couldn't connect with life support either. In a corner, he saw a transparent tube full of suit kits. He walked over and took two.

"Look," Rene whispered.

Mig handed her one of the inactivate suit kits and turned. Several desiccated corpses—men and women in crew uniforms—were heaped in the corner, with a tar-like substance leaking from their noses. His heart lurched. He had expected some sort of resistance, the people in charge to question them about their sudden appearance, or even trying to detain them. But he wasn't prepared for what he saw.

"This place gives me the creeps," Rene said. "Call the ship and let's get out of here."

"No." Mig lifted his hand, looking at the platform's schematics on a holoscreen his augment generated. Biosensors showed no humans alive anywhere, but there was an odd flicker of life reading in the control room. "There were sixty-eight crewmembers here. I want to know what killed them." He headed towards the control center.

Cleaning bots crawled on the floor, and repair scarabs scuttled out of their way. A large rat scurried into an air duct, naked tail twitching. Mig found a galley with a food assembler unit, its once gleaming sides covered by grime. Feedstock from it stood in puddles on the inert floy deck, some dried into moldy patches.

He passed several sleeping cubicles, with soiled clothing piled on bunks.

"It's a ghost station," Rene said. "This kind of system failure is . . . impossible, especially on a DXL-2000 research platform. I recognize the configuration because I've worked on a similar one."

Mig agreed; stations were programmed with thousands of redundant safety systems. Sabotage? A dreadful notion occurred to him. He contemplated whether he should discuss it with Rene, but decided against it. She seemed frightened enough already.

They entered the access way encircling the control center and faced an open door. Mig stepped back a pace, gagging from the stench. He breathed through his mouth and walked into the control center.

Rene followed. The hexagonal control column was lit up, and holoscreens of strange symbols flickered before the instrument panels. The two variform control couches visible from their vantage were empty, but Mig heard a faint sound from the other side. He walked around the control column and stopped.

A woman sat in one of the variforms, head tilted at an odd angle, mouth open. A black tarry substance oozed from her mouth and nose. Her gray-tinged face was twitching, flowing, like—

Mig shuddered. Like the hide of the alien in Barton's files.

"What's that in her hands?" Rene pointed to an undulating black cloth, like a tightly beaded shawl, covering the woman's fingers.

Mig shrugged and leaned closer to look, then jumped back suddenly as the black mass surged towards him. He stumbled backward, pushing Rene behind him, while he activated his far vision. The augment clicked and he saw thousands of flea-sized black burrs, spherical and connected to each other by microscopic spikes, moving on the cloth. No, they *were* the cloth. A hole formed in the burr-woven structure, attenuated, and began to ooze down the woman's lap. Mig recognized it; it was the hide of the alien, perhaps some kind of a symbiont. As the images from his eyes transferred to his augment, preliminary analyses flooded his mind: hostile takeover, datavores, collective, mental patterns, human template, strategy.

"Back out, slow and easy," he whispered, moving in carefully measured steps towards the door and keeping his eyes on the alien infestation. If it weren't for Barton's augment, he wouldn't have seen the things.

The burrs reached the woman's shin, then a few jumped off and bounced towards Mig and Rene.

Mig turned and pushed Rene out, then quickly sealed the door behind them. He groped for the Cobia's code in his augment, cursing himself for not doing it before. "Let's get away from here and activate the suits." They should have done that too, before they had ventured into the platform's depths.

"You think it can get out?" Rene's lips trembled but she kept pace as they dashed through the passages.

"Eventually," he said. "*They*, there are thousands of them, hundreds of thousands." He wondered how they got aboard the platform, and whether the alien that carried them was lurking around. He kept glancing over his shoulder, even though his augment registered no life signs in any direction.

Once they reached the living areas, they found a relatively clean sleeping cubby. Mig inspected it for burr infestation, then closed the door. He quickly undressed and unsealed the skinsuit. Rene turned her back and did likewise.

When the filmy material unfurled, Mig stepped into the leg parts. They flowed up over his body in a continuous motion, covering him from foot to chin. He pulled up the head flaps and they began to fuse, the dull film turning skin color.

Rene turned, eyes casting left and right. "Is the ship coming?"

Mig nodded, checking the vitals of the suit on his retinal screen.

"You think the burrs can penetrate the skinsuits?"

"I don't know. But I don't plan to stand still to find out."

Mig dressed and latched his boots, grappling with conflicting emotions. His instinct told him to run and hide, far from here, but his conscience said otherwise. He couldn't help the prisoners down below, even if any had survived the quake, because Barton's ship could only transport two people. Unless the burr infestation had reached that too. But he refused to consider that possibility. Though it was obvious that the platform crew had died from the neural infestation, the burrs couldn't have invaded the Cobia; it was equipped with DI chameleophage and parked at the moon.

"We'll find an airlock and jet over to the Cobia," he told Rene. Then he linked with the Cobia's AI and advised it not to dock at the platform. "This place should be quarantined." More than quarantined, he thought, according to DI protocols. *And if I decide to finish Barton's mission—*

"Who cares what happens to this place after we leave?"

—then I must do something for the survivors down below.

Mig was relieved to find that the umbilical they had come through was safe. He used the augment to study the lander's subroutines until he found a way to cancel the emergency lockdown of its controls. "I'm sending the lander down to wait for survivors."

"Don't—"

Mig lifted his hand to forestall her objections. This had ceased to be an opportunistic escape from a prison world. Along with Barton's augment, he had also inherited his mission. "If someone makes it out of the caves, they can hole up in the lander. There's food and water for weeks."

Rene glared. "You're making a mistake. If any of the guards survived, they would call the Patrol." She turned her back on him, unsealed the door, and looked out into the corridor.

Mig walked around her. "Let me go first, I have augmented vision."

While they retraced their route to the storage area, he linked with the Cobia's AI and, using Barton' encrypted DI code, transmitted the records his augment had made of the platform's condition. In an attempt to cut the tension, he grinned at Rene. "I could get used to an aug like this."

"I suppose it's yours now."

Mig detected a slight envy in her voice, so rather than listing the capabilities of a military augment, he quickly changed the subject. "Let's see if there are jet belts we can use." He approached the storage racks, all the while scanning for burrs.

Rene followed. They opened containers and found the propulsion belts, which they fastened around their waists. "There's a shieldlock at the end of this corridor." He pointed to their left. "We can wait there for the ship."

Beyond the flickering shieldlock, space stretched into infinity. When Mig saw the Cobia stop two hundred meters from the platform, he turned to Rene and nodded. They sealed up the head flaps of their suits and stepped through the shieldlock. He activated the belt and aimed himself in the direction of the craft.

Mig admired the system as he jetted across, getting the data feed from Barton's augment. The white star of 1.3 Solar mass showed a disk from the distance of Grombar, the third planet and 1.4 AUs from its primary. Grombar was the farthest out, but the other two gas giants were in close orbit.

The Cobia grew, then blocked out the view, its shieldlock shimmering like a fisheye. Mig passed through, and as soon as he landed on the floy deck, a white light enveloped him.

"Welcome aboard, Mig Sloan," said the AI. The light moved over Rene, scanning her, then scanning her again. "Who is your companion?"

"I'm Rene Deveron, if you must know."

"What is your function here?"

Rene gave Mig a fearful look.

"It's none of your business," Mig said.

"Everything aboard is my business, Mig Sloan," said the AI. "But I have satisfied my curiosity for now. Ship and I bear the same name, so you may call me *Scarecrow*."

"Fine, Scarecrow, from now on, curb your curiosity." Mig followed the tracer light to the bridge. "Scan this system for the presence of alien spacecrafts." He sat in the command chair and motioned Rene to take the other variform couch. Now that he was sitting, safely ensconced aboard the *Scarecrow,* fatigue washed over him in waves.

"I have been scanning," said the AI. "There are no spacecrafts in this system, human or alien."

Rene grinned. "That should make our getaway easier. I thought we might have to dodge Patrol ships. What are you waiting for, *Scarecrow*? Head for the transgate, whichever takes to Hubble Hole." She tilted her head for a second, then added, "I have friends on Harmony, we could—"

"What is your command, Mig Sloan?" asked the AI.

Rene turned to face him, frowning. "Well?"

Mig compressed his lips and refused to look at her, partly because he was embarrassed by his indecision, but another part of him wondered what crime she had committed. He could ask her but she wouldn't tell him . . . Also, she seemed different since their escape, callous and selfish, not the timid Rene he had known down below.

"If you'd rather take Newton Nexus, I know some people on Bator."

Mig shook his head but didn't tell Rene that he would not stay with her. And even before he thought about his own future, there was something he had to do first. "What do you have in the way of weapons?" he addressed the AI. The alien had blown up Larana Station because it had failed there and didn't want to leave the burrs behind for humans to study, but here, the burrs had obtained data. So had he on the burrs, and since they were hostile, he couldn't leave the infestation unchecked. If it couldn't be contained—and he was certain the burrs would infest the first spacecraft that docked at the platform—DI protocol called for total eradication. That was Barton's mission directive. One of them; the other one was to deliver data on the aliens to Defense and Intelligence.

"I carry defensive and offensive ordnance. Perhaps you might tell me what you intend."

"We need to destroy the platform. Not just blow it up but completely annihilate it, so that not even a microbe survives."

"That would call attention to our presence!" Rene threw up her hands. "We can't afford to linger here and blow things up."

"Shut up," Mig said without turning.

Rene hit the arm of the variform couch. "You're an idiot! Barton's augment warped your sense of priorities."

An array of weapons lined up on the main screen, things he had never even imagined: plasma cannons, queser guns, nuke-tipped missiles, pulse beam resonator, and a molecular imploder.

"All right," Mig said. "Prepare the nuke-tipped missiles."

"May I suggest we use the plasma cannon first, followed by the nukes?"

"Do it," Mig said, enjoying the comfort of the variform command couch. This part of Barton's mission directive was the easy one to follow; the next one he might regret for the rest of his life. "And after that, head for the Orion wormhole. I believe it would connect us to the nearest DI headquarters."

"No!" Rene's arm shot out and hit him on the side of his head.

Mig cursed and touched his temple, then he saw that the variform was restraining Rene. She struggled in vain as the couch wrapped around her, using the crashweb to pin her arms.

"I have taken the liberty of blocking the message she'd tried to send to a merchant fleet," said the AI.

Mig narrowed his eyes as the realization hit him. Rene, it was Rene all along, spying on him in case he escaped, so she could learn the location of the stolen cargo. Disappointment filled him, because he'd thought she was a friend, just like he'd thought that Gheet Riff the pirate was a business partner. He had also misjudged Barton, and perhaps he was making another mistake now, but he shrugged and waited for the ship to carry out his commands.

Mig glanced at the main screen. White plasma roiled, followed by a brief flare as the nuke-tipped missiles reached the platform. As he watched the radioactive cloud diminish behind the ship, he felt relieved. "Scarecrow, head for the nearest headquarters of Defense and Intelligence."

Author's note: From another, as of yet titleless, series in which I've written half a book.

Harvest

SOME SAY THE DEAD DON'T CARE, but they do, Almion thought. Could she bear that much anguish? She breathed in and opened her clenched fists, following the orderly down to the hospital's basement. She worried that she would be late for the Vtara tournament.

The orderly turned into a short corridor and then stopped before a steel door. "In here, please," he said and left.

She hesitated, staring after his suit-clad back. The plague was upon Xilora again, and though no one knew how it spread, it didn't seem to spread by contact. She entered the cold room where two medical mobiles stood in the center, each holding a body covered with a decon sheet.

"I'm Rilo Costel," said a short man. "The Planetary Council asked me to assist you."

His muscular physique was unusual, and the shaggy black hair was so outdated that she wondered which island or continent he came from. She stared brazenly. "And you're assisting by diverting me from the tournament?"

Piercing blue eyes met hers. Almion looked away and felt her face tattoos throbbing.

"You're the Johannist necromancer."

She winced at the derogatory term often used for the Johannists, quantels whose talents manifested in various ways. "I'm Almion Jenna Forsythe, an SEF reader."

"Sorry," he said and uncovered one of the bodies. "Read them. They both died of the plague just minutes ago."

She walked over to the body - a Human - and shuddered at the sight of his blistered skin and contorted expression. Almion closed her eyes and probed the particles around the departed mind. To her dismay, it was blank. "There are no echoes of memories imprinted on quantum packets." With one hand, she rubbed her eyes.

Rilo looked at her; fear showed in his eyes. "How could that be?"

Almion shook her head.

"Now the Xil," Rilo said and uncovered the other body.

It was a female, her eyes oozing the purple blood of her species, lavender skin scabby and lacerated. Her face tentacles resembled a pile of tangled ropes. After scanning the quantum packets around the Xil's mind, Almion shook her head. Her lips trembled. "She's the same. They're . . . as if they were never born, never lived, and never died."

If she couldn't find the memory imprints of the plague victims, how would she perform her assigned task? *"The fate of our people and that of the Xil depend on your abilities,"* Almion recalled the parting words of the Ponticess before she had left Temple, the small island on Xilora where the Johannists lived.

"Let's go to the stadium now."

"Fine," she said, annoyed by his taciturn nature.

They walked out and rode the droptube up, exited the hospital, and crossed the street to a shimmering dome. Flocks of birds speckled the azure sky. They circled the dome, iridescent plumes bright with the borrowed light of the force field. Occasionally one would fly into the field and rebound, then plummet to the ground. Just birds to the Vtara. Her face flushed with anger at the callous wasting of life.

They passed through the force field and entered the stadium. Deadly particles bounced off her skinsuit. Some crackled and discharged, and others were absorbed and converted into energy to power the machines in her suit. How safe was the suit?

Don't think about that, she berated herself.

"Have you ever wondered why the Vtara always erect their stadium near a hospital?" Rilo asked. He led her to the first tier and they took their reserved seats.

"No," she said and sank into the variform. Her task was to read the SEF, Synorphic Energy Field, and record her findings for the Planetary Council. *After all this time, they want our help.* For centuries, the Johannists had been aware of the SEF deterioration during tournaments, but they had had no inkling what the Vtara did under the guise of the tournaments.

All worlds where sentient beings lived were surrounded by a Synorphic Energy Field, a repository of the psychically, philosophically, and organically recorded experiences of a population, lives coded into bits and embedded inside quantum packets. Even on planets where sentience had barely begun to emerge, an SEF was present. However passively, the SEF interacted with living beings and provided a psychological comfort zone, and it was vital to the evolution of a species. *So how can the Vtara interfere with the SEF?* It terrified her, and Almion didn't want to think about that; she needed to concentrate on her mission.

Not yet accustomed to her AI interface, a wetware resembling a worm inside her brain, she tested it now. None of the other Johannists used implants, as they did not interact with the main colonists.

Through her neural interface, she asked the AI to record a full sensorium of everything she encountered, saw, or felt. She needed to prove beyond any doubt that the SEF deterioration and the Vtara tournaments were connected.

Understood, the AI sent.

Almion soaked up the experience of being among so many strangers. She had never been away from Temple; few among the Johannists traveled. She felt isolated, but also sensed the curious glances that flew in her direction, of Human and Xil. When Almion turned her head, a woman smiled at her. She returned the smile awkwardly and felt her face flush at the warm feeling that coursed through her body. *Don't get distracted,* she berated herself. She was sent here to serve a common cause and her mission didn't include socializing. Tall and thin, with her living face tattoos now covered by makeup, and her newly-grown hair, she felt less like an outsider and watched with more than her eyes. As someone who studied ancient history, she had often wondered about the fear her kind had instilled in others and led to the banishment of all quantels from Earth thousands of years ago. Humanity's grudging acceptance of her people had been a slow process, kick started by the discovery of the Synorphic Energy Field. Since then, a group of Johannists accompanied every colony ship that set out for new worlds. On Xilora, however, the segregation continued. After centuries, it had simply become habit. By now, Johannists preferred the isolation. Despite past injustices, she embraced her duty to serve the orphaned colony to the best of her abilities because she was incapable of doing otherwise. Almion sighed, wondering if her best would be enough.

The Xil warbled in liquid sounds. Contrary to their fluid grace, they gesticulated with all four of their sinuous arms in jerky motions. The Humans whispered and cast furtive glances at the buzzing surveillance wasps.

A sudden fearful doubt gripped her as she thought of the enormity of her task. Only a handful of Johannists had the ability to retrieve data from the SEF. If she succeeded, there might be repercussions from the alien Vtara. If she failed, the people of this lonely planet, both the native Xil and the Human colonists, were doomed.

The crowd fell silent, but it was not out of respect for the Vtara tournament. Some Humans looked away from the stadium; others yawned, not even feigning the slightest interest. Xil youths fluttered their face tentacles in impatience, four-fingered hands covering their speaking mouths in an effort to stifle sounds. She suspected they would rather watch Xil-Human games, where they could cheer and hoot. But noise violators were fined here.

A female Xil let out a high-pitched howl and crumpled, then fell out of the variform seat, her face tentacles twitching. Her eyes oozed purple blood and her skin began to crust and peel off in flaky sections. Total cell death would follow in minutes. Almion shuddered as the pain of a nearly spent life tore through her.

People looked at the Vtara with hatred, and despite her mental shield a fleeting thought of outrage reached her from somewhere in the crowd - *If I must die from the plague, I don't want to spend my last hours watching the Vtara tournament.*

A man and two Xil carried the stricken female out.

Another victim of the plague. After centuries of study, scientists still didn't know what caused it. Almion contained her fear and took solace in the fact that if the Johannists could prove the Vtara was culpable, no people of Xilora would ever be forced to attend another tournament. They could tackle the plague after.

The field above the stadium expanded, and the tiny plasma sphere serving as a miniature sun spat out violet rays. Heat shimmered in waves. A faint hum registered in her teeth as the gravity generators cut in and pressed her down into the variform seat. Her eyes widened for a second, but then she felt her suit adjust to the extra pull of weight.

Almion imagined the mute whistle of gamma rays as the plasma sphere overhead spun faster, generating heat and radiation that could have killed the spectators instantly without the protection of suits.

Their guests, the Vtara, cavorted at the center of the stadium, showing no sign of concern for the safety of the two species that hosted their cursed tournaments. Silver-gray, four-legged Vtara moved around with stiff deliberations. Slabs of hard armor plates covered their bodies, glinting with the harsh light of the stadium. Four neon-blue eyes glowed in a horizontal row on the blunt head of each, and the gaping hole of a mouth seemed rigidly frozen into permanent immobility.

"What could be the purpose of that insane frolicking?" Almion heard someone whisper in the row behind. She tuned out the crowd and expanded her senses into the SEF.

With ponderous steps, each Vtara lumbered onto one of the octagonal crystal slabs placed randomly around the arena. They rubbed the black wart-like eruptions that circled their necks, using two of their four hands, and with a swiftness that belied their physique, all four of their legs began to tap on the crystal slabs.

Some Vtara ejected raw brains through their mouth. The apple-sized gray masses sizzled and pulsed with urgency. The adults hastily lowered them onto the slabs, which began to resonate, throwing off beams of colorful shards.

Almion stiffened as four minds were ripped from the SEF. She felt them clutch desperately at the quantum matrix before they died. Searing waves tore the quantum fabric that normally contained the departed minds before an invisible force shunted them into a dissonant dimension.

Nausea rose in her throat, followed by vertigo as she sensed the dislocation of several souls. Her mind heaved under the onslaught while her instinct screamed for her to tune out. Perspiration drenched her face until her suit absorbed it. This was murder on the deepest level; this was genocide. Her breath came in gasps and her limbs twitched.

"Easy." Rilo touched her arm.

The simple gesture succored her, but her mind whirled with the implications. "The SEF weakens because they're stealing life memories during the tournaments. The raw brains do it, but I don't know how."

Rilo turned white and then his eyes narrowed. "Of course, they're stealing souls. And there's no lack of dead during the plague."

Something nagged at the back of her mind but she couldn't think about it as another wave of soul dislocation seared her mind. Almion grabbed the arm of the variform. She gulped, as the realization hit her. "They . . . the Vtara, *they* cause the plague." Tears sprung to her eyes. She looked away, suddenly embarrassed by her lack of control.

Rilo nodded. "We knew they bring the plague, and now we know why."

Almion faced him. "That's why you wanted me to scan the victims at the hospital."

"I thought a necromancer, sorry—" He gave her an apologetic look. "I thought an SEF reader could find some clues in the mind imprints of recently departed plague victims."

"I see."

Rilo sighed. "I'm sorry we must put you through this. We don't have the technology of the Federation worlds."

"It's nice to know we're needed."

Rilo nodded. "We must expose the Vtara deceptions. According to them, the tournaments allow the next generation of Vtara, the raw brains, to interact with other species. But now we know that they bring the raw brains near other sentient species to steal SEF memory." He laced his fingers together, staring before him. "We told the Council several times that we must stop the tournaments."

So did we, Almion thought, irritated by his arrogance, but even more by his mysterious behavior. She wondered who he was and whom he meant by 'we'.

"And it all makes sense now; think about it," Rilo continued. "The plague precedes the Vtara every eleven years when they come to Xilora. Something in the clouds makes people sick and die. Coincidence?" He shook his head. "Maybe they need the plague because they can't reach into the SEF, but at the moment of death, the raw brains somehow snatch the minds of the deceased. And the raw brains are the offsprings of the Vtara."

Almion recalled reading the work of an ancient sociologist that suggested that a Vtara tournament was a ceremony, a single parent reproductive dance. According to another publication, by a member of the original crew, the tournament was a fraud. The Vtara was a mystery, but so was the original crew, whose members were rumored to be alive after centuries. But after the alien attack that destroyed the wormhole, the colony ship, and the main science lab, no one had heard from the original crew.

Almion sensed Rilo's xenophobia and wondered if he knew how much of his emotions leaked.

The AI intruded upon her thoughts: *I have been monitoring the Humans and Xil. Four hundred sixty-seven people died during the last two hours.*

"Keep monitoring," she responded.

Almion returned her attention to the tournament. Seven raw brains twitched on the crystal slabs now and settled into a rhythmic pulse as another seven dislocated minds howled mutely. She had already lost count, but even one stolen SEF memory weakened the integrity of Human and Xil sentience.

In ancient times, before the Terran Federation, people had called the memories within the SEF soul. They were sacred, mentioned in various literature, religions, and myths. No one had ever proven whether souls had a divine origin, nevertheless, they knew now that the sentience of a species was impossible without souls. And if life was sacred, then sentient life was more so. Following that reasoning, the ancients were certainly right about the sanctity of the soul.

The field above them flickered and shut off, and the gravity generator fell silent. Almion became aware of the crowd moving. It was slow at first, then gained speed like an avalanche rolling down a mountainside.

"We've been hosting tournaments for the Vtara for centuries," Rilo said in a sad tone. He seemed to have shucked his arrogance.

Almion sat in the variform seat with her head bowed, not in a hurry to leave the scene of the crime. Closing her eyes, she reached out to those stolen souls. But it was wishful thinking, for the dissonant dimension where the raw brains took them was closed to her.

Anger intruded upon her grief. "And it's expensive to host tournaments." She spread her arms in a wide sweep. "First to irradiate the entire stadium to their specs, and then to design the reclamation nanites to clean up the radioactive mess they leave."

"Our resources could be better used exploring the outer worlds," said Rilo. "If we used our resources for more rigorous science, to regain what we lost in the collapse, we wouldn't be in this position. But the Council is static. That's why we left."

Almion narrowed her eyes. "Who are you?"

"No one important."

Could he be one of the original crew? His appearance seemed . . . outdated. She tried to recall the names of the starship crew that had survived the collapse of the wormhole. Rumor said they were still alive, as they enjoyed a special cellular treatment, another technology which had been lost to the rest of the colonists. The Masters from Temple had been trying to contact the crew. Perhaps they had succeeded. Curiosity was eating away at her but she was too polite to force the issue.

"Well, at least the Vtara helped us after the wormhole collapse," she said to change the subject.

"Most of the technology they gave us was useless," Rilo said. "Their aid was designed to put us in their debt. To repay them, we agreed to host their tournaments."

For decades, the Johannists had been telling the Planetary Councilors that the Vtara tournaments were degrading the SEF. But until now, the Johannists hadn't known how the degradation was achieved. They still didn't know the aliens' reasons. "Go on," she said.

"I was asked not to tell you everything—"

"Who are you?" Almion interrupted. Her irritation had finally overcome her manners. "I know most of the Councilors and not just by telepresence. That can be faked. I know them in the flesh, so don't try to mislead me."

Rilo shrugged. "I suppose you're entitled to know. I'm Garil LaCostel, but everyone calls me Rilo. I'm one of the original crew."

Even though Almion had begun to suspect it, her eyes widened. "One of the navigators. I have a feeling you know *why* the Vtara are stealing SEF memories from Xilora."

Rilo nodded, and then his face creased into worry lines. "Are we doomed?"

"Not yet. But if we don't stop hosting tournaments, the Masters of Temple see no future for us. Genilda Romy Aesophin will call a Council meeting."

"I know," Rilo said. "Your Ponticess contacted us."

"We've been trying for decades and none of you ever responded."

"We needed more evidence. The old Council didn't believe us after the wormhole collapse." His tone was weary. "It might be different now. I've found an intact Vtara in the desert. It's on Temple. Johannist scientists have been studying it for a few six-days. Their findings will be released to the Councilors."

"We're holding a live Vtara on Temple?" Almion was shocked, and disappointed that the Ponticess had kept her in the dark. "That's incredible. The Vtara never allowed us to examine them."

"It's not alive and it's not dead. It's inactive. We don't have all the answers, but we know for certain that the Vtara are biological constructs."

"Constructs?"

"Yes, self-replicating engineered organisms so sophisticated that they've been deceiving us for over three centuries. We don't know how they became what they are. One theory is that they killed off their creators. Another is that they've been abandoned. Whatever the case is, it seems that they've realized the importance of the SEF and designed a way to get souls to create their own Synorphic Energy Field. Every person that dies during a tournament, his or her soul is directed to one of the Vtara systems."

It made sense. Although difficult to prove, both the energy field that held the captive SEF memories during transit and the increased death rate brought on by the plague during tournaments pointed to the aliens' duplicity.

She narrowed her eyes. "How long have you known this?"

"That they bring the plague we've known for a long time. We became suspicious because of the death toll increase at every cycle. Some of us investigated and discovered that it's a sophisticated biotech."

"If we refuse to host their tournaments, we might instigate a war."

"That's true," Rilo said. "But after centuries, we finally have a bio template of a defunct Vtara, which Todd is using to develop disassemblers to render them all inactive."

"Todd Berger, the biologist," she whispered, not bothering to hide her awe at the sudden appearance of these historical figures.

She sensed that there was more behind the Vtara issue than Rilo was telling her. "Tell me the rest."

"You'll find out at the Council meeting."

"There can be no other decision," Genilda Romy Aesophin said. "If we want to survive, we must end the Vtara tournaments." The Ponticess stood in the booth reserved for the Johannists, regal in her plain white robe. Her hairless head was uncovered, face tattoos shimmering in rainbow colors. That she had left Temple at all and attended in person emphasized how serious the situation was.

Almion sat behind the Ponticess, palms perspiring. She stared at the Planetary Councilors. They had already experienced the senso record she had made at the tournament.

A few Councilors moaned quietly as they felt the soul dislocations still resonating within them, others held their heads and rocked back and forth. Fear and indecision rode the psychic waves. The faint rustling of silk robes and the crackling of the recording sensors embedded in the walls seemed loud.

Rilo stood up and walked to the interface module. "Here's the final incriminating evidence." He placed a small senso cube into the receptacle. "Feel free to experience it, but feel free to ignore my brashness. I was young then." He grinned and returned to the seat next to Delanin Wagner, a tall, lithe woman, the xenobiologist of the original crew.

Almion picked up the biogel cap and placed it on her fuzzy head. Its slick insides oozed over her scalp, covering her from nape to temples. She closed her eyes and gave herself up to the ancient record of Garil LaCosta, navigator of the colony ship that had brought her ancestors to Xilora.

A scroll of data appeared before her eyes.

Federation year: 4493

Local year: 1

Location: Wulf Nexus, 3189 light-years from Earth.

She skipped the local astro data, as well as the planetary data of Xilora and plunged into the senso record of Rilo's memories.

Rilo felt Virid tugging at the *Husky Lady*. Interfacing with the EI of the lander, he navigated between the gas giant and one of its moons. Massing three times that of Jupiter, Virid had a monstrous gravity well, but this vector was the shortest to the second world. A small moon showed its icy face, an oblate gray surface that had melted and refrozen countless times during its dance around the gas giant.

Rilo was glad that the colony was nearly established and only a few more runs remained to ferry the science modules and the scientists still aboard the *Brunhilda*. He was tired of overseeing the all the transfers from the starship to the colony, but they had only three landers. The largest, one of them the *Husky Lady*, were used for transporting the science modules. Unlike ordinary homes and public buildings, the coreminds of the research stations couldn't be assembled from pre-designed seeds because the Human Neuron EI systems were leased. They were a patented design guarded by safety disassemblers and grown only in the Federation.

Starlight glinted off the hyperdiamond protrusions of the *Brunhilda*, her lozenge shape barely illuminated this far out. More prominent were the actinic beacon lights of the wormhole, tracing a circular mouth at the edge of the system and held stable by negative energy. Rilo's instruments detected nothing from the throat, but he knew that inside was an impossibly steep gravitational gradient kept open by antiparticles.

Closer toward the inner system but still beyond the orbit of Virid, a faint arc hung in the black void, a lacy trellis of growing girders and struts, as the Von Neumanns assembled the station. No other colony ship would be sent through the Wulf Nexus until they had a station built. After biohazard tests, traders and merchant ships would follow. The Federation was cautious, but more than that, the wealthy demanded comfort. Around newly settled worlds, only the stations could provide that.

Rilo pulled his mind out of the interface and opened the xeno files on the Xil. He shuddered. A slight biped with four arms, and thought the large indigo eyes hinted at humor, the alien face writhed with a mass of tentacles. Rilo couldn't believe that fifteen thousand colonists had been mingling with the Xil for months now. The natives of the second world were friendly, too friendly. For some reason, they genuinely *wanted* Humans to settle their world. That was unnatural for any species.

Delanin glanced at the image on the screen and shook her head. "You're a xenophobe."

"Suspicious."

"That they have an ulterior motive?"

"Either that or they're crazy."

"They're just guileless."

"Whatever." Discussing the altruistic nature of the Xil bored him. Time would tell.

"I heard the Johannists negotiated to settle on a small island," Delanin said. "They named it Temple."

Rilo laughed and stood up, stretching. "What, a few hundred of them and they establish another Temple?" He shrugged. "I suppose we'll feel more at ease once they're out of the way."

"They don't ever scan uninvited."

"How do we know? *They* claim that."

"Rilo, you're not only a xenophobe but paranoid as well." Delanin laughed. She stood behind him, wrapping her arms around his waist.

Her laughter didn't have its usual calming effect. He felt restless and troubled. Peeling her arms off him, Rilo began to pace the foam alloy deck.

"You're jumpy." Delanin's eyebrows rose. "What's wrong?"

"I don't know." He looked at the outside view. "Lady, run a full system check."

"Commencing full system check," said the female voice of the *Husky Lady*.

Delanin looked puzzled. "You did that before we left the *Brunhilda*.

Rilo watched the scrolling data on one of the screens and made no reply. All was well, and yet he felt a hard knot in his stomach.

"This is Seamus Morigan, to all Federation landers," the voice came from the *Brunhilda*. "We have visitors."

"Lady, enlarge the image around the wormhole," Rilo said.

Hundreds of charcoal-colored lumpy shapes had materialized around the Wulf Nexus and the *Brunhilda*. Some surrounded the colony ship, but the bulk of them accelerated at incredible speed and took up position near the beacons.

"Jesus sweat, these ugly mothers didn't come from the wormhole," Morigan said. "They . . . they must have FTL. They just popped out of nowhere."

"Give me the *Brunhilda*'s bridge," Rilo said.

Morigan's face appeared on the *Husky Lady*'s bridge, floating before the curved bulkhead of the sensor board beside the outside view of the wormhole. "Gomez is hailing the aliens," he said.

Rilo felt his stomach clench as several alien ships popped onto the pristine void. And it seemed that they were indeed faster-than-light spacecrafts. "Lady, scan the new arrivals at all wavelengths. I want a full analysis."

"Most objects move in excess of eighty gees," the *Husky Lady* said. "They all employ an unknown form of energy shield."

"They don't acknowledge our signals," Gomez said aboard the colony ship.

"Keep trying." Morigan's face was covered with perspiration.

"Lady, start moving behind Virid but keep recording," Rilo said. "Head for Tahor." He was hoping the larger moon would hide them. Exactly from what he didn't know, but the sour churning in his stomach would not be denied. He always heeded his gut feelings.

Delanin glanced at him, eyes wide with alarm.

"I record energy surges aimed at the wormhole nexus," the *Husky Lady* said. "Their composition is unknown. I also detect gravity waves directed at the wormhole."

"It's buckling!" Morigan's eyes darted from screen to screen.

Plasma jets sprouted from the wormhole, while the charcoal alien crafts pelted it with pencil-thin white beams. The beacons winked out one by one, but the mouth remained visible as exotic energy bolts danced upon it, fighting for dominance. A rainbow ripple shook the structure, followed by a crimson flicker.

"Morigan, move the *Brunhilda*!" Rilo shouted into the com. Mouth pressed into a thin line, he watched in horror. "Head for the inner moon, maximum speed."

"Maximum speed," the *Husky Lady* said.

The crash web lowered over him and the gravity plates shifted. They canceled out the inertia up to twenty gees, but they needed more now. The gel cocoon activated automatically, its squishy surface cold against his body. It quivered, as if sensing his revulsion. A red haze filled his vision for a second, then the gel slithered up his neck and face, flowed into his mouth and nostrils. Rilo suppressed his gag reflex and flexed his implant to interface with the *Husky Lady*. Green nanocilia entered his optic nerves, and then his vision cleared.

His heart pounded as he took in the outside view. The wormhole looked like a tortured white cone, cerulean bolts crackling and sizzling. Thin threads spun rapidly into a swirl, spitting out gobs of plasma. The entire structure bulged, as if pushed from within and torn from outside. The *Brunhilda* was moving now but not fast enough; her shield flickered from the unleashed energies, snapped back and flickered again.

Rilo cursed silently.

Frenzied alien particles halted suddenly and then rushed toward the center of the wormhole. In a few moments, it turned into an intensely brilliant white point. It held, searing and stable, as if local space held its breath. The next instant the wormhole disappeared. Black space roiled like an ocean of tar, a tidal wave of destruction.

Rilo dreaded what was coming next; a silent howling gathered in his throat, vibrating the acceleration gel that filled his mouth and nose, as he watched the *Brunhilda* buckle under the gravity waves. Her flow-alloy double hull cracked like a squashed egg, spilling atmosphere and engine pieces in a white brilliance, that salted the obsidian sky.

"You fuckers!" Rilo gurgled into the acceleration gel. "Suck void and die." For long seconds, he stared at the point where the colony ship had been, unaware of his tears mingling with the gel that surrounded him.

He swallowed his grief and concentrated on reaching Tahor's shadow. The moon might protect them from the gravity waves. He was still wondering whether this was the beginning of an invasion when the charcoal spacecrafts suddenly disappeared from local space.

When the invisible tide reached the partially assembled station—light minutes from the collapsed Wulf Nexus—it crumbled like a worm-riddled fruit.

Almion removed the gel cap and looked at Rilo. Grief flooded her, whether his or hers it didn't matter. That it had happened centuries ago didn't matter, either. Humanity had been victimized. Rilo and the other crew of the *Brunhilda* had lost so much. More than half of them had been killed in the wormhole collapse.

Others stirred in the Council chamber; most looked stunned and some stared off into a distance.

Natalie Lertoix, one of the Councilors, cleared her throat and faced the semicircle of Councilors, her seamed face concerned. "We all saw that the black ships were Vtara ships. They destroyed the wormhole."

"We can't jump to conclusions," Councilor Dietz said.

"The same ships appeared on Xilora three six-days later," Natalie said. "That was not a coincidence."

Rilo stood up and walked to the interface equipment. He removed his senso cube and turned to the Councilors of Xilora. "We showed the same record to the Councilors three hundred twenty years ago, a copy, mind you." He indicated the tiny green cube. Then he closed his hand around it and put it in his pocket. "That copy disappeared and the Councilors did nothing about the Vtara attack. Maybe they were afraid, or maybe they wanted the technology the Vtara offered. Whatever their reason was, they quickly agreed to host the Vtara tournaments. Back then I'd assumed that our Councilors were in league with the Vtara, but now I think they were just incompetent."

"No," said Throminoh, the Xil Councilor. "Your Councilors were helpless. They had no choice in the matter."

Rilo pivoted, staring at the Xil.

"You see," Throminoh continued, "the Vtara have been harvesting Xil long before you Humans landed. My ancestors have known that my species was dying, but they knew not what caused it. That is why they were happy when your ships arrived."

"But . . ." Rilo said, face twisted into a sneer. "The Human Councilors knew that the Vtara was responsible and they did nothing?"

The Xil Councilor nodded. "There was nothing they could do. They didn't want to cause panic, because they had no cure for the plague. Also, you have to remember that the Vtara is a powerful race, and that Humans have lost most of their technology along with the *Brunhilda*." His secondary arms coiled around his narrow torso, indicating extreme stress.

"That makes the situation even worse," Councilor Dietz said. "If they've been having the tournaments for that long, they won't leave without a fight."

An argument erupted among the Councilors.

Without a word, Rilo turned and left the chamber, followed by Delanin.

"If we show them this record," said the Xil Councilor. "They may acknowledge their crime and not resort to violence. At any rate, even war is better than no future at all," he added in a resigned tone, nodding to himself in a very Human manner. "I vote to bar them from Xilora."

We're leaving, Genilda sent and stood. *We've done all we can. I'm afraid the ancient Johannists were right. These are a bunch of bureaucrats.* Her mental resonations were filled with contempt as she strode toward the door, her robes swishing around her long legs.

Almion followed silently. Genilda opened the droptube door and they entered. If the Council voted to do nothing, it would doom them all eventually. No one knew how long that would take, but the decline would come as sure as death.

When the droptube hissed open, Rilo's smile greeted them. He stood in the large hall, leaning against the wall. "I knew you'd leave them to sort it out."

The Ponticess kept walking.

"Care for a lift to Temple?" he asked. "We have to take the defunct Vtara back to our headquarters, so we can design the disassemblers."

Genilda nodded, but it was clear that she didn't relish losing the alien bioconstruct, and with it her access to superior technology. "Perhaps later, we might borrow it again. Since the Vtara are constructs, I'm sure my scientists could find some use for them."

Rilo burst into laughter. "You're just like the rest of us."

The Ponticess smiled but didn't reply.

We're only human, Almion thought, her heart full of gratitude. Despite centuries of prejudice against her kind, the Johannists still belonged. She smiled at her companions. "I suppose we're users, but as long as we do it with dignity, we'll be fine."

Rilo laughed again, but then he sobered. "I hope the Council makes the right decision."

Almion nodded. "I'm sure they will. I have a feeling the majority would vote to stop the tournaments."

"Good enough for now." With an arm around her shoulder, Rilo guided her to his flyer.

Author's note: This story is from *The Dhyany* universe, from Book 2 in the series.

The Last Outpost

JOANNE RESISTED THE URGE TO LOOK over her shoulder as she hurried across the dry grass to a secluded bench. She brushed off the moldy leaves and sat down, anxious to start the final phase of her plan.

"Sizzle, pop, click."

Without turning her head, Joanne moved her eyes. A surveillance wasp detached from a trash bin; alien sensors clicking, it approached and circled above her head. With her jaws clenched, she schooled herself to endure the scrutiny and silently cursed the Kwel. Even out here, near the recycling plant where surveillance was at a minimum, she had to be careful. Despite the possibility of getting stung, she preferred them to the microscopic gnats inside the living quarters.

Screams reached her, and the wasp moved off toward a group of running people. Joanne slid down and hid under the bench. People were fleeing from the torques, human security guards using machetes and electric whips. The aliens needed more workers, or test subjects. With a shudder, she recalled the torqued child she had seen accompanying one of the aliens. Joanne had wanted to intervene, but knew that the Kwel's body armor would protect it from her small needler gun. No one knew why the Kwel needed children now. Soon after they had taken the children, resistance members had launched an attack, but they'd all been massacred by drones before they even reached the tunnels leading to the alien compound.

Soon, Joanne thought, as the stench of burnt flesh coiled in her nostrils. *Is that how they killed Roy?* She hated the Kwel, and even though she pitied the torques, sometimes she hated them too. Her dreams were nightmares of Roy's death, her mind filling in the unknown with gruesome images of torture. He'd disappeared like so many others, and all he'd left behind were his hidden equipment. Roy, who had lied to her to protect her, Roy who'd whispered her name with so much passion in their tight cubby, Roy, who'd promised her freedom. She would finish what Roy had started, now that she had acquired the Kwel tissue samples—a dangerous endeavor even by preprogrammed probes.

She crawled out from under the bench and activated her augment, holding her breath until T-6, her secretary software, appeared in her view. "Your recipes are safe."

Relief surged through her. Although the Kwel didn't monitor the human net, there was a slight chance they could have discovered them. All she needed now was a nanolab and a delivery system, perhaps a simple droid like the Kwel used, and then she could assemble their downfall.

"Send out the snares, T-6," Joanne subvocalized.

Her view focused, showing her spy nits spreading out over the net, taking off on their errands. Joanne resigned to wait. T-6 would find the resistance, the only source for high-tech hardware, leftover from the war. She suspected that Roy had been a member of the resistance and killed by the Kwel. Perhaps he had discovered that the repairs of the *Carnival Queen,* a crashed starship of the Transalliance, were nearly complete, like Joanne had discovered it months ago. She didn't have much time and prayed that she wasn't too late. Cyrano, once a supply outpost during the war, was the last world the Kwel had taken over, and for all she knew it was the last human settlement in this sector—no one had arrived in the past nineteen years.

"Snooper nodes," T-6 said.

Joanne sat up straight and wiped her sweaty palms on her pant leg. She had been naive to assume that the resistance would rely only on encryptions and firewalls; it was reasonable that they used snoopers as deterrent. "Encapsulate them."

The virtual muscles of T-6 bulged from the effort of controlling several shield walls. "It's big. Whatever sent them is hiding in the net. Got it, but I used up most of your shields. It's not the resistance."

Joanne swallowed and cautiously tapped the dungeon icon, letting just a small part of her awareness through. Thousands of nodes lit up in her view, and data swirled in encrypted segments. Then her view shifted to the snooper's and the world spun before her, missile carved trenches and leveled mountains. Amidst a buzz of alien machines, *Carnival Queen,* the human starship stuck out of the ground, her burnt and dented hull patched up by shiny new metal. A grid of the tunnels below lit up in her view.

An aerial view, projected by an intelligent system, she thought with a stab of fear. T-6 was right; it was not the resistance, and she could see it was nothing remotely like what the Kwel used. Could it be a ship in orbit, perhaps Kwel reinforcement? Humanity's oppressors were few, and their home world was nine thousand years distant, according to tales two decades old.

"What the hell are you?"

"I am the Cyrano mainframe." The feminine voice that came through her augment sounded indignant.

Joanne snorted. "The planetary AI was destroyed during the war."

"I was not destroyed. Furthermore, I control a couple of satellites, Joanne Foxx."

Joanne almost fell off the bench. The AI knew her name. Was it really the Cyrano AI? Maybe it was helping the resistance. On second thought, she didn't think so, because the resistance would have used it to defeat the Kwel. Cyrano outpost had fought under Commander Jenny Meade, and it was possible that the planetary AI had survived the war.

"Prove it."

"If you release my nodes from this trap."

Her eyes narrowed; it was a compromise, but maybe she could blackmail the AI instead of looking for the resistance members. Time was short. "I need some equipment." Joanne held her breath as the shield walls of the capsule swelled with the AI's struggle.

"I can give you information."

"I need more than info, but you can start by telling me about Roy Iman."

"He was a member of the resistance and the Kwel killed him. They were close to finishing the ship drive and didn't want anyone to interfere, so they sent out sniffers to hunt down resistance members that could harm them."

Joanne stiffened, hands trembling. "You know all this and you didn't help the resistance?"

"I couldn't help them without calling attention to my existence."

'Don't call attention to yourself,' she recalled Roy berating her because she had designed miniature alife on his nanolab and could

have been discovered by the Kwel. She doubted it, because the Kwel bioscience was not very sophisticated; they relied mostly on robotics. But Roy had been over protective of her. Grief clouded her thoughts, and memories: Roy's absences and the occasional whisperings she'd caught when she'd come in unexpectedly. Joanne had complained that Roy had always been at work or out with friends, but she knew now that those friends were other resistance members. His death had left a void in her heart. She had also lost the use of Roy's nanolab, which he'd taken when he disappeared. Sweat trickled down her back. She must stop the Kwel, and she couldn't afford to botch it. For nineteen years, since Jenny Meade had destroyed the Kwel starship near the gas giant, the aliens had been working on repairing *her* ship, the *Carnival Queen*. Joanne had seen it through her clouds' eyes that the aliens were nearly finished.

I have to stop them without getting the ship destroyed.

"I have been watching them and have some records of their human experiments," said the AI. "The earlier ones, well . . . the human test subjects died in horrific agony. But they worked out that children tolerated their torque much better. They plan to use them to interface with the *Carnival Queen*."

So that's why they needed the children. At least it wasn't something gruesome.

"Are you going to release me?"

"Not yet." Joanne scowled. "I'm going to kill them. With your help."

"If the resistance can't kill them, no one can. I'm not risking myself helping you."

Joanne shrugged, feigning nonchalance. "Then consider your nodes destroyed, and without them you don't have access to the net."

"In time, I will develop new nodes."

Joanne thought furiously. She needed to convince the AI that it was in its best interest to help her. "If the aliens take the *Carnival Queen*, we're all in danger. They'll either bomb us from orbit or leave us stranded on this world, cutoff from the Transalliance. They would certainly not leave you functional."

"They may not find me," said the AI.

"They would find you," Joanne said, though she wasn't so sure. "Soldiers of the Transalliance died to give us a chance to regroup and fight." Though she'd been only nine years old, Joanne remembered the war and Commander Meade's sacrifice, that after she had destroyed the alien starship and sustained damage herself, she'd crash landed and kept fighting with her ground troops rather than limping away in a crippled ship. Afraid to lose her edge, she continued in a hurried tone, "They knew that they couldn't defeat the Kwel, but they fought anyway. You either help me or I wipe these memory storages I'm holding." Joanne wouldn't, not unless she was forced to, but it didn't hurt to bluff. "How *did* you survive?"

"Jenny Meade designed a failsafe. Before the Kwel bombed the grid, I fragmented into small systems. I have been dormant for over a decade, then reassembled into the mainframe. I have been obeying her last command to repair the damages of the war and make Cyrano habitable for the survivors. I'm working on reclamation designs, with the help of her alife creations."

Joanne smiled. Of course, the war effort had commandeered every starship in the Transalliance, even ships owned by the Planetary Engineering Corps. The AI could supply what she needed to accomplish her goal. "Here's the deal: I need a nanolab and one of those alife creatures, a small humanoid. I'll release one of your nodes for the task. Here's where you can deliver them." She squirted an image of her hiding place to the node she released from the dungeon capsule.

"I don't know," the AI said.

"You have twelve hours to think about it. After that, I'll start destroying your nodes."

Five made sure the stealth mode was on as he flew over blasted craters and shiny metal lakes. Under thick smog, the remaining human dome was a dirty blister, a pocket of survivors he had been designed to serve.

The reclamation module descended vertically over a clear patch of ground, and Five stepped through the irising door. With short quick steps, he walked to the edge of the trees and plunged a telescopic rod into the ground to pick up soil samples. By flexing his eye circuits, he activated his photocell screen and checked the sensor's alignment with Cyrano's satellite. The work was slow, and Five didn't know when it would bear fruition. Sadness filled him, and he wondered whether his ilk should feel guilty when he sensed his neural interface twitching.

Cyrano.

"There is a biohacker in the dome," the AI said. "She needs you."

Five shivered. "For what?"

"To kill the Kwel."

"I can't get into the dome without being seen."

"Go through the catacombs. Joanne Foxx will take care of the details."

Five shrank away, but there was no place to hide on the blighted valley. Rebellion glinted in his eyes. "But the torques would find me."

"You are a pathetic coward."

"I, we. . ." He wanted to say that the PICCOs were not engineered for courage, but he realized that no argument would sway the AI. Through his multi-sensors, he sensed Cyrano's massive mind churning with selfish motives of self-preservation. Five feared that it was truly insane, its quantum parts entangled.

"If need be, I can replace your kind."

"No, no. Please don't replace us." He turned a dark shade of green, fear coursing through his vegetal blood. The PICCOs were the best alife for planetary reclamation work, but he knew Cyrano had other templates in its memory storage. "I'll leave at once." He bowed, ropy neck straining to hold up his large head.

"Stay near the dome to receive instructions."

"Yes, Cyrano—" Five began, but realized that the AI had already withdrawn.

Joanne plodded through the sludge of the catacombs and kicked at the scurrying rats under her feet. She clutched the handle of the case that contained her newly acquired nanolab, and under her arm, she carried the bundle of child's clothes she had stolen from the crèche. Furtive shapes and murmuring voices followed her, but no one interfered with her progress.

A cluster of figures wrapped in shadows scattered as she stepped into the next branch, refugees who rather lived down here than work under the yoke of the aliens. She wondered if any of them were resistance members, but it was too late to inquire. With a shrug, she followed the tracer into a declining, narrow corridor. Wet patches rippled on the walls, white slugs the size of her fingers, sucking on the slime noisily. She shuddered and hunched her shoulders to avoid contact with the walls.

Joanne felt uneasy. Though the AI had given her the equipment, she suspected that it was less than honest. She could still back out, but then the aliens would get the *Carnival Queen*. Her first priority was to prevent that, and perhaps after that she could find out why the AI was lying. The tracer led her through a rough-hewn chamber. She squinted through the murk and discerned movements.

"Greetings, Joanne Foxx." A small figure stepped out of the shadows. "I'm a PICCO Five. Cyrano sent me to help you."

Joanne sucked in her breath, staring at a short, green-skinned creature with large olive eyes. Though the AI had sent her the creature's cell samples to work with, it hadn't included a visual. "What's a PICCO?"

"Photonic Integrated Chloroplasmic Cybernetic Organism. Call me Five." The creature waved a bamboo arm, clothed in a tight smartfabric coverall. We must begin at once." He turned around and walked to the other side of the chamber. Thin fingers traced a pattern on the stone, forming an oval opening, of which he passed through. He stood on the other side, waiting.

Joanne hesitated.

"We mustn't keep the door open too long. It's an abandoned cell of the Transalliance, and the torques frequently patrol this area."

Joanne stepped inside and the door closed behind her. Lights came on. She placed her equipment on the single chair and gave Five the clothes. "They're not made of smartfabric—"

"Thank you," Five said and clutched them to himself. "I've never worn human clothing." He gingerly placed them on the chair's arm, green fingers lingering over the coarse fabric.

Joanne looked away, embarrassed by the strange behavior. She opened the case of the nanolab and feasted her eyes on the gleaming tubes, plaz vials, assembler plate, and support structures. And she would be using it to assemble a weapon. Maybe she was not prepared to kill the Kwel. Granted that the list of their crime was long, they had enslaved humans, murdered Roy and other resistance members, but . . . there were so few of them left. Joanne didn't know anyone who knew why the Kwel had traveled such a great distance to attack human worlds, or the reason there were so few of them. Even before the Transalliance had decimated the Kwel ships, there was only a handful of aliens aboard each. She was surprised to find her hands shaking.

"What's wrong?"

Joanne looked at Five. "If these are the only Kwel left in the galaxy, I'd be committing genocide."

Five shrugged. "They couldn't have sent all their people into war. There must be more of them where they come from. Jenny Meade designed us to cherish life, all life, but my actions would save millions of humans, even at the cost of killing some Kwel. Humans die in their mines and tunnels, day after day, and many died in their experiments."

Five was right. "Let's get to work." Joanne activated her augment. She uncoiled a hair-thin optic cable and plugged one end into the port behind her ear and the other end to the nanolab port.

The two sets of recipes she had designed appeared. "Start the un-masque procedure," she said and projected an image.

Five squatted down beside her and watched the masq program, disguised as a folded protein. Layers unfurled and peeled back one by one, until only a small core remained, full of data squiggles.

Joanne checked the bio templates of Five. It was very sophisticated. She wanted to quiz the alife about the AI and its base, but she didn't want to risk losing his trust. She took out a two-liter plaz bottle and plugged its feed cable into the nanolab. "Pure bio-feedstock, it's faster than using the sludge in the catacombs." She looked at Five. "Ready?"

"Ready," Five said and removed his coverall. He plopped down onto the stone floor, picked up the bio-attachment snaking out of the assembler plate, and stuck it to his rubbery green chest.

Joanne tried not to stare at the sexless thin body; instead, she calculated the volume of the feedstock. "Just about enough for a small person." Then she started the recipe running for the Kwel skin.

She opened the other recipe and unmasked the program. The template for the dust looked like a tiny brush, with bristles gyrating and shooting off nanoscopic particles. The feed for this one was in a shielded bottle and contained a microscopic atomic pile—mined by some unfortunate humans—which the lab would incorporate into the dust. She inspected the sequences and the alien polymerase chains engineered to attach to receptor molecules in the Kwel's chromosome analog, and the artificial enzyme that would convert them to dust. The dust would force every cell in the Kwel to copy it, and then self-destruct. She checked the self-destruct command and the attachment of the plate, and gave the command to begin the assembly. Then she sat back to wait, leaning against the hard stone of the chamber. "This'll take a couple of hours. Sleep if you want."

"PICCOs never sleep."

"That's convenient." All the things she could accomplish if she didn't have to sleep. She would have time to master all that was contained in the hidden files, old knowledge that had to be re-learned if Humanity was to survive. Ever since she could remember, she was always interested in biological systems. And if people didn't have to sleep—she recalled Roy's constant fatigue and lack of attention when they were together—maybe he wouldn't have been so exhausted; he would have been more vigilant and . . . Pain clawed her middle, but she couldn't allow grief to distract her now.

After a long stretch of silence, Five shook his arms. Like two bamboo sticks with odd joints, they began to twitch.

"Are you in pain?" Joanne reached into the program to shut it off.

"No, I'm just experiencing . . . warmth." From Five's chest, a network of faint purple arteries spread out, covering his shoulders and upper arms. "Meat warmth," he whispered. "This is how meat life must feel. Dense alien meat. It's warm, much warmer than terrestrial life."

Joanne swallowed - engineered Kwel skin. Would her plan work? There was a lump of ice in the pit of her stomach. But she refused to yield to fear, instead she forced herself to stare at Five's chest. Wet skin began to form in charcoal sections from the frothy nanofactured chain molecules the lab churned out through the attachment. They adhered to the network of arteries, making tiny spattering sounds like rain pattering on soggy clothes. Joanne found the process fascinating, but she finally tore her eyes away and looked at Five's face. The large eyes had no sclera or iris, just an olive, oval-shaped chlorophyll crystal. The mouth was small and thin-lipped, and the large head was out of proportion to the child-sized body.

"I like how meat life feels. I wish Jenny Meade used meat to design us."

Joanne nodded. "Jenny Meade."

"She was the most brilliant in all the Transalliance."

"I know. But I don't trust the AI." Joanne was surprised that she admitted that to this small creature who was in the service of the AI now.

"Cyrano's loyalty is to humans. Even though the AI is not operating at optimum, it retains the original programming."

"The fragmenting damaged it."

"Slightly," Five said.

In Joanne's opinion, more than slightly, but she let it pass. The Transalliance had lost the war, and so had the Kwel, but it was still being fought by the resistance members, if there were any alive. It was an impasse, and she had taken it upon herself to eradicate the enemy. A weight pressed upon her, and she wished she had consulted the resistance leaders before she decided upon this action. They may not have gone along with her plan.

She snorted. Who was she kidding? The Kwel had killed billions of humans, thousands of resistance members on Cyrano, Roy among them. No, she was sure the resistance leaders would jump at a chance like this.

The charcoal froth of alien skin tissues continued to adhere to Five's body in scale-sized sections, covering his torso, upper legs, and arms by wet skin. Whorls of iridescent purple were beginning to stand out. Five wiggled his long toes, staring mesmerized at the process, as the epidermal membranes filled in the jagged edges on his foot and finally knitted together. He spread his hands in front of his face, waved his fingers, and nodded. "You did a great job. Wearing my new clothes, I'll be covered twice." He made a chirping sound that she supposed was laughter. "And once I'm inside the Kwel sector it won't matter."

Joanne grinned. "You'll certainly fool the Kwel security sniffers." She hoped that on their way there, Five would pass for a skinny child with a slightly large head. "But don't look people in the eye on our way there."

"I don't intend to." Five began to pull on the loose trousers and baggy shirt. He donned a sleeveless jacket over these and sealed it all the way to his neck, then clipped on the defunct torque. The cap was a tight fit, but he adjusted the visor so it nearly covered his eyes. He picked up the dust sphere and put it in his pocket. "Let's go."

They passed through the lower levels without trouble, but Five was beginning to limp in the tight shoes. Joanne held the four-fingered hand and they plodded along. They were almost at the terminal when a voice boomed from behind, "Stop!"

Torques, Joanne thought. With heart in her throat, she leaned down and quickly picked up Five, burying the PICCO's face into her shoulder. She adjusted Five's cap and took a few more steps. "My brother . . . wandered out of the crèche. I was in charge of the children—"

"I said stop."

A thick arm spun her around, followed by a fist to the side of her head. Joanne swayed, ear ringing from the blow. Five almost fell out of her arms, but Joanne grabbed him. The small body quivered and clung to her. Joanne's legs shook, and blood trickled down her face, but she stared into the eyes of the men, hoping that the torques controlling them would fail, willing them to let her go.

"These tunnels are off limits," the taller one said and reached a gloved hand for his scanner to ID her. With a ripping sound, the scanner parted from the tacky belt wrapped around his coverall.

"He's only three," Joanne said, clutching Five and watching the scanner pass along her body. She cringed inwardly. The synthetic skin she had sprayed on herself would only gain her a short time, until the alien scanner found the inconsistencies. Slowly, she slid one hand under her jacket for Roy's cobweb she had been hiding inside the thrash chute for months and closed her hand around it gingerly. Once activated, she had five seconds to move out of its radius.

"What's this nonsense?" demanded the taller man. "No ID comes up."

"Lemme see." The shorter one reached for the scanner.

"Damned rats!" Joanne jumped back several paces, pulled out the cobweb, and threw it at the two men.

The web unfurled and spread in a ten-cubic-meter area, shooting out filaments as it expanded. One man reached for his weapon, but a thick translucent coil ensnared his arm. Joanne retreated further and watched them struggle. They stiffened, cursing as the web wound around them, securing them to walls and floor.

"Run," Five whispered.

Joanne turned and dashed off, almost slipping on the scum covering the ground. She wondered if an alarm sounded inside the Kwel tunnels and dared not slow down until she reached the tunnel train terminal. Glancing left and right, she spotted a service door a few meters away. She carried Five there and leaned into the shadowed recess of the doorframe, panting.

After what seemed like an eternity, a train pulled in. Joanne detached herself from the gloom and boarded, with Five clinging to her like glue, gray hands clasping her neck.

"Relax," she whispered.

Joanne went to the rounded end of the train and turned her back on two sleeping men, smelters, by the looks of the burn scars on their arms. From her pocket she withdrew a package of bugeat and threw four on the floor. "Step on them, one foot on each." She put Five down and stepped on the other two bugeat. When their weight cracked the tiny capsules open, they sizzled, and she glanced over her shoulder, grateful for the snoring of the men. The muck on their shoes dissolved and turned into small piles of ash, which she trampled under her feet.

Five did the same and gave her a toothless smile, one hand still holding hers. Joanne grinned back. She was glad that the major part of Five's path to the alien sector led through the ducts, as his appearance didn't bear close scrutiny. Still, she was concerned about the PICCO's safety.

"Maybe we shouldn't go through with this," Joanne whispered.

"We can't stop now." Five stomped a little foot clad in human shoes.

"I . . . I'm worried about you." Though the aliens' security mites didn't pose a threat, for the Kwel skin Five was wearing was in their security files, there were some torqued human guards that could spot that Five was not a human child.

"Please don't worry. I only have to cross a short distance after I emerge from the central duct. And I have my exit route planned."

Joanne nodded reluctantly. The rest of the trip passed in silence, neither of them keen on talking. Besides, Five's voice was not exactly like a human child's.

When the train reached the last stop, they exited and walked to the elevator. It carried them down to the supply hub, and from there they crossed over to the miners' residence. Joanne walked fast and looked ahead, grateful for the crowd. "Wish I could go with you," she said from the side of her mouth.

"You wouldn't fit."

An ear-splitting screech issued from a cargo tube. Joanne felt Five startle, and she squeezed the small hand. "After you're finished, wait a couple of days and come back. You don't have to sneak through the catacombs, you can use the front door. We'll celebrate." She smiled, though she knew Five couldn't see her, as he too, was looking at the floor. "Better yet, I'll invite everyone from my building and we'll throw a big party."

"I would like that." Five squeezed her hand. "I . . . I've never been to a party. Thank you, Joanne."

People jostled them, and she held Five's hand tighter, glaring at a burly man and his cargo pallet that nearly run them over.

"Remember," Five said after they navigated through the crowd. "My exit route is outside near the lake, so don't linger here."

"I know."

"And once we reach the end of this concourse, you go right."

Joanne looked up and saw they were near. Five, of course, had the map in his eye lenses. Suddenly, she felt reluctant to part from the alife. But she had no time for second thoughts, because Five pulled his hand out of hers and turned left. Joanne stopped, and for a moment Five turned back, olive eyes full of sadness. He waved once, and then the crowd swallowed him.

Two weeks later, most of the chaos had settled in the dome. No torques patrolled the buildings now; a few had been killed by angry people, but the majority had taken up communal lives within various enclaves. Joanne had finally tracked down the leader of the resistance and told her what they had done. Word spread quickly among the vastly diminished resistance members.

Joanne was lounging on her bed, cubicle sealed, and waited for Cyrano to appear, whose nodes she had released a few days after the incident. Except for the two large ones she had kept, she wasn't sure for what purpose, but she still didn't trust the AI. The messages she had left through various routes went unanswered, so when the AI appeared in her view, she felt elated.

"Where's Five?" she demanded. "We have some celebrating to do. I want to introduce him to the resistance members."

"You did it, Joanne. All forty-seven of the Kwel are dead."

"I know, but Five did it, not me. Where is he?"

"The PICCO miscalculated. You know, POCCOs are quite stupid. Release the rest of my nodes now."

Anger ballooned inside her, threatening to pop. "I. said. where. is. Five."

"I am sorry. Five expired during the mission."

Expired? Joanne felt as if someone had punched her in the gut. "He . . . he had his exit route planned. Five promised to come see me after—"

"Do not fret about him. He is not important."

Anger and pain coiled into one, and her voice came out a hoarse growl. "You knew he wouldn't make it, you murderous rust bucket."

"Your churlish remarks offend me."

"I don't give a shit!"

"I fail to understand your reaction to the demise of an alife. Five's ilk is disposable, and Cyrano is free now. It was a small sacrifice. And besides, if anyone killed him, it was you."

"What?" Joanne sat up.

"Don't be an idiot. The alien skin you grew for him disintegrated just like the Kwel skin disintegrated. While that didn't do him in, it weakened him enough that his escape became impossible."

It was true. Her stomach lurched and her eyes filled with tears. She'd been too intent on victory, too hasty to think it through. Of course, the AI hadn't bothered to inform her, but she should've known. "Go away. Leave me alone." Joanne buried her head in her arms. She should've known not to trust the AI. Joanne recalled Five thanking her for the party, the sad look in his eyes, and she suddenly realized that Five had known.

Music seeped in from outside, people celebrating their newly gained freedom while Joanne was mourning the passing of a friend.

Author's note: I find artificial life fascinating and wanted to explore the fine line between a friend and a pet.

About the Author

Sophy was born in Budapest and spent a couple of years in Italy before she moved to the United States. As a child, she read everything in sight. Her interest in science and art compelled her to write speculative fiction. She lives in Florida with her husband and two daughters, where she is currently working on a novel.

Her short stories have appeared in anthologies such as *Warrior Wisewoman2*, *Origins*, *The Tangled Bank*, *Desolate Places*, and *The Book of Exodi.*

Her website is: www.zsadani.com.

Copyright Acknowledgments

www.ingramcontent.com/pod-product-compliance
Lightning Source LLC
Chambersburg PA
CBHW030426310726
48979CB00009B/1636/J

* 9 7 8 0 9 8 2 9 4 6 7 6 3 *